SOROCHINSKY FAIR ✲ THE COACH

TALES

CHRISTMAS EVE ✲ NEVSKY PROSPECT

FROM

HOW THE IVANS QUARRELLED ✲ THE NOSE

GOGOL

Translated by Rosa Portnova

SYLVAN PRESS ✲ LONDON, W.C.1

Illustrated by Robert Turner

First Published 1945
Reprinted 1945
This book was produced in conformity
with the Authorised Economy Standard
Printed by Richmond Hill Printing Works, Ltd., Bournemouth
for the Sylvan Press, 24-25, Museum St., London, W.C.1
Made in Great Britain

Contents

Introduction

By JANKO LAVRIN

I

RUSSIA'S great contribution to world literature consists above all in her peculiar realism, the roots of which go back to Pushkin and Gogol. Both were responsible for that "natural school" of Russian fiction, which was first championed by the critic Belinsky and led to an astonishing harvest of masterpieces in the second half of the nineteenth century. Yet it would be difficult to find a bigger contrast than that between Pushkin and Gogol. Pushkin was a classical realist whose genius was one of clarity, economy and simplicity. Gogol, on the other hand, was a hidden and rather complicated romantic even when he pretended to be a realist *par excellence.* He could be primitive, archaically primitive at times, but he was never simple. In fact, he can be regarded as the first enigmatic personality in modern Russian literature: a questioner and a seeker for whom writing became a process of self-examination, self-defence and catharsis in one.

The paradox of Gogol was that he could combine (at least in his later works) a realistic method with the temperament of a typical romantic who never felt at home in the world he lived in. Hence the two alternatives open to Gogol the artist. One was frankly escapist and the other aggressively realistic. It was with the first that he started his literary career, but he finished it with the second. This was however logical, because far from contradicting each other, the two attitudes are actually complementary. An author who is haunted by certain aspects of life to such an extent as to be unable to find an escape even in his art, can easily turn art itself into a "realistic" and satirical weapon for self-defence. And the greater his romantic rancour against the reality he is unable either to accept or to alter, the stronger will be his realism of indictment and the bitter laughter, by means of which he will try to take revenge upon reality, i.e., to show it up and to prove that it is unworthy of acceptance.

The simultaneity of these two attitudes in Gogol's writings, as well as his subsequent transition from the first to the second, marks his work as a whole and can even be studied in Gogol's style. For, in contrast to Pushkin's calm and disciplined clarity, the style of Gogol is agitated, emphatic, and always ready to pass from the solemn, at times almost hypnotic lyrical exuberance, to a realism of small but significant details. If his lyrical passages verge on rhetoric (which is redeemed by his uncanny sense of verbal pattern, rhythm and music), his accumulation of the realistic *petits faits* and grimaces of life is unforgettable in its grotesque concreteness.

In short, Gogol is one of the most interesting and puzzling figures between the romantic and the realistic periods in European literature. And he is puzzling not only as a writer, but also as a personality, since in his case the two are so closely intertwined that it would be impossible to separate one from the other. This is why a few biographic data may be helpful in our approach to both.

II

Born in 1809 into an impoverished Ukrainian gentry family of Cossack origin, Gogol spent his childhood in the idyllic countryside near Poltava. From 1821 until 1828 he was educated at the Grammar School in Nyezhin. During the next eight years he lived in Petersburg, which represented the greatest possible contrast to his sunny Ukraine. The years between 1836 and 1849 he spent abroad—chiefly in Rome, which appealed to his romantic temperament. In 1849 he returned to Russia and stayed for the most part in Moscow, where he died in February, 1852.

Small, nervous and not very prepossessing in appearance, Gogol was always shy and reserved by disposition. As though under the weight of a social and moral "inferiority complex," he became introspective and always ready to attack in others those very defects from which he himself suffered, or thought he suffered. This fostered not only his gift of observation (confined, as a rule, to negative features), but also that satirical and ridiculing vein which became most prominent in some of his writings. At the same time he was anxious to counter, even as a schoolboy, the feeling of his own inferiority by a corresponding strong day-dream of his future greatness.

While still at Nyezhin, he was sure that a brilliant career was in store for him in Petersburg, and under a career he understood in those days, first of all, civil service.

It was with some such hope that he came to Petersburg. But it did not take long for a provincial youth of nineteen to discover that without money and connections he had no prospects in that cold, inhospitable city. He tried his luck again and again, without success. In the end he decided to flee to America. He took a boat to Lübeck, but since the little sum at his disposal would take him no farther he returned to the Russian capital, where he renewed his efforts. This time he obtained at last a miserable underpaid post in one of the Government offices. A victim of circumstances, poverty and disillusionment, Gogol—like so many sons of the gentry—was in danger of becoming a failure, a social *déclassé*. But, all at once, chance intervened, and with rather unexpected results.

As it happened, it was during those months of despondence that Gogol took up literature, chiefly as a means of escape from the dreary reality which preyed upon him. And where indeed was there a better escape than in the reminiscences of the gay and happy Ukraine—the Ukraine of his boyhood? The yarns and tales he had once heard from his Cossack grandfather, the picturesque traditions and superstitions of the people, the sun-drenched landscape of the south, the banks of the Dnieper, the expanse of the steppes—all this came back to his memory in a romantic halo. He shaped the material into a number of bracing narratives and the outcome was his *Evenings on a Farm near Dikanka*, with which Gogol started his literary career.

III

The two volumes of stories which appeared under this title in 1831-32 were an immediate success, partly on account of the subject-matter and partly because of the style. These stories are an amazing blend of fancy and humour, of folklore and folk-life, sprinkled with lyrical passages and quaint gruesome touches, while the general atmosphere is decidedly romantic. Yet in spite of the occasional reminiscences of Tieck and Hoffmann, Gogol's romanticism was not imported from abroad as had been so often the case before him. It was the colourful native romanticism of the Ukrainian countryside, and its aroma was unmistakable. No wonder Gogol wanted to drown in it his melancholy, as he was anxious to drown it also in the impetuosity of his own style, with its rhythms, its "purple patches" and verbal embroideries.

But escapism of this kind provided only a temporary shelter. In his next collection of four narratives, under the title of *Mirgorod* (two volumes, published in 1835), he was already wavering between romance and that realism of indictment which can perhaps best be termed romanticism from the other end. The romance of the Cossack past, *Taras Bulba* (partly inspired by Scott and often referred to as the Cossack *Iliad*), is a gorgeous example of an author's flight from reality into the idealised past brimming with life, adventure and colour. His *How the Two Ivans Quarrelled**, on the other hand, is—with all its fun and grotesque realism—the work of a man anxious to ward life off by ridiculing it, by showing up its vulgarity and meanness. This double attitude is illustrated also by Gogol's miscellany, *The Arabesques* (1835). One of its two stories, *A Portrait,* is ultra-romantic, even redolent of Hoffmann, whereas the very structure of *The Nevsky Prospect* is built on the contrast between what one expects from life and what one gets from it.

It was the disappointed romanticist in Gogol who wanted to punish life, as it were, by means of his realism, his grotesque fun and "laughter through the tears." He did this in two masterpieces in particular, *The Inspector General* (1836) and *Dead Souls* (1842). The first is a satirical comedy of manners; the second is a novel. In both we see, as though in a crooked mirror, the two social strata Gogol knew best—the corrupt officialdom and the petty gentry types—in the process of their mental and moral disintegration. The effect of these two works was all the stronger because of Gogol's ridicule. His gift for grotesque caricature (often reminiscent of Dickens, but without Dickens's benevolence and faith in life) made him attack above all through aggressive laughter. And since laughter of this kind was coupled with moral indignation, it was bound to work upon the moral sense of Gogol's readers and listeners. His "realism" certainly made people think and wish for something better. Aware of this, Gogol soon fell into the delusion that God had endowed him with literary genius for the sole purpose of bringing his country on to the path of righteousness. Gogol, the moralist and "teacher," thus began to encroach upon Gogol, the artist.

Always preoccupied with his own inner problems, and

* The Russian title is *The Story of the Quarrel Between Ivan Ivanovitch and Ivan Nikiforovitch.*

fighting his own "sins," Gogol was the more tempted to preach virtue to others the more he intended to practise it himself. So he came to the conclusion that it was no longer enough to show to his countrymen the sub-human caricatures of man, to laugh and make people laugh at them. What he now wanted to do was to perfect himself in order to depict good and truly perfect characters on whom the readers could model their own lives. He actually embarked upon such a task in the second volume of his *Dead Souls,* little suspecting that his artistic power was derived, not from his moral resolutions, but from the fury of his romantic disgust and criticism of life. No sooner had he tried to shape "positive" paragons of virtue than he became stilted, while his inspiration began to flag, or even abandoned him altogether. This may perhaps explain why the pace of his creative process was now slowed down. So much so that upon the second volume of *Dead Souls* he worked for quite eleven years, and the results were far from satisfactory. He felt how difficult it was to reconcile art with preaching, but at the same time he was so anxious to preach that he decided to publish his moral and didactic ideas in a separate volume for the benefit of Russia, or even humanity at large. The volume appeared in 1847, and its title was *Selected Passages from Correspondence with My Friends.*

This work was the greatest mistake Gogol ever made. Apart from being pretentious and highfalutin', it betrayed his ignorance, since he discussed in it with complacent self-assurance things he knew little about. Moreover, his didactic homilies were imbued with the conservative or even reactionary spirit of a man who had been brought up in the "patriarchal" atmosphere of autocracy and serfdom. The impression it made upon its readers can be imagined. It was not only the progressive intellectuals, but also some of his best friends that turned against him with consternation. His former admirer, the critic Belinsky, even addressed to him a personal letter which was so frank and indignant, *morally* indignant, that it became something of a landmark in the development of modern Russian consciousness.

Gogol was depressed by it all, but could no longer change. With the ascendance of the moralist, the artist in him was on the decline. A prey to misunderstandings, to bad health, to the disgusting vulgarity of contemporary life, and to growing doubts of himself, he was at the mercy of his own despondency. To make things worse, he began to suffer from an atavistic fear of death, or even of hell (as a punishment for his own "wickedness"). He preached and prayed, indulged in ascetic practices, went (in 1848) on a pilgrimage to Palestine, but it was all to no purpose. He could no longer come to terms either with himself or with the world around. During the last two or three years of his life he was hardly normal. In a fit of semi-madness he burnt the completed second volume of his *Dead Souls*, the first five chapters of which have been saved by mere chance. Ten days later he died, on February 21st, 1852. Or, rather, "he burnt himself out to ashes," as one of his modern critics put it.

IV

Gogol's work, like the work of Pushkin, is part and parcel of the mental baggage of every educated man or woman in Russia. Yet his international reputation still lags behind. Partly because he is much too Russian, or, rather, Ukrainian, to be duly appreciated by readers outside his own country. On the other hand, this native flavour only adds to his originality. And so a reliable approach to his work is more than worth while and can best be made through a selection of his stories, reflecting as far as possible the various stages of his literary development. Such, incidentally, is one of the tasks of the present volume, which includes two stories (*Sorochinsky Fair* and *Christmas Eve*) from *Evenings on a Farm near Dikanka*; one, *How the Two Ivans Quarrelled*, from *Migorod*; and one, *The Nevsky Prospect*, from *The Arabesques*. In addition, *The Coach* and *The Nose* illustrate some further aspects of Gogol, the writer.

Sorochinsky Fair deserves to be widely known since the composer Moussorgsky based on it his famous opera under the same title. The story itself is hardly more than an intensified anecdote about a village lad who resorts to a gypsy's tricks in order to fool his sweetheart's pigheaded but superstitious father, and to win her hand. It opens with a solemn lyrical description of the Ukrainian summer, after which there is a sudden transition to comic scenes and dialogues—leading up to the pageantry of a country fair, with its lively mix-up of fun, mystification, buffoonery and grotesque portraiture so dear to Gogol. Even this early product of Gogol's pen betrays his propensity to observe, not as a mere describer, but as a potential actor who wants to mimic and impersonate his characters, especially his comic characters. Otherwise the comicality of the story is mainly one of situations, and its gaiety sounds spontaneous from the first to the last line.

The same can be said of *Christmas Eve,* which is considerably more varied and more richly articulated in construction. It is based on an Ukrainian folktale about a not particularly sagacious devil who wanted to ruin the soul of the pious village blacksmith, Vakula, but was himself cheated by the sly Ukrainian instead. The story reads like a delightful joke for its own sake. Peasants and Cossacks, devils and witches, the love between Vakula and his capricious Oksana, Vakula's journey on the devil's back to Petersburg and his triumphant return (by the same means of transport) with the golden slippers of Catherine II as a present for Oksana—all this is told in a bracing tempo and with that whimsical inflection which was one of the most enviable gifts of Gogol, the impersonator.

As for *How the Two Ivans Quarrelled* it is above all an example of Gogol's grotesque realism. Both the portraiture and the background are contrived in such a way as to produce in the reader the mood which was typical of Gogol himself. The principal characters—two worthies of the same petty gentry class to which Gogol belonged—are examples of the senseless, fat and vulgar existence he was so afraid of. Fast friends at first, the two Ivans quarrel for no reason and ruin each other from sheer inner emptiness and stupidity. While telling us the story, Gogol, the impersonator, puts himself, of course, on the level of the characters described. At the end, however, he rises to a height from which he can pronounce his verdict and refute the whole of this mean and squalid way of life.

Realistic in manner, but romantic in its temper, is *The Nevsky Prospect.* The amorous adventures of the two comrades portrayed in it represent, by their very contrast, the height of romantic irony in the sense of utter incompatibility between the ideal and the real planes of life. This narrative in one of Gogol's Petersburg stories, which, besides it, include his famous, *Greatcoat, The Portrait, Memoirs of a Madman* and *The Nose.* The most puzzling of them is, of course, the last one. Written in 1835, it may have been suggested to Gogol by the "nosological" passages in *Tristram Shandy* (he knew it from a Russian translation) ; yet the story itself develops like a confused dream behind the apparent nonsense of which one can easily detect certain phobias and peculiarities connected with Gogol's sexual life. Like *A Cruel Vengeance,* this story, too, is of great value for anyone interested in the meeting point between psycho-analysis and literature.

Entirely different is *The Coach,* although it was written in the same year as *The Nose*. Here Gogol returns, once again, to the gentry class types, but in a somewhat more tolerant, humorous mood. This perfectly worked out anecdote links Gogol with some earlier things by Chekhov.

The influence of Gogol upon subsequent Russian literature was enormous. Whereas Pushkin was responsible for the directness, clarity and straightforward simplicity of Russian realism, Gogol bequeathed to it its questioning and searching current—its "vexation of the spirit." In this respect he was a precursor of both Tolstoy and Dostoevsky. He, too, suffered —like Tolstoy— from the inner division between the artist and the moralist. And, like Tolstoy again, he often turned his literary works into a confession in disguise.* As for Dostoevsky, it is a well-known fact that he wrote his first two narratives under the influence of Gogol.

A strong mark was left also by Gogol's vindictive attitude towards existing reality : the attitude of a frustrated idealist and romantic. This is particularly true of such authors as Pisemsky and Saltykov-Shchedrine. The latter even took up Gogol's laughter as something unique in its social and moral importance. Combining the grotesque satire of Gogol with the rancour of a Swift, he became the most vehement critic of Russian life in the second half of the last century.

Even Gogol's agitated and nervous style was continued by Dostoevsky and, recently, by the modernist Andrey Bely, who was one of the best interpreters of Gogol's technique and craftsmanship. The latter exercised (through Bely and Remizov) a certain influence also upon Soviet literature. Such works again as *A Cruel Vengeance, Memoirs of a Madman* and *The Nose* bring Gogol into contact—in spite of the distance in time—with both psycho-analysis and *surréalisme*.

This, however, is but a further proof of the importance of Gogol's writings for readers interested in Russian literature, or in literature in general. They will certainly be glad to welcome a selection of stories which provides an introduction to Gogol's work as a whole.

UNIVERSITY COLLEGE,
NOTTINGHAM.
1945.

* The parallel can even be carried farther, since Gogol's personal *Confession of an Author* is a counterpart of Tolstoy's equally personal *Confession*.

Sorochinsky Fair

1

How intoxicating, how wonderful is a summer's day in Little Russia! How lanquishingly hot are the hours, when at noon the day sparkles in silence and sultriness, and the blue and infinite ocean of sky, bent over the earth like a voluptuous dome, seems to have fallen asleep steeped in tenderness, clasping lightly the beautiful earth in an airy embrace! No cloud in the sky, no voices in the field. Everything seems to have died, only above, deep in the sky, the lark trembles and silvery songs float down to the enamoured earth and from time to time the sea-gull's cry or the resounding voice of the quail echoes in the steppe. Lazy and oblivious, idle and aimless, the oak-trees stand under the clouds and the dazzling blows of the sun enflame picturesque masses of leaves, casting on others a shadow as dark as night, which gusts of wind sprinkle with gold. Clouds of ethereal insects, like emeralds, topazes, sapphires, pour over multi-coloured kitchen gardens, shadowed by stately sun-flowers. A camp of grey hay-ricks and golden sheaves of corn is scattered in the field and wanders its infiniteness. Wide boughs of the wild cherry, the plum tree, the apple and the pear—bent under the weight of the fruit; the sky and its clear mirror, the river in its green, proudly raised frame . . . how full of voluptuousness and abandon is summer in Little Russia!

With such splendour glittered one of the days of a hot August in the year one thousand eight hundred . . . eight hundred . . . yes, it must have been about thirty years ago, when the road for about ten verst from the small town of Sorochintsy, teemed with people hurrying from all the hamlets, adjacent and remote, to the fair. From early morning waggoners with salt and fish dragged along in an endless procession. Mountains of pots, wrapped up in straw, moved slowly and appeared to be weary of their imprisonment and darkness.

Only in some places a vividly painted basin or pot boastfully displayed itself above the wattle crowded high on the cart and attracted admiring glances from lovers of luxury. Many passers-by cast envious glances at a tall potter, the owner of these valuables, who slowly followed his merchandise, carefully wrapping up his clay dandies and minxes with the straw so odious to them.

Lonely and apart, dragged a cart, pulled by weary oxen, piled up with sacks, hemp, linen and various household goods. Behind it rambled its owner in a clean linen shirt and dirty loose linen trousers. With a lazy hand he wiped from his swarthy face the profuse perspiration which trickled even from his long moustache, powdered by that inexorable hairdresser, who appears unbidden to the beauty and the deformed and has been forcibly powdering the whole of mankind for a few thousand years. Next to him walked a mare tied to the cart, whose meek appearance disclosed her good old age. Many passers-by, young men especially, took off their caps as they drew near to our peasant. But it was not the grey moustache or the dignified gait which compelled this courtesy; you only had to lift your eyes a little to see the cause of such reverence. A pretty daughter sat on the cart, round faced, with black eyebrows raised in even arches over hazel brown eyes, with pink lips smiling unconcernedly, with red and blue ribbons tied on her head which together with long plaits and a bunch of field flowers, rested like a rich crown on her charming little head. Everything seemed to entertain her, everything appeared strange and new . . . and the pretty eyes continually flashed from one object to another. How could she help being entertained? This was her first visit to the fair—an eighteen year old girl for the first time at the fair!

But none of the passers-by knew what it had cost her to persuade her father to take her with him. He would have done it gladly, with all his heart, if it were not for the angry step-mother, who had learned to handle him as skilfully as he handled the reins of his old mare, which in return for her long service was now being dragged to the fair for sale. The turbulent wife . . . But we have forgotten that she too sat here on top of the cart in a flashy green woollen jacket, on which little tails were sewn, as on ermine, save that these were red in colour, and who wore a rich skirt, vividly chequered like a chess board and had a chintz headdress on her head, which added some special importance to her fat red face; but something so unpleasant and wild stole from time to time over it, that everyone with alarm hurriedly turned his glance to the daughter's gay face.

The town of Psel already appeared before our travellers' eyes, and even from the distance there emanated from it a sense of coolness the more perceptible after the languishing and destroying heat. Through the dark and light green leaves of the poplars and birches, negligently scattered over the field, the beautiful river dazzlingly bared her silver breast, on which the green curls of the trees dropped luxuroiusly. Rows of watermills lifted wide waves on their heavy wheels and threw them powerfully down, smashing them to atoms and covering them with dust. The cart, with whose passengers we have become acquainted, had by that time reached the bridge and the river like a long looking glass stretched below there in all its grandeur. The green and blue woods, people, carts of pottery, windmills, everything reversed, stood and walked upside down without falling into the wonderful light blue abyss of sky.

Our maiden fell into a reverie looking at the magnificent view and even forgot her sun-flower seeds, which she had been shelling throughout the journey, when suddenly the words "What a girl!" roused her from her day-dream with a start. Turning round, she saw a crowd of young men standing on the bridge, one of whom, dressed more elegantly than the others in a white short jacket and wearing a grey lambskin cap, stood with his hands on his hips staring impudently at the passers-by. She could not help noticing his sunburnt handsome face and his fiery eyes, which seemed to try to pierce through her and she cast down her eyes at the thought that the words might have been uttered by him.

"Lovely girl!" continued the youth in the white jacket, without removing his glance from her, "I'd give all I have for a kiss from her, but there rides the devil in front!" Laughter rose from all sides; but the irate wife of the peasant who walked with slow steps in front of the cart, did not particularly appreciate such a greeting. Her red cheeks turned purple and a torrent of choice words began to pour at the rakish young man. "May you choke, you ill-bred clown! May a pot knock your father on his head! May he stumble on ice! Cursed antichrist! May the devil burn his beard in hell!"

"See, how she swears," said the young man, opening his eyes wide at her as if nonplussed by the forceful volley of unexpected compliments. "The witch is a hundred years old and her tongue can still speak such words without hurting her!"

"Hundred years old!" took up the weathered beauty, "You heretic! Wash your dirty face first! You filthy good-for-nothing! I haven't seen your mother, but I know she's a pig and your father is a pig and your aunt is a pig. A hundred years old! His mother's milk still hasn't dried on his lips . . . !"

Here the cart began to descend the bridge and it was impossible to distinguish the last words; but the young man apparently did not want to leave it at that. Without hesitation he snatched up a piece of mud and threw it after her. The blow was more successful than was to be expected. The new chintz headdress was completely spattered with mud and the laughter of the gay hooligans redoubled with renewed vigour. The overdressed stout beauty began to boil with fury, but by this time the cart had driven on and her wrath was switched to her guiltless step-daughter and her phlegmatic sleeping partner, who long accustomed to such incidents, kept stubborn silence and listened unmoved to the seditious talk of his infuriated wife. In spite of that, her tireless tongue chattered and rolled in her mouth until they reached the suburbs and the house of their old acquaintance and relation, the Cossack Cibulya. This meeting with relations, whom they had not seen for a long time, temporarily drove this unpleasant incident from their minds as our travellers had to talk about the fair and have some rest after the long journey.

2

You will probably have heard somewhere a distant waterfall, when the startled surroundings are filled with din and a chaos of strange indistinct sounds whirls before you. Is it not true, that the same feelings are roused in you by the whirligig of a country fair, when all the crowd grows into one huge monster, which moves its whole body on the market place and in the narrow streets and shouts, gabbles, thunders? Noise, swearing, bellowing, bleating, braying—everything merges into discordant buzzing. Oxen, sacks, hay, gypsies, pots, women, gingerbread, caps—everything tosses in vivid colourful disorderly heaps and flashes before your eyes. Voices in different keys drown each other and not a single word will free itself and escape this deluge, not one cry will be shouted clearly. Only the striking of hands as the dealers conclude their bargains is heard from all sides at the fair. A cart breaks, iron clanks, planks are thrown to the ground with a clatter and the giddy head wonders where to turn.

Our newly arrived peasant with his black-browed daughter had been pushing his way in the crowd for some time ; he approached one cart, felt the goods in another and took stock of the prices, but his thoughts continually turned to the ten bags of wheat and the old mare, which he had brought to the fair for sale. It was apparent from his daughter's expression that she found little pleasure in rubbing shoulders with carts of flour and wheat. She would much rather have gone where under linen tents were decoratively displayed red ribbons, earrings, pewter and brass crosses and coins. Nevertheless, here, too, she found many objects which attracted her attention ; it seemed to her extremely funny to see how a gypsy and a peasant struck hands over a bargain so hard that they shouted with pain, how a drunken Jew smacked a woman's behind, how the quarrelling saleswomen threw swear words and crayfish at each other, how a thief stroked his goat-like beard with one hand, and with the other . . . But suddenly she felt somebody pulling at the embroidered sleeve of her blouse. She turned round—and the youth in the white jacket and with the fiery eyes was standing in front of her. Her heart contracted and began to beat as it had never done before, either in joy or in sorrow, and it seemed strange and lovely to her and she could not understand what was happening to her.

"Don't be frightened, sweetheart," he said and continued softly, "I shan't say anything bad to you."

"Perhaps you won't, indeed," thought the young beauty, "but I feel queer. It is probably the devil himself ! I seem to know full well that I shouldn't allow this . . . but I haven't the strength to take my hand away from his !"

The peasant turned round to tell his daughter something, but then he heard a word said from aside : "WHEAT." This magic word immediately caused him to join two loudly talking merchants and once his attention was drawn to them nothing else could distract it. This is what the merchants were saying about wheat.

3

"What do you think, neighbour, will our wheat go badly or not ?" one man, who looked like a newcomer and an inhabitant of some small town, and who wore striped loose trousers, dirtied with tar and stained with fat, was saying to another in a short blue jacket, patched in places and with a huge bump on his forehead.

"There's no doubt about it. I'm ready to put a rope round my neck and hang from that tree like a sausage from a house at Christmas if we sell a single measure."

"Listen, friend, you're having a joke with me, aren't you? No one has brought any wheat to the fair, except us," contradicted the man in the striped trousers.

"Well, you can say what you like," thought our beauty's father, who had not missed a single word of the conversation between the two merchants, "but I've got ten bags in reserve."

"That's what happens when the Devil himself is mixed up in things. You can expect as much profit as you'd make out of a starving cat," said the man with the bump on his forehead.

"The Devil?" exclaimed the man in the striped trousers.

"Haven't you heard what the crowd's talking about?" continued the one with the bump on his forehead, looking at him askance.

"What?"

"What, that's just it—what. The assessor—may he never be able to raise his lips to his master's brandy bottle—assigned a cursed site for the fair; even if you burst, you won't sell any grain here. Can you see that old dilapidated barn, the one standing at the foot of the mountain over there? (here the curious father of the beauty moved even nearer and seemed to have turned into attention incarnate). In that barn, devilish pranks are played and not a single fair in this place has been held without some trouble. Yesterday the district scribe passed it late at night, when suddenly a pig's head looked out of the window and grunted at him in such a manner that he was covered with goose pimples. Just wait and see, the red jacket will appear again!"

"What's that—the red jacket?"

Here our attentive listener's hair began to stand on end. Filled with fear he looked back and saw that his daughter and the youth were unselfconsciously embracing each other and singing love songs into each other's ears, oblivious of all the jackets in the world. This dispersed his fear and restored his courage.

"Well, well, well, my boy, you're an expert at embracing! I only learned to hug my Chveska (may she rest in peace) four days after our wedding, and even then thanks to my best man, who put me wise."

The youth immediately saw that the father of his beloved was a simple man and began to plan how to win his favour.

"You don't seem to recognise me, but I knew you immediately."

"May be I don't."

"If you like, I'll tell you your name and surname and various other things : your name is Salopy Cherevik."

"That's right, Salopy Cherevik it is."

"Well then, have a good look, don't you recognise me ?"

"I don't. I don't want to hurt your feelings, but I have seen so many snouts in my time, that the Devil alone could remember them all."

"It's a pity you don't remember Golopupenkov's son."

"Will you be Ochrimov's son ?"

"Who else's ?"

Here the new friends took off their caps and kissing began, but Golopupenkov's son decided not to lose time and to lay siege to his new acquaintance.

"Well, Salopy, as you see, your daughter and I have fallen in love so much that we'd like to live together for ever."

"May be, Paraska," said Cherevik, turning to his daughter and laughing. "Perhaps you should indeed, as the saying goes, graze in the same meadow ? What ? Shall we strike hands on that ? Now then, new son-in-law, let's wet the bargain."

And the three of them found themselves in the fair's famous eating-place under a Jewess's tent, which was bedecked with a large flotilla of flat bottles, round bottles and flagons of various kinds and vintages.

"Good chap, I love you for that," the slightly merry Cherevik was saying, seeing how his future son-in-law filled a pint-sized mug and without batting an eyelid, drained it and then smashed it to smithereens. "What say you, Paraska ? Look what a bridegroom I've got you ? See, how he takes his drink —like a man."

And laughing and swaying he trotted back with her to his cart and our youth departed to the stalls where the luxury goods were displayed, some of them sold by merchants who came even from Gadyach and Mirgorod, two famous towns of the Poltava district, where he intended to look out for a good wooden pipe in an elegant brass mounting, a flowery scarf with a red background and a cap, as wedding presents for his father-in-law and others to whom they were due.

4

"Well, wife, I've found a bridegroom for my daughter."

"Just the right time to look for bridegrooms now! Fool, idiot! You're likely to remain one, too! Where have you seen or heard of such a thing as a decent man running after bridegrooms? You'd better think how to get the wheat off your hands. The bridegroom should be good, too! I should think he is the most ragged of all the beggars."

"That's what you think. If you had only seen him! What a youth! His jacket alone costs more than your green one and your red boots put together. And how well he drains his brandy! The Devil take me and you too if in all my life I've seen a young man drink nearly a pint at a gulp without so much as knitting his eyebrows."

"That's it. If he's a drunkard and a vagabond that should be up his street. I bet it's the same scoundrel who trailed after us on the bridge. It's a pity I haven't come across him yet. I'd show him!"

"Well, Chivrya, and if it is the same fellow, why is he a scoundrel?"

"Why is he? You nit-wit! Have you heard anything like it—why is he? Where were your idiotic eyes when we drove past the mill? He wouldn't care if his wife was dishonoured right under his very nose, stained with rotten tobacco as it is."

"I still can't see anything bad in him, he's a fine chap, that's what he is. All he did was to plaster your dial with dung and then only for a moment!"

"So that's what we've come to. You won't let me get a word in! And what's the meaning of it? You haven't done this before. You must have been boozing instead of trying to sell your goods."

Here our Cherevik realised that he had gone too far and immediately covered his head with his hands, assuming, no doubt, that his infuriated sleeping partner would now proceed to attack his hair with her wifely claws.

"To hell with it! There goes the wedding," he thought, backing away from his wife who was now attacking him fiercely. "I'll have to refuse a good chap, for no reason at all. God Almighty, why have you sent this misfortune to us sinners? There's enough misery in the world as it is and you have to breed wives."

5

The youth in the white jacket sat near his cart gazing absent-mindedly at the noisy crowd around him. The tired sun was leaving the world after blazing steadily throughout the morning and afternoon and the dying day was flushed enticingly and vividly. The tops of large and small tents glistened dazzlingly, tinged with touches of fiery pink. The glass of the heaps of window frames was aflame, the green flagons and goblets on the tables of the publicans had turned to fire, the mountains of melons, water-melons and pumpkins seemed moulded of gold and brass. The talking noticeably decreased and became duller and the tired tongues of the dealers, peasants and gypsies moved more lazily and slowly. Somewhere a small fire began to sparkle and the pleasant steam of boiling dumplings wafted into the streets which began to grow silent.

"Why so mournful, Grizko!" exclaimed a tall sunburnt gypsy, slapping his shoulder. "What about it ? Will you sell the oxen for twenty ?"

"All you think of are oxen. Your tribe are full of greed, you'll trick and deceive a good man."

"The Devil ! You've got it badly. Annoyed at being tied to a bride ?"

"No, it's not that, I keep my word. I gave it once and I'll keep it for ever. It's the old fool Cherevik. He's got no conscience it seems. He promised and now he takes everything back. Still, it's no use blaming him. He's just a block-head. This is the old witch's trick, the one we made fun of good and proper on the bridge. If I was a king or a grand-duke, the first thing I'd do would be to hang every fool who let a woman put a saddle on him."

"Will you let the oxen go for twenty if we make Cherevik give us Paraska ?"

The perplexed Grizko looked at him. There was something wicked, malicious and evil and, at the same time, haughty about the dark features of the gypsy : after one glance at him one could see that this strange soul harboured fierce emotions for which there was only one reward on earth—the gallows. His mouth, completely sunk between his nose and his sharp chin, was twisted into a permanent smile at once taunting and malicious ; expressions of cunning and calculation flashed in lightning succession from his narrow eyes piercing as a flame—all this seemed to demand an equally strange apparel, of the very kind he wore. The short dark brown jacket, which looked as if it would turn to dust if touched, the long black hair, falling in tufts over his shoulders, the shoes worn on bare sunburnt feet—all these seemed to have become part of him.

"You shan't have them for twenty—I'll let them go at fifteen, but only if you're not lying," answered the youth without removing his scrutinizing look from the man's face.

"For fifteen? All right! It's a deal. And don't you forget it. For fifteen it shall be. Here's a deposit."

"What if it's a lie?"

"If I'm lying—the deposit is yours."

"All right, let's strike hands."

"Strike."

6

"Here, Aphanasy Ivanovitch! The hedge is lower here, lift your leg, no need to be afraid. This fool of mine has gone for the whole night with his kinsman to stay under the carts in case thieves pinch something."

Thus Cherevik's stern sleeping partner tenderly encouraged the priest's son, who clung cowardly to the fence and then quickly mounted the hedge and for a long time stood on it perplexed like a tall horrible spectre, measuring with his eyes how best to jump off and, finally, noisily slumped down into the high grass.

"What a shame! Have you hurt yourself, or, God forbid, broken your neck?" lisped Chivrya anxiously.

"Sh! It's nothing, nothing at all, dearest Chavronya," painfully whispered the priest's son, getting on his feet, "if you leave out the stings caused by the nettles, that serpentiform grassy tribe, to quote the archpriest, may he rest in peace."

"Let's go into the house now, there's nobody there. I began to worry, Aphanasy Ivanovitch, I thought perhaps you had scabies, or stomach-ache, I have not seen you for such a long time. And how are you? I heard that your honourable father has done very well in many ways."

"A mere trifle, Chavronya Nikiforovna, dear father received during the whole of the fast only about fifteen sacks of spring corn, about four sacks of broom-corn, about a hundred loaves of white bread, and if you counted the hens, they won't even amount to fifty, and the eggs are mostly rotten. Indeed, the truly sweet gifts are to be expected only from you, Chavronya

Nikiforovna," continued the priest's son, casting tender looks at her and sidling nearer.

"And there is a gift for you, Aphanasy Ivanovitch," she murmured, putting on the table some dishes and mincingly buttoning her blouse, pretending that it had unbuttoned by chance, "dear little curd-dumplings, wheat dumplings, and various other dumplings."

"I am prepared to wager a bet that it is all made by the the cleverest hands of Eve's sex," said the priest's son attacking the wheat-dumplings with one hand, and pushing nearer the curd-dumplings with the other. "Nevertheless, Chavronya Nikiforovna, my heart hungers for food from you, sweeter than all the curd or wheat-dumplings."

"I really don't know what other food you desire, Aphanasy Ivanovitch," said the obese beauty, pretending not to understand.

"It is your love, to be sure, incomparable Chavronya Nikiforovna," whispered the priest's son, holding a dumpling in one hand and embracing her wide waist with the other.

"God knows what you are up to, Aphanasy Ivanovitch," said Chivrya, casting her eyes down coyly. "For all I know, you will contrive to do some kissing."

"With regard to that, even I, let me tell you," continued the priest's son, "when I used to be at college, so to speak, I can remember quite vividly . . ."

Here barking was heard in the yard and a banging at the gates. Chivrya hurriedly ran out and returned quite pale.

"Well, Aphanasy Ivanovitch, we've been caught ; a crowd of people is knocking at the gates, and I seemed to hear the kinsman's voice . . ."

The dumpling stuck in the throat of the priest's son. His eyes bulged out, as if some emigrant from the other world had just visited him.

"Climb up here," cried the frightened Chivrya, pointing to the planks, which lay under the ceiling on two crossbeams and on which were heaped household utensils of various kinds.

Danger gave courage to our hero. Slightly recovering his senses, he jumped on the stove-couch and from there crawled cautiously on to the planks ; and Chivrya, having almost lost consciousness, rushed to the gates, as the knocking increased in strength and impatience.

7

A strange incident had occurred at the fair; a rumour was abroad that somewhere among the merchandise the red jacket had been seen. Satan, in the shape of a pig, had appeared to the old woman who sold cracknels. This pig kept incessantly bending over carts as if searching for something. The rumour quickly spread to all the corners of the fair-encampment, which by that time had become quiet, and everybody thought it a crime to disbelieve the story, although the cracknel-woman's mobile store was situated next to the alekeeper's tent and she bowed to people the whole day for no apparent reason and scraped with her feet likenesses of her appetising merchandise on the ground. To this report were added exaggerated tales of the miracle witnessed by the district scribe in the dilapidated barn, so that by nightfall people pressed closer and closer to each other; the calm was broken and fear drove everybody's sleep away and those, who were not of the bravest and had provided themselves with sleeping accommodation in houses, departed there. To the latter belonged Cherevik with his kinsman and daughter, who, together with guests who had begged for shelter in the house, were the ones who made the loud noise, which had so frightened our Chivrya. The kinsman was somewhat far gone. It was obvious from the way he drove his cart twice round the yard before finding the house. The guests too were in a gay mood and, not standing on ceremony, entered the house before the host. Our Cherevik's wife sat on pins and needles, while they began to rummage in all the corners of the house.

"What is it, sister?" exclaimed the kinsman on entering, "are you still shaken by fever?"

"Yes, I'm not very well," answered Chivrya, listlessly looking at the planks under the ceiling.

"What about getting the flask from the cart, woman?" said the kinsman to his wife, who had arrived with him. "We'll sample from it with the good people here. Those cursed women frightened us so much that I'm even ashamed to admit it. By God, brother, it was silly to come here," he continued sipping from a clay mug, "I'll bet you my new cap that the women took it into their heads to play a joke on us. And even if the pig was the devil, what of it? You just spit at his head. And had he decided this very moment, for example, to stand up here in front of me—I'd be a dog's son if I didn't shove my fist under his nose."

"Why have you suddenly gone pale ?" shouted one of the guests, a head taller than the others and who always tried to appear brave.

"I ? God be with you ! Dreaming, are you ?"

The guests laughed, a pleased grin spread on the face of the talkative braggart.

"How could he get pale ?" shouted another. "His cheeks are blooming like poppies. He's no longer Cibulya, but a beetroot, or even better—the red jacket itself, which has frightened people so much."

The flask went around the table and made our guests even gayer than before. Here our Cherevik, whom the red jacket had been tormenting for a long time and giving his curiosity not a moment's peace, approached his relative.

"I keep on asking," he said, "what is the story of the cursed jacket, but nobody will tell me."

"Ah, brother, it shouldn't be told at night, unless it be to do a favour to you and these good people (here he turned to the guests), who I notice want to know about this strange thing as much as you do. So be it then."

Here he scratched his shoulder, wiped himself with the lapel of his coat, put both his hands on the table and began :

"Once upon a time, strike me if I know why, a devil was driven out of hell."

"How is that, brother," interrupted Cherevik, "how can a devil be driven out of hell ?"

"Can't be helped, brother, they threw him out, just as a peasant throws out a dog from his house. May be he was foolish enough to perform a good deed ; well, they showed him the door. Poor devil, he began to long, to long so much for Hell, he was ready to hang himself. What should he do ? From sorrow he took to drink. He made his home in that broken-down barn under the mountain which you saw and which no good man will pass without first protecting himself with a holy cross ; and the devil became such a gadder-about, as you won't find among the young men ; he'd sit in the pub from morning till night ! . . ."

Here Cherevik again interrupted the story-teller severely :

"Heaven knows what you're talking about, brother ! How could it be that anybody would let the devil into the pub ? After all, God be praised, he has claws on his paws and small horns on his head."

"The trouble was, he had a cap and gloves. Who could recognise him ? He gadded about and gadded about and finally it came to this—he drank through everything he had on him. The publican chalked everything up for a long time and then stopped. The devil had to pawn his red jacket at barely a third of its value to a Jew, who kept a pub at the Sorochinsky Fair at that time. He pawned it and said to the Jew: 'Remember, Jew, I shall come to you to redeem the jacket in a year's time: guard it!' and vanished as if the earth had swallowed him. The Jew had a good look at the jacket, the cloth was such as you won't get even in Mirgorod and its red colour seemed to burn like fire—you couldn't take your eyes away from it! It seemed to the Jew tedious to wait for the term to be up. He scratched his whiskers and made a stranger pay through the nose for it—no less than five chervonec. The Jew completely forgot about the term. But one day, towards evening, a man arrives. 'Well, Jew, give back my jacket,' he says. The Jew didn't recognise him at first and then when he did, pretended that he had never set eyes upon him before. 'What jacket are you talking about? There's no jacket here. I know nothing about your jacket.' And the man left, but after nightfall, when the Jew, having locked his miserable hole and counted the money in his trunks, threw a sheet over himself and began to pray in the Jewish way—he hears a rustle. He looks up and sees pig's snouts in all the windows."

Here some indistinct sound was heard, not unlike grunting. Everybody became pale. Sweat appeared on the story-teller's face.

"What was that?" said the frightened Cherevik.

"Nothing," answered the kinsman, whose whole body was shaking.

"Ah," said one of the guests.

"Did you say anything?"

"No!"

"Who grunted then?"

"God knows, why we're all alarmed, there's nothing there!"

They all began to turn around apprehensively and to rummage in the corners. Chivrya felt neither dead nor alive. "You women! women!" she said loudly. "You're the ones to be Cossacks and husbands. You'd better be off with a spindle in your hands. Perhaps one of you, may God forgive him, made a sinful noise, or the bench squeaked and you all toss about like half-wits."

This shamed our brave men and gave them courage. The relative swallowed from the flagon and continued his story.

"The Jew fainted, but the pigs on legs as long as crutches crept through the windows and revived the Jew in a jiffy with cat-o'-nine tails, forcing him to dance higher than this beam. The Jew fell on his knees, confessed everything . . . but it was impossible to return the jacket in a hurry. Some gypsy had robbed the stranger on the way and sold it to a dealer. She brought it again to the Sorochinsky Fair, but from that time on nobody bought anything from her.

"The dealer wondered and wondered and at last tumbled to it : it was probably the fault of the red jacket, not in vain did she feel something crush her when she had it on. Without much thought or delay she threw it into the fire—the demon's clothing would not burn ! 'Eh, this is the devil's present !'

"She tumbled to it at once and managed to push the jacket into the cart of a peasant, who had brought butter for sale. The fool became overjoyed, but nobody even asks for his butter. 'Eh, bad were the hands which threw in the jacket.' He grabbed an axe and hacked it to pieces : the pieces creep up to each other and the jacket is whole again ! He crossed himself, hacked it again, threw the pieces all over the place and drove away. But when the fair is on, from that time, every year the devil disguised as a pig, walks about the whole square grunting and picking up pieces of his jacket. They say that only the left sleeve is missing now. Ever since then everybody has avoided that place and it will be about ten years since the last fair was held there. The devil must have now made the assessor fr . . ."

The other part of the word died on the story-teller's lips, the window crashed noisily, the glass flew out jingling, and a terrible pig's snout pushed through, moving its eyes as if asking "and what are you doing here, good people ?"

8

Horror chained all present in the house. The relative turned to stone, his mouth agape, his eyes protruding as if they wanted to shoot out, his fingers remained motionless and spread out in the air. The tall braggart in an unconquerable fear jumped up to the ceiling and hit his head on the beam, the planks moved and the priest's son thundered to the ground.

"Ai, ai, ai," desperately screamed someone, falling heavily on a bench with terror and swinging on it with his hands and legs.

"Help !" yelled another, covering himself with his coat.

The relative, whom the second shock returned to life, crawled under the skirt of his spouse. The tall braggart crawled into the oven, in spite of the narrow opening and pulled the door to behind him. And Cherevik, as if scalded with boiling water, grabbed a pot, put it on his head instead of his cap, dashed to the door and ran through the streets like a madman, not seeing the ground under him. Only exhaustion forced him to reduce the speed of his flight. His heart was pounding like a mill wheel, and perspiration streamed from him in torrents. He was already prepared to drop to the ground in exhaustion when he seemed to hear somebody racing after him. He held his breath . . .

"The Devil ! The Devil !" he shouted almost senseless and, losing strength, fell to the ground in a faint.

"The Devil ! The Devil !" something shouted behind him and then he heard that something throw itself on him with a roar. Here his senses left him entirely and like a terrible occupant of a narrow coffin, he remained numb and motionless in the middle of the road.

9

"Can you hear it, Vlas ?" asked one of the crowd who were sleeping in the street, raising himself during the night. "Somebody mentioned the Devil near us ?"

"What business is it of mine ?" grumbled the gypsy lying near him as he stretched himself, "let him mention all his relations !"

"But he was screaming as if he was being crushed."

"A man will lie about many things in his sleep."

"As you say, but one should have a look. Give us a light !"

Another gypsy, grumbling to himself, rose to his feet, twice illuminated himself with sparks as if by lightning, blew with his lips on the tinder and with a lamp in his hands, an ordinary lamp of Little Russia consisting of a piece of a broken jar filled with mutton fat, went off lighting up the road.

"Wait ! There's something lying here. Throw some light here !"

Here a few more people joined him.

"What's lying, Vlas ?"

"Looks like two people on top of each other. Which of them is the Devil I can't make out at all !"

"And who's on top ?"

"A woman."

"Ah well, that will be the Devil!"

The laughter which followed awakened nearly the whole street.

"A woman climbed on a man, well, probably the woman knows how to travel," said one of the crowd that had gathered round.

"Look here, brothers," another said, lifting a piece of the pot, only half of which remained on Cherevik's head, "look at the cap this brave fellow has put on himself."

The increased row and laughter revived our corpses. Salopy and his wife, still stricken with fear, looked for a long time with fixed gaze filled with undiminished terror at the swarthy faces of the gypsies. By the light of the tremulous, flickering lamp they seemed in the darkness of the night like a wild crowd of gnomes, surrounded by a heavy subterranean mist.

10

The freshness of the morning wafted over the awakened town. Clouds of smoke from all the chimneys rushed to meet the rising sun. The fair filled with noise. Sheep bleated, horses neighed; the screams of geese and saleswomen again swept over the whole encampment—and frightening rumours about the red jacket, which had so intimidated the crowd in the mysterious hours of darkness, vanished with the appearance of morning.

In his kinsman's barn, covered with straw, Cherevik, yawning and stretching, lay half awake among oxen, sacks of flour and wheat and apparently had no desire to part from his dreams. Suddenly he heard a voice as familiar as that refuge of his laziness, the blessed stove-couch of his cottage or the pub of his distant relative, not more than ten steps from his threshold.

"Get up, get up!" his tender wife was shouting into his ear, pulling with all her strength at his arm.

Instead of replying, Cherevik blew out his cheeks and began to wave his hands, imitating the beating of a drum.

"Lunatic!" she screamed, averting herself from his waving hand, which nearly caught her face.

Cherevik raised himself, rubbed his eyes a little and looked around.

"May my enemy overpower me, my little pigeon, if I did not imagine your snout to be a drum, on which they forced me to beat a tattoo. The same pig's snout, about which my kinsman says . . ."

"Enough, enough of that rubbish! Go on, take the mare quickly for sale. We are a laughing stock. We came to the fair and haven't even sold a thing."

"How can I do that, dearest?" exclaimed Salopy, "they will laugh at us now."

"Go on, go! They laugh at you in any case."

"Can't you see, I haven't washed yet?" continued Cherevik, yawning and scratching his back and trying in the meantime to gain some time for his laziness.

"This is no time for you to start having such fancies! Cleanliness indeed! When was that a habit of yours? Here's a towel. Wipe your muzzle!"

Here she grabbed something crumpled up in a ball and threw it away from herself in terror. It was the red cuff of a jacket!

"Go on, attend to your business!" she repeated to her husband, summoning up courage, seeing that fear paralysed his legs and that his teeth were chattering.

"What a sale there's going to be now," he grumbled, untying the mare and leading her to the market place. "Not for nothing was my heart as heavy as if somebody had thrown a dead cow at me, when I got ready for this cursed fair, and the oxen turned home twice of their own will. Yes, and didn't we leave on Monday, too? I remember now. What a misfortune! And the cursed Devil won't calm down: he could have worn a jacket without one sleeve. But no, he won't leave good people in peace. Were I a devil, for example—which God forbid—would I roam about at night looking for cursed rags?"

Here our Cherevik's philosophising was interrupted by a thick piercing voice. In front of him stood a tall gypsy.

"What are you selling, my good man?"

The salesman looked him over from head to foot and then said calmly, without stopping or releasing the reins from his hands:—

"You can see what I'm selling!"

"Straps?" asked the gypsy, glancing at the reins in Cherevik's hands.

"Yes, straps, if the mare is a strap."

"But, the Devil take it, brother, you probably fed her on straw."

"Did you say on straw?"

Here Cherevik was about to pull the reins to show the mare and to accuse the shameless slanderer of lying, but his hand, with an unexpected lack of resistance, had struck his chin. He looked—he held a cut rein and to the reins was tied—oh, horror! his hair stood on end—a piece of the red sleeve of a jacket! He spat and crossing himself and waving his hands, ran from the unexpected present and, quicker than a boy vanished in the crowd.

11

"Catch him, catch him," some men shouted in the narrow end of the street and Cherevik felt himself grasped suddenly by strong arms.

"Tie him! He's the one who stole a mare from a good man."

"God be with you! Why are you tying me?"

"He's the one to ask! And why have you stolen a mare from the newcomer peasant Cherevik?"

"You've gone off your heads, boys! Where have you heard that a man should steal anything from himself?"

"That's an old joke! An old joke! Why were you racing along, as if Satan himself was at your heels?"

"You can't help running, when the Devil's clothing . . ."

"Ah, brother! Cheat somebody else with this tale. You'll get it from the assessor for frightening people with devilry."

"Catch him, catch him!" a cry was heard at the other end of the street. "Here's the runaway!"

Here before our Cherevik's eyes appeared his relative in a most pitiable state, with his hands tied behind his back and led by several men.

"Miracles will happen," one of them was saying. "You should have heard what this rogue says. If you only glance at his face you see thief written all over it. When he was being asked why he was running like a madman—'I put my hand in my pocket'—he says—'to get some snuff and instead of the snuffbox I dragged out a piece of the Devil's jacket, from which flashed out red fire,' and he took to his heels."

"So that's what it is, is it? Two birds of one feather. Tie them both together."

12

"Perhaps, brother, you really stole something?" asked Cherevik, lying tied with his kinsman under a straw tent.

"You too, brother! May my hands and feet rot off, if I've ever stolen anything, except perhaps sour cream dumplings from my mother, and then I was only ten years old."

"Why then, friend, have we been so accursed? It's not so bad for you. They accuse you at least of stealing from someone else. But why should I, miserable one, be so unjustly accused of stealing the mare from myself ? Probably, brother, it was written in the books for us not to have any luck !"

"Woe to us, poor orphans !"

Here both relatives began to sob loudly.

"What's the matter with you, Salopy," said Grizko, who had entered at that moment. "Who has tied you up ?"

"Ah ! Golopupenko, Golopupenko !" shouted Salopy with delight. "Here, kinsman, that's the same fellow, I was talking to you about. Ach, dear friend ! May God strike me dead here and now, if he didn't gulp down a mugful of drink bigger than your head, without even turning a hair."

"Why then, brother, haven't you honoured such a nice chap ?"

"As you see," continued Cherevik, turning to Grizko, "God has punished me probably for the wrong I've done you. Forgive me, good fellow. By God, I'd be glad to do anything for you . . . Just command me . . . There's a devil in the old woman."

"I'm not spiteful, Salopy ! If you wish I'll free you !"

Here he winked at the young men and the same ones who had been guarding the peasant rushed to untie him.

"For this do what you ought to do : arrange a wedding ! And let's celebrate so that feet will ache for a whole year from dancing the kopak."

"All right, that's fine," said Salopy, striking hands with him. "I've become as gay now, as if my old woman had been stolen from me ! Don't want to think—is it good or bad—we'll have a wedding to-day, and let everything be forgotten."

"Don't forget then, Salopy, I'll be in your place in an hour, and now off you go home. Buyers are waiting for your mare and wheat."

"What, has the mare been found ?"

"It has."

Cherevik stood still with joy, looking at the departing Grizko.

"What about it, Grizko, have we done badly ?" said the tall gypsy to the hurrying youth. "Are the oxen mine now ?"

"Yours ! Yours !"

13

Alone in the house, Paraska fell into deep thought, resting her pretty chin on her elbow. Many dreams floated around her fair head. A fleeting smile would suddenly touch her red

lips and some happy thought raise her dark eyelashes, or a cloud of thoughtfulness cause them to drop over her hazel brown eyes.

"And what if it does not happen as he said?" she whispered with an expression of doubt on her face. "What if they will not give me to him? If . . . No, no, it will not be! My step-mother does everything that comes into her head. Can't I do whatever comes into mine? I too am stubborn enough for that. And how good he is! How beautifully his black eyes burn! How lovingly he says 'Paraska, little pigeon!' How his white jacket suits him! If he only had a more colourful belt! But, of course, I shall weave him one, when we move into our new house. Can't think of it without joy!" she continued, taking out from the bosom of her dress a small mirror in a red paper frame purchased by her at the fair, and looking into it with secret pleasure. "Then, if I ever meet her, I won't even bow to her, whatever happens, even if she bursts. No, step-mother dear, you've finished beating your step-daughter. Sand will sooner grow on stone or the oak tree bend to the river like a willow, than that I will bow before you. But I've quite forgotten—let's try on the head-dress, although it's step-mother's. How will it suit me?"

Here she got up holding the mirror in her hands, bent towards it and cautiously walked as if afraid to fall, seeing in the mirror instead of the floor beneath, the ceiling with the planks under it, from which the priest's son had recently tumbled, and the shelves crammed with jars.

..."Am I a child after all," she then exclaimed laughing, "that I'm afraid to put my feet down?"

And she began to stamp her feet—the longer the braver and at last her left arm slid down and was on her waist akimbo, and she began to dance, tapping her heels, holding the mirror before her and humming her favourite tune.

Green leaves
Spread low,
My dear dark-browed,
Come near.
Green leaves,
Spread lower,
And you dear dark-browed
Come nearer.

Some time before, Cherevik had glanced through the door and, seeing his daughter dance before a mirror, stopped to look at her. He looked for a long time, laughing at the girl's strange mood, who, engrossed in her thoughts, did not notice anything, but when he heard the familiar sounds of the song, his muscles began to move and, proudly putting his hands to his hips, he stepped forward and began to dance, forgetting all his business affairs. The kinsman's loud laughter startled them both.

"That's good, father and daughter have started the wedding ! Come on, the bridegroom has arrived."

Hearing the last words, Paraska blushed redder than the red ribbon tied around her head, and the irresponsible father remembered why he had come home.

"Well, daughter, let's hurry," he said, looking nervously in all directions. "Chivrya, overjoyed that I sold the mare, ran out to buy some skirts and cloth. That's why it's necessary to finish everything before she comes back."

Hardly had Paraska crossed the threshold, when she felt herself lifted in the arms of the young man in the white jacket, who had been waiting for her in the street with a crowd of people.

"God bless you," said Cherevik, putting their hands together. "Let them live as they garlands weave."

Here a noise was heard in the crowd.

"I'd rather burst than allow this !" shouted Salopy's wife, but she was pushed back by the laughing crowd.

"Don't feel mad, don't feel mad, wife," said Cherevik coolly, seeing that a pair of hefty gypsies had taken possession of her hands. "What's done is done, I don't like changes."

No, no, it shall not be !" shouted Chivrya, but nobody listened to her. Several young people surrounded the young pair and formed an impenetrable dancing wall around them.

A strange inexplicable feeling would have filled the spectator at the sight of how at one stroke of the bow of the musician in a rough grey jacket and with a long twisted moustache, everything was spontaneously transformed into a harmonious whole. People with morose faces, which had seemingly never known a smile, tapped their feet and jerked their shoulders. Everything whirled round, everyone danced. But even stranger and more inexplicable would be the feeling roused in his heart at the sight of shrunken old women, whose ancient faces were marked with the indifference of the grave, dancing shoulder to shoulder with young, laughing, living humanity. Carefree ! With none of the gaiety of youth, without a spark of emotion, only alchohol like the mechanism of a lifeless automaton can turn them into a semblance of human being ;

yet they rocked their heads wordlessly as if intoxicated, and hopped with the gay crowd, without even turning their eyes towards the young couple.

The thunder, laughter, songs, grew quieter and quieter. The fiddler's bow was dying, getting weaker and loosing indistinct sounds in the emptiness of the air. Some stamping was still heard in the distance, somehow reminiscent of the murmur of the distant sea and soon all was empty and silent.

Does not thus joy too, that lovely and fickle guest, fly away from us and a lonely sound try in vain to express gaiety? In its own echo it hears sadness and solitude and wildly listens to it. Do not thus lose themselves in the world the frolicsome friends of our turbulent and carefree youth, singly, one by one, and at last leave one old brother of theirs behind? Lonely is he who lingers on. And heavy and sad grows his heart and there is nothing to relieve it.

Christmas Eve

THE last day before Christmas had passed. Wintry lucid night had arrived. The stars looked out. The stately moon rose in the sky to shine for good people and the whole world, so that everyone might be gay and sing carols praising Christ. The frost was sharper than in the morning, but everything was so quiet that its crunching under the boot could be heard half a verst away. No gathering of young men yet appeared beneath the windows of the houses. Only the moon peeped into them stealthily, as if tempting the girls to hurry with their dressing up and run out on to the creaking snow.

From the chimney of one house a column of smoke arose and spread in a cloud over the sky and with the smoke rose a witch riding on a broomstick. If the assessor from Sorochinsky had been passing at the time, driven by all his three horses, wearing his Lancer-like cap with a sheepskin band, and his blue coat lined with sheepskin, with his whip devised by the devil which he uses to urge on his driver, then he would surely have noticed her. For there is not a witch in the whole world that can escape from the Sorochinsky assessor. He can remember the number of piglets the peasant woman's pig delivered, how much linen lies in her trunk and exactly what piece of his clothing or of his household goods a citizen will pawn in the tavern on Sunday. But the Sorochinsky assessor was not travelling by and, after all, what business of his are strangers—he has his own district.

Meanwhile, the witch had risen so high, that she flashed by above like a mere black speck. But wherever the black speck appeared there the stars, one after the other, disappeared from the sky. Soon the witch had collected a sleeve full of them. Three or four still sparkled. Suddenly, from the opposite direction, another speck appeared. It grew, began to expand and was no longer a speck. A shortsighted man, even had he put on his nose the wheels of the commissar's carriage instead of spectacles, still could not have discerned what it was. In front it looked exactly like a German. The tip of its small narrow snout, which turned about incessantly sniffing everything it came across, was round like a pig's. Its legs were so thin that, if the Mayor of Jareskovsh had possessed such, he would have broken them during the first "kazachok." On the other hand, from behind, it looked quite like a district lawyer in uniform, its hanging tail being as sharp and long as the flaps of the modern uniform. It was perhaps only by the goatlike beard under its snout and the smallish horns sticking out of its head and the fact that the whole of it was not whiter than a chimney sweep, that one could see it was neither a German nor a district lawyer, but just a devil with one night left to roam the wide world, instructing good people in sin. To-morrow, when the first bells peel the morning service, he will tuck in his tail and, without looking back, run straight into his den.

Meanwhile the Devil stealthily drew up to the moon and had already stretched out his hand to seize it, when he suddenly jerked it back as if burnt. Sucking his fingers, he shook his leg and ran to it from the other side and again jumped away withdrawing his hand. But, despite his failures, the sly Devil did not cease his pranks. Running up to it, he suddenly grasped the moon with both hands. Grimacing and blowing, he kept throwing it from one hand to the other like a peasant who has taken a live ember with his bare hands for his pipe. Finally, he quickly hid it in his pocket and ran on as if nothing had happened.

Nobody in Dikanka heard how the Devil stole the moon. It is true that the district scribe, when leaving the pub on all fours, saw the moon dancing in the sky for no apparent reason and tried, on his oath, to convince the whole village of what he saw. But the villagers shook their heads and even made fun of him.

And why did the Devil embark on such lawless business? This was the reason. He knew that the rich Cossack, Chub, had been invited by the Deacon to a party after the Mass for the dead, which would be attended by the Mayor, a relation of the Deacon (a bishop's chorister who had arrived in a blue jacket and could sing the lowest bass), the Cossack, Sverbiguz, and somebody else. There, in addition, to the kutya*, would be mulled wine, vodka distilled with saffron and a multitude

*A dish made of barley or rice with raisins, and eaten after the Mass for the dead.

of various edibles. Meanwhile, Chub's daughter, the prettiest girl in the village, would remain at home, and to her would probably go the blacksmith, a very muscular and powerful young man who was more odious to the Devil than the sermons of Father Kondrat. In his spare time the blacksmith engaged in painting and was famous as the best painter in the whole neighbourhood. L . . . ko himself, the Captain of a hundred Cossacks, who was alive at that time, had called him to Poltava expressly to paint the deal fence near his house. All the basins from which the Cossacks of Dikanka gulped their borsch, were painted by the blacksmith.

He was a godfearing man and often drew pictures of the saints, and, even now, his evangelist Luke can be found in the Church of T . . . The triumph of his art, however, was a picture painted on the church wall in the main entrance. In that he had depicted Saint Peter on Doomsday, with keys in his hands, evicting the evil spirit from hell. The frightened Devil was tossing in all directions, having a presentiment of his perdition, and sinners, released from imprisonment, were thrashing him and chasing him with whips and sticks and anything else they could get hold of. When the painter was labouring over this picture, painting it on a large wooden board, the Devil had tried with everything in his power to hinder him. He invisibly pushed the painter's hand and, raising cinders from the furnace of the smithy, scattered them over the picture, but, despite everything, the work was finished and the board carried into the church and fixed to the wall of the entrance. From that time on the Devil swore to take vengeance on the blacksmith.

Only one night remained for him to roam the wide world, but, during that night, he was seeking somehow to avenge his wrath on the blacksmith. That was why he resolved to steal the moon. He knew that old Chub was lazy and disinclined to move, that his house was not too near to the Deacon's, that the road stretched behind the village past the mills and the graveyard and wound round a ravine. On a moonlit night mulled wine and vodka distilled with saffron might have tempted Chub, but, in complete darkness, hardly anyone would manage to drag him from the stove and tempt him out of the house. And the blacksmith, who had been on bad terms with Chub for a long time, would never dare, despite his strength, to visit Chub's daughter in his presence.

Indeed, as soon as the Devil had hidden the moon in his pocket, it at once became so dark all over the world that few men could have found their way to the pub, let alone to the Deacon's. The witch, finding herself suddenly in the dark screamed out. At this the Devil drew up alongside, fawning, caught her arm and began to whisper into her ear the things usually whispered to all the feminine species.

Strangely is our world arranged. All living things strive to imitate and copy each other. In the past, in Mirgorod, only the Judge and perhaps the town Bailiff would walk in winter wearing sheepskin coats covered with cloth. All the minor officials wore them simply bare. But now the Assessor and other officials cover themselves with new lambskin coats with a cloth finish. The Chancery clerk and the district scribe, about three years ago, bought some blue nankeen at six griven an arshin.* The sexton made himself loose nankeen trousers for the summer and a waistcoat from striped worsted yarn. In short—everybody tries to rise in the world! When will people stop being vain! I would wager that many will think it strange that the Devil should try to do the same. What is most annoying is that he probably thinks himself handsome when, as far as his appearance is concerned, one is ashamed to look at him. His muzzle, as Phoma Grigorievich used to say, is an abomination of abominations. Nevertheless he too makes love!

But, in the sky and under the sky, it became so dark that nothing further could be seen of what transpired between them.

*

"Then you haven't been to the Deacon's new house yet?" Cossack Chub asked this question, as he left the threshold of his house, of a tall emaciated peasant in a short sheepskin coat, whose overgrown beard showed that the fragment of scythe, with which the peasants usually trim their beard for lack of a razor, had not touched it for more than two weeks.

"There's going to be some good drinking there," continued Chub, a grin spreading over his face, "Only we mustn't be late."

Saying this, Chub straightened out his belt, which closely embraced his overcoat, pulled his cap more firmly over his eyes and tightened his grip on his whip which frightened and menaced the troublesome dogs. But, glancing up, he stopped.

"What the Devil! Look! Look, Panas."

"What?" said his kinsman lifting up his head also.

*A length of twenty-eight inches.

"What do you mean what ? The moon's not there."

"The Devil ! You're right, there's no moon."

"That's it, there isn't," said Chub, with some annoyance at his kinsman's invariable indifference. "Doesn't mean a thing to you, probably."

"And what can I do about it ?"

"Some Devil," continued Chub, wiping his moustache with his sleeve, "had to interfere. May he, the dog, have no glass of vodka to drink in the morning ! It's as if he did it to mock us . . . I purposely looked through the window when I was sitting in the house. The night was a miracle ! The snow shining in the moonlight, everything visible, like daytime. Hardly do we leave the door and there, he might just as well have put my eyes out. May his teeth be broken on a dry oatcake !"

Chub continued to grumble and swear for a long time and in the meantime pondered what to do. He was extremely eager to chatter at the Deacon's about all sorts of nonsense, where, without any doubt, the Mayor was already sitting with the foreign bass and the tarrer Mikita, who travelled every two weeks to Poltava to auctions and who played such tricks that all the villagers held their sides with laughter. Chub could already visualise the mulled wine standing on the table. All this was enticing, true, but the darkness of the night reminded him of that laziness which is so dear to all Cossacks. How good would it be to be lying now on the stove, with his feet drawn up, calmly smoking a pipe and listening drowsily to the carols and songs of the gay young men and girls, thronging in crowds under the windows. Had he been alone, no doubt, he would have decided on the latter course, but now, for the two of them, it would not be so dull or frightening to walk in the dark night. Moreover, after all, he did not want to appear lazy or cowardly to others. Having finished swearing, he again turned to his kinsman.

"Well, then, isn't there a moon, kinsman ?"

"No."

"It's very strange, really. Give me a pinch of tobacco. Yours is nice tobacco, brother, where do you get it ?"

"Nice, my foot," answered his relative, closing his birch bark snuff box, pricked with a design : "It won't make an old hen sneeze."

"I can remember," continued Chub in the same tone, "the deceased publican Zuzulya once brought me some tobacco from Nyezhin. Ech, that was some tobacco ! That tobacco was good. Well then, brother, what shall we do? It's dark in the yard."

"Well, perhaps we'll stay at home," uttered his relative, grasping the handle of the door.

Had his kinsman not said this, then Chub would have probably decided to stay, but now something seemed to drive him to do the opposite.

"No, friend, let's go. Impossible, we've got to go!"

Having said this, he became annoyed with himself for having said it. It was very unpleasant for him to trail along on such a night, but he was consoled by the thought that it was his own deliberate decision and that he was not following anybody else's advice.

The relative, without showing on his face the slightest trace of annoyance, like a man to whom it makes absolutely no difference whether he sits at home or drags himself out of it, looked around, scratched his shoulders with the handle of his whip—and the two kinsman departed on their journey.

*

Now let us see what is happening to the beautiful daughter, who had remained alone.

Oksana was not quite seventeen, yet in almost all the world, on the other side of Dikanka as well as this side of Dikanka, there was nothing but talk about her. The young men declared unanimously that there had never been a finer girl in the village and that there never would be. Oksana knew and heard everything that was said about her, and was as temperamental as behoves a beauty. Had she worn neither petticoat nor blouse, but just a dressing gown, she would still have surpassed all other girls. The young men pursued her in crowds, but, losing patience, left the wilful beauty one by one and turned to others not so spoilt. The blacksmith alone was stubborn and did not stop trailing after her, although he, too, was dealt with not in the least better than the others.

After her father's departure, Oksana dressed herself up for a long time and preened herself before a small mirror in a pewter frame and could not admire herself enough.

"Why have people got it into their heads to praise my beauty?" she was saying, as if absentmindedly and merely for the sake of having a chat with herself, "People are lying, I'm not beautiful at all."

But the reflection in the mirror of a fresh, lively face of childlike youth with gleaming black eyes and an inexpressibly sweet smile, which burnt the soul, quickly demonstrated the contrary.

"Are my black brows and eyes then," continued the maiden, without relinquishing the mirror, "so beautiful that there are none equal to them in the world? What is good about this turned-up nose? And these cheeks? And these lips? Are my black plaits really pretty? Uch, they could be frightening in the evening: like long snakes they are coiled and twisted round my head. I can see now that I'm not beautiful at all!"

And removing the mirror a little further from herself, she exclaimed:

"No, I am beautiful! Ach, how beautiful! Wonderful! What joy I'll bring to him whose wife I shall be! How my husband will admire me! He'll forget himself with joy! He'll smother me with kisses."

"Strange girl," whispered the blacksmith who had entered quietly. "How little vanity she possesses! She stands for hours looking into the mirror and can't see enough of herself, and praises herself aloud in addition."

"Yes, boy, am I not too good for you? Look at me!" continued the pretty minx. "How gracefully I walk! My blouse is embroidered with red silk. And what ribbons are on my head! You won't see a richer braid in all your life. All these have been bought for me by my father, so that the best young man in the world shall marry me."

And smiling she turned around and saw the blacksmith. . .

She screamed and then stopped with a stern expression before him. The blacksmith became quite crestfallen. It is difficult to describe the expression on the girl's slightly tanned face. There was sternness to be seen and contempt for the confusion of the blacksmith and a faintly perceptible blush of annoyance. All this was so blended and was so indescribably lovely, that you could have kissed her a million times, which would have been the best thing to do.

"Why have you come here?" began Oksana. "Do you want me to drive you out with a spade? You're all masters at driving up to us. You'll soon ferret out when our fathers aren't at home. Oh, I know you. Tell me, is my trunk ready?"

"It will be ready, sweetheart, it will be ready after the holiday. If you only knew what pains I've taken over it.

I haven't left the smithy for two nights. Not even a parson's wife will have such a trunk. I've used iron on the ironwork, such as I didn't even use on the captain's two-wheeled cart, when I worked in Poltava. And how it will be painted ! Even if you walked the whole district on your little white feet, you wouldn't find anything like it. It will be covered with red and blue flowers. It will shine like a flame. Don't be angry with me ! Allow me at least to talk to you, at least look at you."

"Who's stopping you ? Talk and look."

With this she sat down on a bench and again glanced into the mirror and began to straighten out the plaits on her head. She looked at her neck, at her new blouse embroidered with silk. A subtle expression of self-satisfaction showed itself on her lips and her fresh cheeks and was reflected in her eyes.

"Allow me to sit next to you," said the blacksmith.

"Sit down," said Oksana, preserving on her lips and in her pleased eyes the same expression.

"Wonderful, lovely Oksana, allow me to kiss you," said the encouraged blacksmith and pressed her to him, with the intention of gleaning a kiss. But Oksana turned away her cheek as it almost touched the blacksmith's lips, and pushed him away.

"What else do you want ? When he has honey he wants a spoon as well ! Go away, your hands are harder than iron. And you smell of smoke. I should think you've stained me with your soot."

Here she held up the mirror and again began to preen herself before it.

"She doesn't love me," thought the blacksmith to himself, hanging his head. "It's all a game to her, and I stand before her like a fool and can't take my eyes off her. And I could go on standing before her and would never remove my eyes from her. Strange girl. What I'd give to find out what's on her mind. Whom she loves. But no, nobody matters to her. She admires herself, tortures me, wretched that I am, and I can't see the world through my longing. And I love her so much, as no man in the world has ever loved or will ever love."

"Is it true that your mother is a witch ?" asked Oksana and began to laugh. And the blacksmith felt that inside him everything began to laugh. This laughter seemed to echo simultaneously in his heart and in his veins and then annoyance rose in his heart, that it was not in his power to cover this lovely laughing face with kisses.

"What do I care about my mother? You are mother and father to me and everything that's dear in the world. Had the Tsar summoned me and said: "Blacksmith Vakula, ask me for the very best in my empire, I'll give it to you. I'll order you a golden smithy and you shall forge with silver hammers." I'd say to the Tsar: 'I don't want either precious stones or a golden smithy or your empire. Just give me my Oksana.'"

"So that's what you're like! But my father isn't a fool either. You'll see, if he doesn't marry your mother." Oksana said, smiling roguishly. "But the girls haven't come . . . What does it mean? It was time for carol-singing hours ago, I'm getting bored."

"Leave them alone, my beautiful."

"Certainly not. The boys will probably come with them. Then it'll become gay. I can imagine the funny stories they'll tell."

"Are you merry with them then?"

"Merrier than with you. Ah! Somebody knocked, probably the girls and the boys.

"Why should I wait any longer," the blacksmith was talking to himself. "She mocks me. I am as dear to her as a rusty horseshoe. But if it's so, then at least I won't let someone else laugh at me. If only I can find out for certain who pleases her more than me, I'll teach . . ."

A knock at the door and a loudly sounding voice in the frost: "Open up," interrupted his meditations.

"Wait, I'll open it myself," said the blacksmith and left for the hall in a fury, intending to break the ribs of the first man he came across.

The frost increased and up above it became so cold, that the Devil skipped from one hoof to another and blew on his fists, seeking somewhat to warm his freezing hands.

It is small wonder that he should freeze, who knocks around Hell day and night, which, as we know, is not so cold as our Russian winter, and where, with his night-cap on and standing before the fireplace like a real eating-house keeper, he fries sinners with the same satisfaction as a peasant woman frying sausages for Christmas.

The witch herself began to feel the cold, although she was warmly dressed. Therefore, raising her hands, she lifted up a leg and in the posture of a man sliding on skates, she descended, without moving a muscle, through the air as from a steep icy mountain and landed straight in the chimney.

The Devil departed after her in the same manner. But, as this creature is more agile than any dandy in stockings, it is no wonder that he landed on the neck of his mistress at the very entrance of the chimney, where they both found themselves in the spacious stove among the pots.

The lady-traveller quietly pushed open the stove door to see whether her son Vakula had not invited some guests into the house. Perceiving that there was nobody there except some sacks which lay in the middle of the floor, she crept out of the stove, threw off her warm peasant coat and straightened herself up, and nobody would have guessed that a minute before she had been riding on a broom.

The mother of the blacksmith Vakula was not more than forty years old. She was neither handsome nor plain. After all, it is difficult to be beautiful at her age. Nevertheless, she was so bewitching to the steadiest Cossacks (to whom, there is no harm in remarking, beauty mattered little), that she was visited by the Mayor and by the Deacon Osip Nikiforovich (of course, if the Deacon's wife was not at home) and the Cossack, Krnyo Chub, and the Cossack, Kasyan Sverbiguz. And, let it be said in her honour, she could manage them cleverly. Not one of them even dreamed that he had a rival. Both pious peasants and noblemen (as the Cossacks call themselves), who went dressed in cloak and hood to church on Sunday, or, if the weather was bad, to the pub—saw nothing amiss in calling on Solokha, eating fat curd-dumplings with sour cream and having a chat in a warm house with that talkative and attentive hostess. The noblemen, especially for that purpose, made a long detour before reaching the pub and called it dropping in on the way. And when Solokha went to church on a feast-day, wearing a nankeen blouse with a bright petticoat and over it a blue skirt, with golden tassels sewn on at the back of it, and stood near the right choir, the Deacon would be sure to begin to cough and blink involuntarily in her direction, and the Mayor would stroke his moustache, wind his tuft of hair around his ear and say to his neighbour: "Ech, that's a good woman! A devil of a woman!" Solokha bowed to everyone, and each thought that she was bowing to him alone.

But anybody who loved poking his nose into other people's business would have noticed at once that Solokha was most affable of all to the Cossack Chub. Chub was a widower. Eight cornstacks always stood before his house. Two pairs of strong oxen pushed out their heads from his wattle-barn into the street and lowed, when they saw their approaching relative—the cow, or their uncle—a fat bull. The bearded buck-goat climbed to the very roof from which he bleated in a sharp voice like a town bailiff, teased the turkeys, which strutted about the yard, and exhibited his posterior when he saw his foes—the small boys—who jeered at his beard. A lot of linen, thick overcoats and ancient Polish surcoats with golden galoons lay in Chub's trunks ; his deceased wife had been an elegant woman. In addition to poppies, cabbages and sunflowers, two rows of tobacco were sown every year in his kitchen garden.

All this Solokha thought no harm in adding to her own household and, reflecting in advance how it would be arranged when it fell into her hands, she redoubled her benevolence towards old Chub. And to prevent her son Vakula from successfully courting Chub's daughter and grabbing everything for himself—when he would probably not allow her to interfere with anything—she resorted to the usual method of all forty-year-old-widows—making mischief between Chub and the blacksmith as often as possible. It was perhaps due to these very guiles and to her shrewdness, that the old woman began to gossip about her, especially when they had drunk a little more than usual in some gay reunion, saying that Solokha was certainly a witch, that the young man Kizyakolupenko had seen a tail behind her back no bigger than a woman's spindle, that two Thursdays ago she had run across the road in the shape of a black cat, that a pig had once rushed up to the priest's wife, crowed like a cockerel, put Father Kondrat's cap on its head and had run away.

It so happened that when the old women were gossiping about it, a cowherd, Timish Korostyovi, arrived. He did not refrain from mentioning how in summer, before the very fast of St. Peter, when he lay down to sleep in the cattle shed, having propped up his head with straw, he had with his own eyes seen the witch, with her hair falling loose over her shoulders and wearing only her night shirt, begin to milk the cows. He could not move—he was so bewitched—and she greased his lips with something so horrible, that he kept spitting the whole of the next day. All this, however, is somewhat dubious, for only the Sorochinsky Assessor can see a witch. And therefore all the leading Cossacks waved their hands when they heard such talk. "The bitches are lying," was their usual comment.

Having crept out of the stove and straightened herself out, Solokha, as behoves a good housewife, began to tidy up and put everything in its place, but she did not touch the sacks. "Vakula brought these in, he can carry them out."

In the meantime the Devil, when he was still in the process of flying into the chimney, somehow happened to turn around and see Chub arm in arm with his relative, when they were still a long way from the house. He immediately flew out of the stove, ran across their path and began to dig up heaps of frozen snow from all directions. A snowstorm arose. The air turned white. The snow tossed about backwards and forwards like a net and threatened to plaster the eyes, mouths and ears of the pedestrians. The Devil flew back again into the chimney, firmly convinced that Chub and his relative would turn back, would find the blacksmith and would probably deal with him in such a manner, that for a long time he would not have the strength to take the paint brush in his hands and paint insulting caricatures.

Indeed, hardly had the snowstorm risen and the wind begun to sting and hurt his eyes, than Chub expressed repentance and pulling his hood deeper over his head, treated himself, the Devil and his relative to some swearing. As a matter of fact this annoyance was only simulated. Chub was very pleased with the raging snowstorm. The distance to the Deacon's remained eight times as long as they had walked. The travellers turned back. The wind blew at the back of their heads, but nothing was visible through the whirling snow.

"Wait, brother! It seems we aren't going in the right direction," said Chub stepping aside a little, "I can't see a single house. Ech, what a snowstorm! You, friend, turn a little to the side—see if you can't find the road, and in the meantime I'll look here. What demon drove me to roam about in such a snowstorm? Don't forget to shout when you find the road. Ech, what a lot of snow the Devil has blown into my eyes."

But the road was not to be seen. The relative, having walked off to the side, wandered back and fro in his high boots and at last stumbled straight on to the pub. This find so overjoyed him that he forgot everything and, shaking off the snow from himself, without worrying in the slightest about his friend who had remained in the street, he entered the hall.

In the meantime, it seemed to Chub that he had found the road. He stopped and began to shout with all his might, but seeing that his relative did not appear, decided to walk on alone. Some time later he saw his house. Snow drifts were lying near it and on its roof. Clapping his hands which froze in the cold, he began to knock at the door and to shout in a commanding voice to his daughter to open it.

"What d'you want ?" sternly shouted the blacksmith who had come out.

Chub, recognising the blacksmith's voice, stepped back a little.

"Ech no, that's not my house," he said to himself, "the blacksmith wouldn't wander into my house. Yet, if you look at it closely, it isn't the blacksmith's either. Whose house can it be ? There ! I haven't recognised it ! It's the cripple Levchenko's house, who recently married a young wife. His is the only house like mine. That's why it seemed a little strange to me at first to find I'd arrived home so quickly. But Levchenko is sitting now at the Deacon's, that I do know. Why, then the blacksmith ? E, hehehe ! He goes to his young wife. That's what it is ! That's good ! . . . Now I've understood everything."

"Who are you and why do you barge into people's houses ?" said the blacksmith more sternly than before and came nearer.

"No, shan't tell him who I am," thought Chub, "for all I know he'll give me a beating, the accursed monster !" And changing his voice he answered :

"It's me, good man ! I came to you to sing a few carols for your entertainment."

"Go to hell with your carol singing !" angrily shouted Vakula. "What are you standing about for ? D'you hear ? Get out of my sight immediately !"

Chub himself had this prudent intention, but it seemed insulting to him to be forced to obey the blacksmith's orders As if some evil spirit pushed him and forced him to bid defiance.

"I don't see what you're shouting so much about !" he said in the same voice, "I want to sing carols and that's all there is to it."

"Ehe ! I see that words have no effect on you !"

Chub felt a very painful blow on his shoulder following these words.

"I see, you're beginning to fight already," he said, stepping back a little.

"Go, away with you," shouted the blacksmith, presenting Chub with another blow.

"What's the matter with you ?" said Chub in a voice which expressed pain, annoyance and fear. "I see, you want to fight seriously and to hurt too."

"Go, go away !" shouted the blacksmith and slammed the door.

"What cheek," Chub said, when he remained alone in the street. "You try and get nearer ! See, what he's like. Who does he think he is ? You think I won't start proceedings in court. No, my good man, I certainly will and I'll go straight to the Commissioner. I'll show you, although you're a blacksmith and a painter. At any rate, I'd like to have a look at my back and shoulders, I bet they're black and blue. They should be. He's battered me, the son of an enemy. It's a pity it's cold, and I don't feel like throwing off my overcoat. You wait, you Devil's blacksmith. May the Devil smash you and your smithy. You'll do some coughing then ! You damned gallows-bird ! Still, he's not at home now. I bet Solokha's sitting there alone. Ahem ! Not far from here, after all, I might go there. Nobody will surprise us at this time. May be, may be one could also . . . Ach, how painfully that blasted blacksmith has beaten me."

Chub scratched his back and departed in the opposite direction. The pleasure which he anticipated from the meeting with Solokha somewhat alleviated his pain and made hardly noticeable even the frost, which raged in the streets unallayed by the whistle of the blizzard. At times an almost sugary smile appeared on his face. His beard and moustache were lathered with snow by the storm more thoroughly than by any barber who tyranically grasps his victim by the nose. If the snow had not obliterated everything, we should have long continued to see how Chub would stop to scratch his back and mutter : "He hit me hard the accursed blacksmith," and again depart on his way.

As the agile dandy, with the tail and goat-like beard, flew out of the chimney and then back again, the pouch, which hung tied to his side and in which he had hidden the stolen moon, somehow accidentally became caught on the stove. It fell open and the moon, taking the opportunity, flew out through the chimney of Solokha's house and gracefully rose in the sky. Everything became light again. The blizzard vanished completely. The snow began to sparkle like a wide

D

silvery meadow and became studded with crystal stars. The frost seemed to become less acute. Crowds of young men and girls appeared with sacks. Songs began to resound and there were few houses before which carol singers were not crowding.

How wonderfully the moon shines! It is difficult to describe how good it is on such a night to jostle among a crowd of laughing, singing girls and young men, only too ready to joke and play tricks, that only such a gaily smiling night can inspire. It is warm in the peasant's tight fitting overcoat; the cheeks burn even more vividly from the frost and the Devil himself is behind, pushing one on to frolics.

A crowd of girls with sacks broke into Chub's house and surrounded Oksana. Shouting, laughter and talking deafened the blacksmith. All of them vied with each other in telling the beautiful girl something new. They emptied the sacks and boasted of the small flat bread loaves, the sausages and dumplings, quite a considerable amount of which they had managed to collect for their carol singing. Oksana seemed full of happiness and joy, chatted to one and to another and laughed without stopping.

With a mixture of annoyance and envy the blacksmith gazed on this gaiety and this time cursed carol singing, although he used to be passionately fond of it.

"Ah, Odarka," said the gay beauty, turning to one of the girls: "You've new shoes on. Ach, how pretty they are, and with gold. You're lucky, Odarka, you have a man who buys you everything, and I have nobody who could get me such nice shoes."

"Don't worry, my darling Oksana," exclaimed the blacksmith, "I'll get you shoes that even a nobleman's daughter rarely wears."

"You?" said Oksana, and quickly looked at him haughtily. "I'd like to see where you'd get shoes, that I would put on my feet, unless you bring me the shoes the Empress is wearing."

"See, what she's got into her mind," the crowd of girls shouted with laughter.

"Yes," continued the beauty proudly, "you're all witnesses; if the blacksmith Vakula brings me the shoes which the Empress is wearing, then here is my word that I'll marry him immediately."

The girls led the capricious beauty away with them.

"Laugh, laugh," said the blacksmith leaving after them. "I, too, laugh at myself! I think and can't make out where my brains have got to. She doesn't love me—well, I'll leave her alone. As if there were only one Oksana in the world. Thank God, there are many good girls beside her in the village. And what is Oksana? She'll never make a good housewife; she's only good at dressing up. No, it's enough. It's time to stop playing the fool."

But just when the blacksmith intended to be resolute, some evil spirit carried past him Oksana's image, which said mockingly: "Get me, blacksmith, the Empress's shoes and I'll marry you." He became agitated and thought only about Oksana and her alone.

The crowds of carol singers, the men separate from the girls, hurried from one street into another but the blacksmith walked and saw nothing and did not take any part in these gaieties which once he used to love more than any others.

*

In the meantime, the Devil's courting of Solokha became downright serious. He kissed her hand with the same mannerisms with which the Assessor pays court to the priest's wife. He put his hand on his heart, sighed and said frankly that if she would not consent to gratify his passion and, as was usual, reward it, then he was ready to do anything; throw himself into the water, and despatch his soul straight to Hell.

Solokha was not so cruel. Moreover, as is known, he played into her hands. Although she indeed liked to see a crowd dangling after her and was seldom without any visitors, she had expected to spend that evening alone, as all the eminent inhabitants of the village had been invited to the dinner at the Deacon's after the Mass for the dead. But everything took a different course.

Hardly had the Devil confronted her with his demands, than suddenly a knocking and the voice of the stout Mayor were heard at the door. Solocka ran to open the door, and the agile Devil climbed into a sack.

The Mayor shook off the snow from his hood and, having accepted from Solokha's hands a glass of vodka and drunk it, told her that he did not go to the Deacon's as a snowstorm had risen and, seeing a light in her house, had called on her with the intention of spending the evening with her.

Hardly had the Mayor managed to say this, than a knock was heard at the door and the Deacon's voice.

"Hide me somewhere," whispered the Mayor. "I shouldn't like to meet the Deacon now."

Solokha thought for a long time where to hide such a thick-set guest. Finally she chose the biggest sack of coal. She emptied the coal into the tub, and the stout Mayor, with his moustache, head and hood complete, crept into the sack.

The Deacon entered, groaning a little and rubbing his hands, and said that nobody had called on him and that he was extremely pleased with this opportunity of having a drink with her and that he had not been frightened by the snow-storm. Then he drew nearer to her, coughed, smiled at her, touched her bare stout arm with his long fingers, and said with a sly and self-satisfied air:

"And what have we here, magnificent Solokha?" and having said that, jumped back a little.

"What do you mean what? It's a hand, Osip Nikiforovich," answered Solokha.

"Ahem! A hand! He-he-he!" said the Deacon, heartily satisfied with this beginning, and strutted across the room.

"And what is this, dearest Solokha?" he said with the same expression, again drawing near, and touched her neck lightly with his hand and jumped back in the same manner.

"As if you didn't see, Osip Nikiforovich," answered Solokha. "It's my neck, and on my neck is a necklace."

"Ahem! On your neck is a necklace! He-he-he," and the Deacon again strutted across the room rubbing his hands.

"And what is this, incomparable Solokha? . . ."

Heaven knows what the lascivious Deacon would have touched next with his long fingers, but suddenly a knock was heard at the door and Cossack Chub's voice.

"Ach, Heavens, a stranger!" shouted the Deacon in his fright. "God in Heaven, if they find a person of my calling here! It will reach Father Kondrat's ears . . ."

But the Deacon's apprehension were of a different kind. He was even more anxious that his better half should not find out, for she, even without this additional pretext, had thinned his thick mop of hair with her terrible hand.

"For God's sake, virtuous Solokha," he said, all his body trembling, "they are knocking, by God, they're knocking! Och, hide me somewhere."

Solokha emptied the coal from another sack into the tub and the Deacon, whose body was not too bulky, crept into it and sat down at the very bottom of it, so that one could have poured about half a sackful of coal on top of him.

"Hallo, Solokha," said Chub entering the house," perhaps you didn't expect me, eh? You really didn't expect me?

Perhaps I've intruded? . . ." continued Chub, his face bearing a gay and significant expression, which indicated that his clumsy brain was working and preparing to release some laboured and intricate witticism. "Perhaps you've been playing around with somebody here! . . . Perhaps you've hidden somebody, what?" and, enchanted by his own remarks, Chub began to laugh, inwardly triumphant that he was the only one to enjoy Solokha's benevolence.

"Well, Solokha, now let me have some vodka to drink. I think my throat has frozen in the cursed frost. Why did God have to send such a night before Christmas! How it started, d'you hear, Solokha, how it started . . . Ek, my hands are numbed; can't open my coat! How the blizzard started . . ."

"Open up!" A voice sounded in the street, accompanied by a push at the door.

"Somebody's knocking," said Chub and stopped.

"Open up!" came a shout louder than before.

"That's the blacksmith," said Chub grabbing his hood, "d'you hear, Solokha, put me where you like. Nothing in the world will make me appear before that accursed monster, the Devil's son. May a pimple, as big as a hayrick, spring up under both his eyes."

Solokha, who had become frightened, rushed around herself like a person possessed and, losing her wits, made a sign to Chub to creep into the same sack in which the Deacon was already sitting. The poor Deacon did not even dare to express his pain by coughing or groaning, when the heavy peasant sat down almost on his head and placed his long frostbitten boots on both sides of his temples.

The blacksmith entered without saying a word or taking off his cap, and almost dropped on the bench. It was apparent that he was extremely out of sorts.

Just as Solokha was closing the door behind him, somebody knocked again. This was Cossack Sverbiguz. He could not be hidden in a sack, because no such sack could be found anywhere. He was heavier in body than the Mayor himself and of greater height than Chub's relative. Therefore Solokha led him into the kitchen garden to listen to everything he wanted to impart to her. .

The blacksmith absentmindedly surveyed the corners of his house, listening from time to time to the songs of the carol singers, which resounded in the village from far away. At last his eyes fell on the sacks.

"Why are these sacks lying here? They should have been

taken away a long time ago. This love affair has made me quite crazy. It's a holyday to-morrow and all sorts of rubbish is still lying in the house. I'll carry them out to the smithy."

The blacksmith crouched down before the tremendous sacks, tied them more firmly and prepared to heave them on his shoulders. But it was obvious that his thoughts wandered God knows where, otherwise he would have heard how Chub began to hiss, when the hair on his head was twisted by the string which tied the sack, and how the corpulent Mayor began to hiccup quite distinctly.

"Won't this wretched Oksana really be driven out of my head ?" said the blacksmith. "I don't want to think about her, but I still do, and, as if on purpose, only about her. Why do these thoughts steal into my head against my will ? What the devil ? The sacks seem to have become heavier than before ! Something's probably been put into them besides the coal. I'm a fool ! I've forgotten that everything seems heavier to me now. Before, I used to be able to bend and unbend a brass coin with one hand and a horseshoe with the other, and now I can't lift a few sacks of coal. Soon I'll tumble down at a whiff of the wind . . . No !" he exclaimed after a silence, having taken courage, "what a woman I am ! I shan't allow anybody to laugh at me ! Even if there were ten such sacks—I'll lift them all."

And bravely he loaded his shoulders with the sacks, which two strong men could not have carried.

"I'll take this one too," he continued, lifting the small one at the bottom of which the Devil lay curled up. "I think I put some of my tools in here." Then he left the house whistling a song :

'I won't be bothered with a wife.'

*

Louder and louder echoed songs, laughter and shouting in the streets. The crowds of jostling people were increased by the arrivals from neighbouring villages. The young men played pranks and ran wild to their hearts' content. Often, in between carol singing, some gay song would be heard which one of the young Cossacks had managed to compose on the spot. Laughter would reward the composer. Small windows would be pushed open and an emaciated old woman's hand (these old women and sedate fathers were the only ones to remain indoors) would emerge, holding a sausage or a piece of pastry. The young men and the girls vied with each other in holding out the sacks and catching the booty. In one spot the young men appeared from all sides and surrounded a crowd of girls. Noise and shouting arose. One threw snowballs at them, another snatched away a sack with a variety of edibles in it. In another spot the girls would be catching a young man, and tripping him up so that he would fly headlong to the ground with his sack. They seemed prepared to spend the whole night in making merry. And the night, as if especially for that purpose, shone wonderfully. The moonlight seemed even brighter through the lustre of the snow.

The blacksmith stopped with his sacks. He seemed to hear Oksana's voice and her delicate laughter in the crowd of girls. All his nerves became alert. Throwing the sacks to the ground, so that the Deacon, who was at the bottom, groaned from the blow and the Mayor hiccupped quite audibly, the blacksmith with the small sack still on his shoulders, joined the crowd of young men who followed the crowd of girls, among whom he seemed to have heard Oksana's voice.

"Yes, it's her ! She stands like a queen and her black eyes are blazing. A handsome man is telling her something, probably something funny, for she is laughing. But she's always laughing."

As if not of his own free will, without knowing how, he elbowed his way through the crowd and stood beside her.

"Ah, Vakula, you're here ! Hallo !" said the beauty with that smile, which almost drove Vakula mad. "Well, have you got much for your carol singing ? Ech, but your sack's small ! Have you got the shoes which the Empress wears ? Get the shoes and I'll marry you." And laughing she ran away with the crowd of girls.

The blacksmith stood as if rooted to the ground.

'No, I can't, I've no more strength left," he said at last. "But my God, why is she so devilishly beautiful ? Her glance and talk, and everything, well, it just sets me on fire, just does . . . No, it's beyond me to master it. It's time to put an end to everything. May my soul perish ! I'll drown myself in the mill pond and disappear."

With resolute steps he went forward, caught up with the crowd of girls, came up alongside Oksana and said in a firm voice :

"Good bye, Oksana. Look for whatever bridegroom you want. Fool whoever you want, but you won't see me again in this world."

The beauty seemed to be surprised, wanted to say something, but the blacksmith waved his hand and ran away.

"Where are you off to, Vakula ?" shouted the young men, seeing the blacksmith begin to run.

"Good-bye, brothers," shouted the blacksmith in reply: "God willing, we'll meet in the next world, but in this one we're not meant to be merry together. Good-bye! Don't bear me any ill-will! Tell Father Kondrat that he should have a Mass said for my sinful soul. I haven't painted the candles for the icons of Christ and the Holy Mother, sinner that I am, because of worldly occupations. All the things found in my big trunk are for the church. Good-bye."

Having said this, the blacksmith again began to run with the sack on his back.

"He's gone mad," said the young men.

"Lost soul," piously mumbled an old woman who passed by, "I'll have to go and tell how the blacksmith hanged himself."

*

In the meantime Vakula, having run through several streets, stopped to get some breath.

"Really, where am I running to?" he thought, "as if everything was lost? I'll try one more remedy, I'll go to the Cossack from Zaporozhye*, Bigbelly Paciuk. They say he knows all the devils and can do whatever comes into his head. I'll go. My soul will be lost in any case."

At this the Devil, who had been lying without moving for a long time, began to jump in the sack with joy, but the blacksmith decided that he had somehow caught at the sack with his hand and caused this movement. He hit the sack with his big fist, shook it with his shoulders and departed to Bigbelly Paciuk.

This Bigbelly Paciuk had indeed been a Cossack a long time ago. Whether he had been cashiered or had run away himself from Zaporozhye, nobody knew. For a long time, for ten years or perhaps fifteen, he had been living in Dikanka. At first he lived like a real Cossack from Zaporozhye, did no work whatever, slept three-quarters of the day, ate enough for six haymakers and drank almost a whole bucketful at one sitting. There was room for it, by the way, as Paciuk, despite his smallish stature, was quite massive in circumference. Moreover, the loose trousers, which he wore, were so wide that, however long his steps, his feet could not be seen and he looked like a distillery vat moving in the street. Perhaps this was why he was nicknamed Bigbelly. Not many

* Country beyond the Dnieper rapids.

weeks had passed after his arrival in the village, before everybody had found out that he was a sorcerer. If anybody had anything wrong with him, he immediately called in Paciuk. And all Paciuk had to do was to whisper several words and the illness would be completely remedied. If it so happened that a hungry nobleman choked with a fishbone, Paciuk knew exactly how to hit his back so skilfully with his fist, that the bone would depart where it belonged, without causing the noble throat any harm. Lately he had seldom been seen anywhere. It was possibly caused by laziness, and perhaps also by the fact that it had become more difficult every year for him to squeeze himself out through the door. Consequently the villagers had to come to him if they had need of him.

The blacksmith opened the door, not without trepidation, and saw Paciuk sitting on the floor in the Turkish fashion before a smallish tub, on which stood a basin with small dumplings. This basin was placed apparently intentionally on a level with his mouth. Without moving a single finger, he slightly bent his head to the basin and sipped the gravy, seizing the dumplings from time to time with his teeth.

"This one," thought Vakula, "is even lazier than Chub, who at least eats with a spoon, while this one doesn't even want to raise his hand."

Paciuk must certainly have been very engrossed in the dumplings, because it appeared that he had not noticed the arrival of the blacksmith, who had hardly crossed the threshold before he made him an extremely low bow.

"I've come to beseech your aid, Paciuk," said Vakula bowing again.

Fat Paciuk raised his head and again began to eat the dumplings.

"Don't be angry with me, they say . . ." said the blacksmith, gathering courage, "I'm not talking for the sake of insulting you—that you're a distant relation of the Devil."

Having uttered these words Vakula became frightened and thought that he had expressed himself too bluntly and had not sufficiently veiled the insulting words. Expecting that Paciuk would grab the tub together with the basin and hurl it straight at his head, he stepped aside a little and covered himself with his sleeve, so that the hot gravy from the dumplings should not bespatter his face.

But Paciuk looked up and again began to eat the dumplings.

The blacksmith, feeling encouraged, decided to continue:

"I came to you, Paciuk. May God grant you everything,

goods and chattels in abundance, bread in proportion! (The blacksmith sometimes could turn out a modern phrase; he had become accustomed to that during his stay in Poltava, when he painted the captain's deal fence): "I have to perish, sinner that I am. Nothing in the world can help me. What is to be, must be. I have to ask help from the Devil himself. So, Paciuk," the blacksmith said, observing his continued silence: "what shall I do?"

"Who needs the Devil, should go to the Devil," answered Paciuk, without raising his eyes and continuing to devour the dumplings.

"That's why I've come to you," said the blacksmith, making a low bow. "I think, apart from you, nobody in the world knows the way to him."

Paciuk, without a word, polished off the remaining dumplings.

"Help me, be kind, don't refuse," urged the blacksmith. "Whether it's pork, or sausages, buckwheat flour, or—if you like—linen, millet meal or anything else, if needs be . . . I know what's customary among decent people . . . I won't be mean. Tell me at least how, for example, I can more or less happen to hit on the right road for him."

"There is no need for him to go far, who has the Devil behind him," answered Paciuk indifferently, without changing his posture.

Vakula gazed fixedly at him, as if the explanation of these words was written on his forehead.

"What's he saying?" wordlessly asked his expression and his gaping mouth, prepared to swallow the first word like a dumpling.

But Paciuk was silent.

At this point Vakula noticed that Paciuk had neither dumplings nor tub in front of him, but instead two wooden basins stood on the floor; one filled with curd-dumplings, the other with sour cream. His thoughts and eyes involuntarily turned to these dishes.

"I wonder," he said to himself, "how Paciuk will eat the curd-dumplings. He probably won't want to bend down and it's impossible to avoid using your hands. You have to dip the curd-dumplings in the sour cream first."

He hardly had the time to think this out, when Paciuk opened his mouth wide, looked at the curd-dumplings and opened his mouth even wider. Immediately a curd-dumpling flapped out of the basin, flopped down into the sour cream, turned over on the other side, jumped up and flew straight into his mouth. Paciuk ate it and again opened his mouth wide, and a curd-dumpling entered it in the same order. He took upon himself only the hard work of chewing and swallowing.

"See, a miracle!" thought the blacksmith, opening his mouth wide in amazement and immediately perceived that a curd-dumpling was climbing into his own mouth and had already smeared it with sour cream. Pushing the curd-dumpling away he wiped his lips and began to reflect on the miracles which occur in the world and the wisdom that the evil spirit brings to man, observing at the same time that Paciuk alone could help him.

"I'll bow to him again. Perhaps he'll explain it better . . . Here, what the devil! It's a fast day and he's eating curd-dumplings, which are forbidden on fast days. What a fool I am to stand here and be infected by sin! Back I go . . ." and the devout blacksmith ran helter skelter out of the house.

But the Devil, who sat in the sack and was rejoicing in anticipation, could not bear to have such nice prey escape from his hands. As soon as the blacksmith put down the sack, he jumped out of it and sat down on his neck.

Goosepimples covered the blacksmith's skin. He became frightened and pale and did not know what to do. He was already on the point of making the sign of the cross . . . but the Devil bent his dog's snout to his right ear and said :—

"It's me, your friend. I'll do anything for a comrade and friend! I'll give you as much money as you want," he squeaked into the blacksmith's left ear.

"Oksana will be ours this very day," he whispered, turning his muzzle again to the blacksmith's right ear.

The blacksmith stood still and pondered.

"So be it," he said at last, "for such a price I'll be yours!"

The Devil clapped his hands and began to gallop with joy on the blacksmith's neck.

"Now, the blacksmith is caught," he thought to himself, "and now I'll revenge myself on you, my friend, for all your paintings and lies which malign us Devils. What will my comrades say now, when they find out that the most pious man in the whole village is in my hands?"

Here the Devil began to laugh with joy at the thought of how he would tease all the long-tailed tribe of hell and how enraged would be the Devil with the limp, who thought himself the best of them all at fibbing.

"Well, Vakula," squeaked the Devil, still without climbing down from his neck as if afraid that he might run away, "you know that nothing is done without an agreement."

"I'm ready," said the blacksmith. "I heard that with you people one signs with blood. Wait then, I'll get a nail from my pocket."

Here he put his hand behind him and seized the Devil by the tail.

"See, what a jester," screamed the Devil with laughter. "Well, that's enough, leave off your pranks."

"Wait, little pigeon," shouted the blacksmith. "And how will you like this?"

As he said the last word, the blacksmith made the sign of the cross and the Devil became as quiet as a lamb.

"You wait," said the blacksmith, dragging the Devil down to the ground by his tail, "I'll teach you how to entice good people and honest Christians to sin."

Here the blacksmith jumped on top of him and raised his hand with the intention of making the sign of the cross.

"Have mercy, Vakula," piteously groaned the Devil. "Everything you need, I'll do it all, only release my soul for repentance, don't put the terrible cross on me."

"Ah, that's a new tune you're singing, you blasted German! I know now what to do. I'll ride on you straightaway. D'you hear? And fly like a bird."

"Where to?" said the sad Devil.

"To Petersburg, straight to the Empress."

And the blacksmith became benumbed with fear, as he felt himself raised into the air.

*

Oksana stood for a long time thinking of the blacksmith's strange talk. Inwardly something was telling her that she had treated him too cruelly.

"What if he really decides on something terrible! He might! Perhaps in his grief he'll take it into his head to fall in love with someone else, and out of spite begin to call her the most beautiful girl in the village? But no, he loves me. I'm so beautiful. He won't exchange me for anything in the world, he's fooling me, pretending. Ten minutes won't pass, probably, before he comes to look at me. Perhaps I have been harsh. I'll have to let him kiss me, as if against my will. Won't he be pleased . . . !"

And the fickle beauty proceeded joking with her girl-friends.

"Wait," said one of them, "the blacksmith has forgotten his sacks. Look what terrific sacks they are. He's got more than we did for his carol singing. I should say a quarter of a sheep's been thrown in here, and there's probably no counting the sausages and the bread. Wonderful! One could stuff oneself throughout the whole of the festival."

"Are these the blacksmith's sacks?" exclaimed Oksana. "Let's quickly drag them into my house and let's have a good look at what he's put in them."

Everybody acclaimed this suggestion with laughter.

"But we can't lift them!" suddenly shouted the whole crowd, straining to move the sacks.

"Wait," said Oksana. "Let's run quickly and get the sledge and we'll carry them away in it." And the crowd ran to fetch the sledge.

The prisoners had become extremely bored sitting in the sacks, in spite of the fact that the Deacon had made quite a considerable hole for himself with his finger. If there were no people about, he might perhaps have also found some means of creeping out, but to creep out of the sack in everybody's presence, to be turned to ridicule . . . that restrained him, and he decided to wait and only groaned slightly under Chub's impolite boots.

Chub himself longed for freedom no less, feeling as he did that something lay under him, on which it was extremely awkward to sit. But as soon as he heard his daughter's decision, he calmed down and did not want to get out, reasoning that at least a hundred, or may be two hundred, steps had to be walked to his house, and having got out he would have to set himself right, button his overcoat, tie his belt—such a lot of work! Moreover, his hood had been left at Solocha's. Rather let the girls drive him up in the sledge.

But it turned out quite differently from what Chub had expected. Just as the girls ran for the sledges, his emaciated relative was leaving the pub, upset and out of sorts. The landlady would on no account take the risk of giving him drink on credit. At first he wanted to wait in the pub, hoping that some pious nobleman might arrive and treat him, but, as if on purpose, all the noblemen remained at home, like honest Christians, among their household. Reflecting on corrupt morals and on the stony heart of the Jewess who sold wine, the relative stumbled on to the sacks and stopped in amazement.

"Look at these sacks somebody has thrown down on the road," he said, looking round. "There's probably some pork in them. Somebody must have had all the luck to get such a lot of odds and ends for his carol singing. What tremendous sacks! Supposing that they're stuffed with buckwheat cakes and biscuits, even that's good. If there are only loaves of bread in them, that, too, is useful—the Jewess gives a small nip of vodka for each loaf. I'd better grab them quickly, so that nobody should see."

Here he heaved the sack containing Chub and the deacon on to his shoulders, but felt that it was too heavy.

"No, it'll be difficult to carry it alone," he mused. But there, as if one purpose, came the weaver Shapuvalenko. "Hallo, Ostap."

"Hallo," said the weaver and stopped.

"Where're you going?"

"Nowhere, I go where my legs go."

"Help me, there's a good chap, to carry the sacks. Somebody did some carol singing and then threw them in the middle of the road. We'll go fifty-fifty."

"The sacks? And what's in them, white or brown bread?"

"I think there'll be a bit of everything there."

Here they hurriedly pulled out some sticks from a wattled hedge, put the sack on them and began to carry it on their shoulders.

"Where shall we carry it then? Into the pub?" asked the weaver on the way.

"That's what I thought, but the accursed Jewess won't believe us. She'll probably think we've stolen it somewhere. In any case, I've just left the pub. Let's carry it into my house. Nobody will disturb us there; the wife's not at home."

"Are you sure she's not at home?" asked the cautious weaver.

"Thank God, we haven't lost our minds yet," said the relative, "even the Devil would not take me where she is. I think she'll be trailing around with the women till daylight."

"Who's there?" shouted the relative's wife, hearing a noise in the hall, caused by the arrival of the two friends with the sack, and opened the door of the house.

The relative was thunderstruck.

"What did I tell you," said the weaver, losing heart.

The relative's wife was a treasure of a kind not unplentiful in this wide world. Like her husband, she hardly ever sat at home. Almost her whole day was spent cringing before gossips and well-to-do old women, praising their food and eating it with a good appetite. She fought with her husband in the mornings only, because it was only then that she occasionally saw him. Their house was twice as old as the loose trousers of the district scribe; the roof in several places was without any straw. Only the remains of the wattle hedge were to be seen, because people, on leaving their houses, never took a stick for the dogs, in the hope that they would pass the relative's kitchen garden and pull out the stick they wanted from his hedge. The stove would remain unlit for three days at a time. Everything that his tender wife managed to scrounge she hid as far as she could from her husband, and often, without any authority, took away from him what he had managed to acquire. That is, if he had not succeeded in drinking it away at the pub. The relative, despite his invariable stolidity, did not care to give in to her and so almost always left the house with a pair of black eyes, while his better half would ramble off groaning, to complain to her cronies about her dissolute husband and the beatings she suffered at his hands.

One can imagine now how nonplussed were the weaver and the relative by such an unexpected apparition.

Dropping the sack on the ground, they hid it by standing in front of it and covering it with their coat tails, but it was already too late. The relative's wife, although she could see badly with her old eyes, had, nevertheless, spotted the sack.

"That's good," she said with an expression which showed a vulture's delight. "It's good that you've got so much for your carol singing. Decent people always do that . . . But no, I think you've picked it up somewhere. Show it to me immediately, d'you hear me! At once! Show me your sack."

"A bald Devil will show you, but we won't," said the relative assuming a dignified air.

"What business is it of yours?" said the weaver. "We've got it for our carol singing, not you."

"No, you'll show me, you rotten drunkard," cried the wife, hitting the tall relative with her fist on his chin and breaking through to the sack.

But the weaver and the relative manfully defended it and forced her to retreat. They hardly had time to recover, when the spouse ran out into the hall with a poker in her hands. Dexterously wielding the poker she struck her husband's hands and the weaver's back and in a moment forced her way to the sack.

"Why did we let her get at it ?" said the weaver, recovering his senses.

"Ech, why have we ! And why did you let her ?" said the relative phlegmatically.

"Your poker's apparently made of iron," said the weaver after a short silence, during which he scratched his back. "Last year my wife bought a poker at the fair, gave twenty-five kopeks ; that's not bad . . . doesn't hurt . . ."

In the meantime the triumphant wife put down the lamp on the floor, untied the sack and looked into it.

But apparently her old eyes, which had perceived the sack so readily, had deceived her this time.

"Ech, there's a whole boar lying here !" she exclaimed, clapping her hands with joy.

"A boar ! D'you hear, a whole boar !" the weaver was nudging the relative. "It's all your fault !"

"Can't be helped," said the relative, shrugging his shoulders.

"And why not ? What are we standing about for ? Let's snatch the sack away ! Come on, attack !"

"Go away, go, it's our boar !" shouted the weaver, stepping forward.

"Get out, get out of here, devilish woman. These aren't your goods," said the relative, coming nearer.

His wife seized the poker again, but in the meantime Chub had crept out of the sack and stood in the middle of the hall, stretching himself like a man who has just awoken from a long sleep. The relative's wife screamed when her hands touched his coat and all of them involuntarily opened their mouths wide.

"What a fool she is ; a boar she says. That's not a boar," said the relative, his eyes protruding.

"See what a man has been thrown into the sack," said the weaver, retreating in his fright. "Say what you wish till you burst, but it can't have happened without the evil spirit. He couldn't have squeezed himself through the window."

"That's my relative," exclaimed the relative, having a good look.

"And who did you think it was ?" said Chub laughing. "Haven't I played a good trick on you ? I bet you probably wanted to eat me instead of pork. You wait, I'll give you a nice surprise, something is lying in the sack, even if it's not a boar, it's probably a piglet or some poultry or other. Something kept on moving under me the whole time."

The weaver and the relative rushed to the sack, the hostess

of the house clawed it from the opposite side and the fight would have been resumed, if the Deacon himself, seeing that there was now nowhere for him to hide, had not scrambled out of the sack.

The relative's wife became stupified and released her hands from the leg by which she had begun to drag the Deacon out of the sack.

"There's another in it, too," the weaver screamed with fear. "The Devil knows what the world is coming to . . . My head's going round . . . Neither sausages nor bread, but people are being thrown into the sacks."

"That's the Deacon," said Chub, who was more amazed than all the others. "There you are! That's what you are Solokha. Puts into sacks . . . That's why I looked—her whole house is full of sacks . . . Now I know everything; in every one of her sacks two people are sitting. And I thought that I was the only one . . . there you have Solokha."

*

The girls were somewhat surprised when one sack was not to be found.

"Nothing to be done, we've enough as it is," lisped Oksana.

They all seized the sack and heaved it on to the sledge.

The Mayor decided to keep quiet. He reasoned that, if he began to shout for them to release him and untie the sack, the silly girls would run away thinking the Devil was in it and he would be left in the street, perhaps till the next day.

In the meantime the girls, all of them holding hands, flew like the wind with the sledge over the crunching snow. Many of them played about and would sit down in the sledge, others would climb even on the Mayor himself. The Mayor decided to bear everything.

At last they arrived, opened wide the doors of the sledge and of the house and, laughing, dragged in the sack.

"Let's see what's lying in it," they all shouted, rushing to untie it.

Here the hi cupping, which had not stopped tormenting the Mayor throughout his sojourn in the sack, had increased so much, that he began to hiccup and cough violently.

"Oh, there's somebody inside it," everyone began to shout, and started to rush out of the house.

"What the devil! Where are you running like people possessed?" said Chub, entering the house.

"Ach, father," said Oksana, "there's somebody sitting in the sack."

"In the sack? Where did you get the sack?"

"The blacksmith threw it in the middle of the road," everybody said in a chorus.

"So that's it. What did I say?" thought Chub, and said, "Why did you get frightened? Let's have a look—Well, villain—forgive us for not addressing you by your full name —get out of the sack."

The Mayor did.

"Ach!" screamed the girls.

"So the Mayor climbed in as well," thought Chub to himself, nonplussed, eyeing him from head to foot, and said aloud, "That's what it is . . . E! . . ." He could not say anything more.

The Mayor himself was not less confused and did not know how to begin.

"It's probably cold outside?" he asked, addressing Chub.

"It's freezing a bit," answered Chub. "And allow me to ask you, what do you grease your boots with, would it be fat or tar?"

He did not want to say this, he wanted to ask, "How did you, Mayor, get into the sack?" and could not understand himself how he pronounced something quite different.

"Tar's better," said the Mayor. "Well, good-bye, Chub," and, shoving his hood deeper on his head, left the house.

"And why did I, fool that I am, ask him what he greases his boots with?" said Chub, gazing at the door through which the Mayor had left.

"Well, well, Solokha. To put such a man into a sack! . . . what a devil of a woman. And I, the fool . . . And where is the blasted sack?"

"I threw it into a corner, there's nothing else in it," said Oksana.

"I know those jokes. Nothing else there! . . . Give it to me. There's someone else sitting in it. Shake it well! What! There isn't? What an accursed woman . . . ! And to look at her—like a saint, as if she never touched meat during Lent."

But let us leave Chub to vent his annoyance at his leisure and let us return to the blacksmith, because it is now probably nine o'clock.

*

At first Vakula was frightened. Especially when he rose from the ground to such a height, that he could no longer see anything beneath him and flew like a fly, under the very moon, so that if he had not bent down a little, he would have brushed it with his cap.

Nevertheless, he soon gathered courage and before long began to tease the Devil . . . He was highly amused by the Devil's sneezings and coughings whenever he removed the cypress wood crucifix from his neck and moved it near him. Purposely he would raise his hand to scratch his head, and the Devil, thinking that the sign of the cross was about to be made over him, flew even faster.

Everything was light, high above. The air was transparent in the light silvery mist. Everything was visible. He saw a sorcerer whizz past them riding on a pot, the stars in whirling crowds playing hide and seek, a swarm of spirits gathered in a cloud. He saw a Devil dance in the moonlight and the latter, preceiving the blacksmith galloping past, raised his cap. He saw a broom speed on its way back, having apparently just conveyed a witch to her destination . . . They met various other scum. Seeing the blacksmith, they all stopped for a minute to look at him and then once more resumed their former occupation.

The blacksmith flew on and on and suddenly Petersburg began to glitter before him, as if on fire. (For some reason or other Petersburg was illuminated on that occasion.) The Devil, having flown over the barrier, turned himself into a horse, and the blacksmith saw himself on a spirited steed in the middle of a street.

Heavens! What a din, roar, glitter; on both sides rose four-storied walls; the clatter of horses' hooves and of wheels echoed like thunder and resounded from all sides. The houses grew and seemed to spring up from the earth at every step. Bridges trembled, coaches flew, cabmen and postillions shouted, the snow whistled under thousands of sledges, which raced along in all directions. Under the houses, studded with lanterns, pedestrians, pressed close, appeared to be squeezed together and their huge shadows twinkled up the walls, their heads topping the chimneys and the roofs.

In amazement the blacksmith gazed around him. It seemed to him that all the houses turned their innumerable fiery eyes at him and stared. He saw so many gentlemen in fur coats covered with cloth that he did not know to whom he should raise his cap.

"My God! How many noblemen there are here!" thought the blacksmith. "I should think everyone who crosses the street in a fur coat is at least an assessor, and those who drive about in such wonderful coaches with glass windows, if they aren't town bailiffs they are probably tax collectors, and perhaps even more than that."

His words were interrupted by the Devil's question :—

"Shall I ride straight to the Empress ?"

"No, I'm terrified of that," thought the blacksmith.

"Somewhere here, I don't quite know where, the Cossacks from Zaporozhye, who passed through Dikanka last autumn, are lodging. They travelled from Secha with some papers to the Empress. It would do no harm to consult them. Hey, Satan ! Climb into my pocket and then lead me to the Cossacks from Zaporozhye."

And in one minute the Devil dwindled and became so tiny that without any difficulty he climbed into the pocket. Vakula hardly had time to look around before he found himself in front of a big house, walked, not knowing how, up the stairs, opened the door, and fell back slightly, dazzled by the glitter of a well-furnished room. But he gathered some courage when he recognized the same Cossacks from Zaporozhye who had passed through Dikanka, now sitting cross-legged on silk couches, their boots smeared with tar and smoking the strongest tobacco, usually called koreshki.

"Greetings, Your Honours. God be praised that we meet again," said the blacksmith, coming closer and bowing to the ground.

"Who's this man ?" asked one, seated right in front of the blacksmith, of another, who sat further away.

"Don't you recognize me ?" said the blacksmith. "It's me, Vakula, the blacksmith. When you passed through Dikanka in the autumn—may God grant you health and long life—you were my guests for nearly two days. I then repaired the front wheel of your coach."

"Ah !" said the same Cossack. "It's the blacksmith who paints so well. Welcome, fellow countryman. Why has God sent you here ?"

"Oh, I just wanted to have a look. They say . . ."

"Well, compatriot," said the Cossack, assuming a dignified air and desiring to prove that he too could speak Russian as well as Ukrainian. "What ? Big town ?"

The blacksmith, too, did not want to disgrace himself and show himself a country bumpkin. Moreover, as we had occasion to see above, he himself knew the cultured tongue.

"Noble district," he answered coolly. "Fine indeed, houses

big, pictures good everywhere. Many houses written on with letter of gold leaf to extreme. Nothing to be said against it, wonderful proportion."

When the Cossacks heard the blacksmith expressing himself so fluently, they drew a conclusion very favourable to him.

"We'll talk to you some more later, compatriot, but now we're off to see the Empress."

"To the Empress? Ah, do me the favour, Your Honours, take me with you as well."

"You?" said the Cossack, with the same expression with which a father talks to his four years old offspring who asks him to put him on a real, on a big horse. "What will you do there? No, it can't be done."

At this his face assumed an important expression.

"Brother, we are to talk with the Empress about our own affairs."

"Take me!" insisted the blacksmith. "Ask!" he whispered quietly to the Devil, hitting his pocket with his fist.

Hardly had he said this when another Cossack said, "Let's take him, brothers."

"Perhaps we really should," said others.

"All right then, but put on the same clothes as ours."

The blacksmith hurriedly pulled on a green jacket, and then suddenly the door opened and a servant in galloons said that it was time to go.

Again it seemed strange to the blacksmith to be racing in a huge coach and to bounce on its springs, while on both sides four-storied houses ran past him and the thundering pavement seemed to unroll under the horses' feet.

"My God, what a world!" thought the blacksmith. "At home it's not as light as this even in the daytime."

The coaches stopped before the palace. The Cossacks stepped out, entered a magnificent hall and began to ascend the brilliantly illuminated staircase.

"What a staircase!" whispered the blacksmith to himself. "It's a shame to walk on it. What ornaments! They say fairy tales lie. The Devil they do. My God! What bannisters! What workmanship! Fifty roubles' worth of iron alone must have gone into it."

Having scrambled up the stairs, the Cossacks passed through the first chamber. The blacksmith followed them timidly, fearful at every step of slipping on the parquet floor. They passed through three chambers, the blacksmith still did not cease to marvel. When they entered the fourth chamber, the blacksmith involuntarily approached a picture hanging on the wall. It depicted the Holy Virgin and the Infant.

"What a picture! What wonderful painting!" he discoursed. "It seems to speak, to be alive! And the Holy Child! It presses its little hands to its heart and smiles, poor little thing! And the colours! God Almighty, what colours! There must be more than a kopek's worth of ochre alone in it. Full of greens and reds. And how the pale blue burns! Magnificent work! The background has probably been painted with the most expensive paint. Still, amazing as this painting is, this brass handle," he continued, approaching the door and feeling the lock, "is worthy of even greater admiration. Ek, what a pure finish! I bet it's all been done by German blacksmiths at an enormous price . . ."

The blacksmith might have continued his discourse for a long time if the lackey in galloons had not nudged his arm and reminded him that he should not lag behind the others. The Cossacks crossed another two chambers and stopped. Here they were ordered to wait. The chamber was crowded with Generals in uniforms embroidered with gold. The Cossacks bowed in all directions and gathered in a group.

A minute later there entered a somewhat heavy man of imposing height, in a Hetman's uniform and dapper yellow boots. He was followed by a whole retinue. His hair was dishevelled, one eye was slightly askew. His face displayed a haughty dignity and his every movement was expressive of command. All the Generals, who had been strutting rather arrogantly in their gold uniforms, began to bustle about. Continually bowing, they endeavoured to catch every word he uttered and studied his slightest movement, prepared to fly immediately to gratify his smallest wish. But the Hetman paid hardly any attention to their efforts, nodded his head briskly and went up to the Cossacks.

All the Cossacks bowed to the ground.

"Are you all here?" he asked with a drawl, pronouncing the words with a faintly nasal accent.

"Yes, father, all," answered the Cossacks, bowing again.

"Don't forget to speak as I taught you!"

"No, father, we won't forget."

"Is that the Tsar?" asked the blacksmith of one of the Cossacks.

"The Tsar! More than that! It's Potemkin himself," he was told.

Voices were heard from an adjoining room and the blacksmith did not know where to look when the room was filled with a multitude of ladies in long trailing satin dresses and courtiers in gold embroidered jackets. His eyes were dazzled by the glitter and he could see nothing else.

All the Cossacks suddenly fell to the ground and began to shout in chorus, "Pardon us, mother, pardon us!"

The blacksmith, too, not knowing why, stretched himself out with all his ardour on the floor.

"Rise!" spoke above them a commanding and, at the same time, charming voice.

Some of the courtiers became agitated and began to nudge the Cossacks.

"We won't rise, mother, we won't. We'll die, but we won't rise," shouted the Cossacks.

Potemkin was biting his lips. At last he came up himself and whispered commandingly to one of the Cossacks. The Cossacks rose.

At this the blacksmith, too, dared to raise his head and saw before him a woman of medium height, almost corpulent, powdered, blue eyed, and with an expression at once majestic and winsome, which nothing could resist and which could belong only to one reigning woman.

"His Highness promised to acquaint me with those of my people, whom I have not yet seen," the lady with the blue eyes said, surveying the Cossacks with curiosity. "Are you well looked after here?" she continued, coming nearer.

"Yes, thank you, mother! Provisions are given good ones, although the sheep here aren't the same as ours in Zaporozhye—why shouldn't we live somehow? . . ."

Potemkin knitted his eyebrows perceiving that the Cossacks were speaking quite differently from what he had taught them . . .

One of the Cossacks, gathering courage, stepped forward.

"Have mercy, mother! What has your loyal people displeased you with? Have we held the hand of the vile Tartar? Have we come to any agreement with the Turks? Have we been disloyal to you in deed or thought? Why, then, are we in disfavour? First we hear that you're ordering fortresses to be built against us everywhere. Then we hear that you want to turn us into foot-soldiers, now we hear of new disasters. What is the crime of the Cossack army? Is it because it led your forces over the Perekop and helped your generals to break the Crimeans? . . ."

Potemkin was silent and with a tiny brush negligently polished the diamonds which studded his hands.

"What is it you wish then ?" solicitously asked Catherine.

The Cossacks looked at each other meaningly.

"Now's the time. The Empress asks you what you want," said the blacksmith to himself and suddenly dropped to the ground.

"Your Royal Highness, don't punish me by death. Pardon me! What are the shoes made of on your feet? May Your Royal Highness forgive me for asking. I should think there's not one shoemaker in any kingdom in the world who can make them like this. My God, if only my wife could have such shoes to put on."

The Empress laughed. The courtiers laughed, too. Potemkin knitted his eyebrows and smiled at the same time. The Cossacks began to nudge the blacksmith, wondering whether he had not gone mad.

"Rise," said the Empress graciously. "If you wish so much to have such shoes, then it is not difficult to procure them. Bring him immediately my most expensive shoes, those with gold! Really, I am very pleased with this sincerity. Here," continued the Empress, directing her look at a gentleman with a fat slightly pale face, who stood aside from the others and whose modest jacket with large mother-of-pearl buttons denoted that he was not to be numbered among the courtiers, "is a subject worthy of your witty pen."

"Your Imperial Highness is too gracious. This requires at least a Lafontaine," answered with a bow the man with the mother-of-pearl buttons.

"Upon my honour, I tell you, I am still enchanted by your 'Brigadier.' You read wonderfully well. However. . ." Turning again to the Cossacks the Empress continued, "I have heard that in your Secha nobody ever marries."

"How's that, mother! You know yourself a man can't live without a wife," answered the same Cossack who had spoken to the blacksmith, and the blacksmith was amazed to hear that this Cossack, knowing the cultured tongue so well, was talking to the Empress, as if on purpose, in the crudest dialect, usually called the peasant's.

"Sly people," he thought, "he probably does it on purpose."

"We're not monks," continued the Cossack, "but sinful people. Like all honest Christians, we can't resist meat in Lent. There are not few among us who have wives, only they don't live with us in the Secha. There are such, who've wives in Poland, there are such who've wives in the Ukraine, there are such who've wives in Turkey."

At that moment the shoes were brought to the blacksmith.

"My God, what ornaments!" he exclaimed joyfully, gabbing the shoes. "Your Royal Highness! How is it when with such shoes on your feet Your Honour, for example, goes skating on the ice. What must the little feet themselves be like? I'm sure they must be made of pure sugar at least."

The Empress, who indeed had the slimmest and most delightful little feet, could not help smiling, hearing such a compliment from the lips of the naive blacksmith, who himself, in his Cossack clothes, would pass as a very handsome man despite his swarthy face.

Delighted with such gracious attention, the blacksmith was on the verge of questioning the Empress thoroughly about everything. Was it true that Tsars ate only honey and pork fat, and such like. But, feeling the Cossacks nudge him, he decided to keep quiet. And when the Empress, turning to the old men, began to ask them how they lived in the Secha, what their customs were, he slipped back, bent down to his pocket and said quietly, "Carry me out of here, quickly," and suddenly found himself outside the city gates.

*

"He has drowned himself. I swear he has. May I never move from this spot if he hasn't drowned himself," lisped the weaver's fat wife, standing in a crowd of Dikanka's women, in the middle of the street.

"What, am I a liar, or what? Have I stolen anybody's cow? Have I cast an evil spell over anybody, that there's no trust put in me?" shouted a woman in a Cossack's jacket, with a violent nose, waving her hands. "May I never thirst for a drink of water, if old Perepertchikha hasn't seen with her own eyes how the blacksmith hanged himself."

"Has the blacksmith hanged himself? You don't say!" said the Mayor, leaving Chub's house. He stopped and pushed nearer to the talkers.

"You'd better wish that you'll never thirst for vodka, you old drunkard." answered the weaver's wife. 'One has to be as mad as you to hang oneself. He's drowned himself, drowned himself in the millstream. I know that, as well as I do that you've just come from the pub."

"You hussy! See what she reproaches me with," answered

the woman with the violet nose in a rage. "She ought to keep quiet, good for nothing that she is! Don't I know that the Deacon visits you every evening."

The weaver's wife turned crimson.

"What Deacon? Who does he go to? Why are you telling lies?"

"The Deacon!" cried the Deacon's wife, who wore a fur coat of rabbit skins, covered with blue nankeen, and pushed herself nearer to the quarrelling women. "I'll show you the Deacon! Who said the Deacon?"

"And that's the one the Deacon visits," said the woman with the violet nose, pointing to the weaver's wife.

"So it's you, you bitch," said the Deacon's wife, ready to attack the weaver's wife. "You're the witch who casts spells over him and gives him an evil potion to make him come to you!"

"Get away from me, Satan," the weaver's wife said, retreating.

"Look at the accursed witch. May she expect children and never see them! Villainness! Tphu!"

Here the Deacon's wife spat right into the weaver's wife's eyes.

The weaver's wife wanted to do the same thing herself, but, instead, spat into the unshaven beard of the Mayor, who, in order to hear everything better, had edged his way right up to the quarrelling women.

"Ach, filthy woman," the Mayor began to shout, wiping his face with his lapel and raising his whip. This movement caused everybody to scatter in all directions, swearing.

"What a filthy woman!" repeated the Mayor, continuing to wipe himself. "So the blacksmith has drowned himself! My God! and he was such a good painter! What fine knives, scythes and ploughs he could turn out! What strength he had! Yes," he continued, becoming thoughtful, "there are few such people in our village. So that's why, when I was still sitting in that blasted sack, I noticed the poor fellow was very much down in the mouth. That's the blacksmith—he was and now he is no more. And I intended to have my dappled mare shoed . . ."

And filled with such Christian thoughts, the Mayor quietly trudged back to his house.

Oksana became confused when the news reached her. She had little trust in Perepertchikha's eyes and the women's chatter. She knew that the blacksmith was sufficiently pious not to want to destroy his soul. But what if he had really gone away with the intention of never returning to the village? She was hardly likely to find another young man like the blacksmith anywhere. He loved her so much! He put up with her tantrums longer than all the others . . . The beauty turned the whole night under her blanket from the right side to the left, from the left to the right, and could find no sleep. Sometimes, stretched out in enchanting nakedness, which the darkness of the night hid even from herself, she scolded herself almost aloud. At times, quietening down, she would decide not to think about anything—and kept on thinking. And was all aglow and by morning had fallen head over heels in love with the blacksmith.

Chub expressed neither pleasure nor sorrow about Vakula's fate. His thoughts were busy with one thing only. On no account could he forget Solokha's unfaithfulness, and did not stop reproaching her even in his sleep.

Morning arrived. The church was full of people even before daylight. Elderly women, with white scarves on their heads and white cloth jackets, crossed themselves piously at the very entrance of the church. The noblewomen, in green and yellow blouses and some even in blue Polish surcoats with golden tassels at the back, stood in front of them. The girls, on whose heads were tied shopfuls of ribbons and round whose necks hung necklaces with crucifixes and ducats, tried to thread their way nearer to the altar. But in front of them all stood the noblemen and plain peasants with moustaches, tufts of hair, thick necks and freshly shaven chins, almost all in cloaks, from under which appeared a white or a blue jacket. On all faces, wherever you looked, a holyday spirit was to be seen. The Mayor licked his lips in advance, picturing how he would break his fast with sausages, the girls thought of how they would skate with the boys on the ice, the old women whispered prayers more zealously than ever before. Over the whole church Cossack Sverbiguz could be heard praying with fervour. Oksana alone stood as if in a daze. She prayed and she did not pray. So many mixed feelings were crowded in her breast, one sadder than another, one gloomier than another, that her face expressed only an intense confusion. Tears trembled in her eyes. The girls could not understand the reason for it and did not suspect that the fault was the blacksmith's. Yet Oksana was not alone in her preoccupation with Vakula. All the villagers noticed that the holiday was not quite a holiday, that something seemed to be missing.

As misfortune willed it, the Deacon, after his journey in the sack, had become hoarse and bleated in a voice that was barely audible. It is true that the newly arrived chorister took the notes well with his bass, but it would have been far better had the blacksmith been there, too. He always stepped up to the choir and led them with the same melody that they sing in Poltava. Matins were already over. Then Mass was said . . . Really, where had the blacksmith vanished ?

*

Throughout the rest of the night the Devil flew back with the blacksmith even quicker than before and soon Vakula found himself near his house. At that moment the cock crowed.

"Where are you off to ?" shouted the blacksmith, seizing by the tail the Devil, who wanted to rush away. "Wait, friend. We haven't finished yet. I haven't thanked you."

Then, picking up a stick, he struck the Devil three times, and the poor Devil began to run like a peasant who has just been thrashed by the assessor. And so, instead of cheating, seducing and fooling others, the enemy of mankind was fooled himself.

After that Vakula entered the doorway, buried himself in the straw which lay there, and slept till midday. When he awoke, he became alarmed to find that the sun had already risen high in the sky.

"I've slept through Matins and Mass !"

At this the devout blacksmith became dismayed, thinking that God, in punishment for his sinful intention of destroying his soul, had probably deliberately sent him the sleep which prevented him even from attending church on such a solemn festival. Then, calming down, reassured by the thought that next week he would confess to the priest and after that would make fifty genuflections daily for a whole year, he looked into the house. Nobody was in it. Apparently Solokha had not yet returned.

Carefully he took out the shoes from inside his shirt and again wondered at the expensive workmanship and the amazing happening of the previous night. He washed himself and, dressing as carefully as possible, put on the clothes which he had obtained from the Cossacks. Then he took out of his trunk a new cap with a black lambskin band and blue top, which he had never worn since the time he bought it during his stay in Poltava, took out also a new multi-coloured belt, wrapped them all, together with a leather whip, in a large scarf and departed straight to Chub.

Chub's eyes began to protrude when the blacksmith entered, and he did not know what to marvel at most. Whether at the fact of the blacksmith's resurrection or at his temerity in coming to him, or at his being dressed up like a dandy and a Cossack from Zaporozhye. But Chub was even more amazed when Vakula untied the scarf and, putting before him a new hat and a belt, such as had never been seen before in the village, dropped to his feet and said in an imploring voice :—

"Have mercy father! Don't be angry with me! Here is a whip, too, for you. Whip me to your heart's content. I surrender, repent everything. Whip me. Only don't be angry with me. After all, you once used to be my dead father's friend. You always liked each other and you used to wet a bargain together."

Not without secret satisfaction, Chub saw that the blacksmith, who did not care a fig for anybody in the village, who could bend coins and horseshoes like pancakes with his hands, that this same blacksmith was now lying at his feet. In order not to lessen his own dignity, Chub took up the whip and struck Vakula three times on the back.

"Now, that's enough for you. Get up! Always listen to older people. Let's forget everything that stood between us. Now tell me, what do you want?"

"Father, give me Oksana."

Chub thought for a short time, looked at the cap and at the belt. The cap was wonderful, the belt no less. He remembered about the faithless Solokha, and said resolutely :—

"Alright. Send matchmakers."

"Ai," screamed Oksana, crossing the threshold and seeing the blacksmith. She fixed her eyes on him with amazement and joy.

"Look what shoes I've brought you," said Vakula. "The same ones that the Empress wears."

"No, no! I don't need any shoes," she said, waving her hand and without removing her eyes from him. "Even without the shoes I'd . . ."

She did not finish and blushed.

The blacksmith came nearer, took her by the hand. The girl lowered her eyes. Never had she been so wonderfully beautiful. The enraptured blacksmith quietly kissed her and her face began to glow even more, and she became even more beautiful.

* * *

The Archdeacon, blessed be his memory, travelling through Dikanka, praised the place on which the village stands. As he passed through one of the streets, he stopped before a new house.

"And whose is this house, which is so beautifully painted ?" asked the Most Eminent of a beautiful woman who stood near the door with a child in her arms.

"The blacksmith Vakula's," Oksana answered, bowing, for it was Oksana herself.

"Nice, nice work," said the Most Eminent, surveying the doors and windows. All the window frames were painted red and on the doors, everywhere, were painted Cossacks on horseback with pipes in their teeth.

But the Most Eminent praised Vakula even more, when he discovered, that in fulfilment of his penance, Vakula had, without charge, painted the whole of the left choir green with red flowers.

Still, that is not all. On the side of the wall, as you enter the church, Vakula painted a picture of the Devil in Hell, so repulsive that no one could pass it without spitting and the women, when the child in their arms would begin to cry, would hold it up to the painting and would say, "Look at the nasty picture," and the child, holding back its little tears, would gape at the picture and press closer to its mother's breast.

How the Two Ivans Quarrelled

1

IVAN IVANOVITCH's winter coat is lovely. Excellent ! And what lambskin ! Hell, what lambskin ! Dove coloured by the frost ! God knows, I'm sure that its like isn't to be found on anyone else ! For Heaven's sake, look at it—especially when he stops to talk to somebody. Look at it from the side ! It's simply delicious ! You can't describe it. Velvet ! Silver ! Fire ! God Almighty ! Holy Saint Nicolas ! Why haven't I such a coat ? He had it made even before Agafya Feodosyevna started travelling to Kiev. Do you know Agafya Feodosyevna ? She's the one who bit off the assessor's ear.

Ivan Ivanovitch is a wonderful man ! What a house he owns in Mirgorod ! It is completely surrounded by an awning on oak poles and under the awning there are benches everywhere. When it becomes too hot, Ivan Ivanovitch casts aside his fur coat and his underwear and, clad only in his shirt, rests under the awning, watching what takes place in his yard and in the street. And what apple and pear trees grow under his very windows ! You only have to open a window—and their branches burst into the room.

All this is in front of the house. If you only saw what he has in his garden ! What hasn't he ? Plums, cherries, wild cherries, various vegetables, sunflowers, cucumbers, melons, pods, even a barn and a smithy.

Ivan Ivanovitch is a wonderful man. He is very fond of melons. They are his favourite dish. As soon as he has finished his lunch and comes out under the awning dressed only in his shirt, he immediately orders Gapka to bring two melons. He cuts them himself, collects the seeds in a separate piece of paper and begins to eat. Then he orders Gapka to bring him an ink-stand and himself, with his own hand, writes an inscription on the paper containing the seeds, "This melon was eaten on such and such a date." If some guest is present at the time, then he writes, "So and so participated."

The deceased judge of Mirgorod always admired Ivan Ivanovitch's house, whenever he looked at it. Yes, the house is not at all too bad. What I like about it is the way the rooms, large and small, are built on to it from all sides, so that if you look at it from a distance, only roofs are visible, planted one on another like a plate of pancakes or a canker of sponge on a tree truck. By the way, all the roofs are thatched with ordinary rushes. A willow, an oak tree and two apple trees lean on them, using their wide branches as elbows. Among the trees shine smallish windows with carved shutters painted white, which protrude right into the street.

Ivan Ivanovitch is a wonderful man! He is known even to the Commissar from Poltava, Dorosh Tarasovitch Puchivotchka. When travelling from Chorol, he always breaks his journey to stay with Ivan Ivanovitch. And the Arch Presbyter, Father Peter, who lives in Koliberda, always says, whenever approximately five people have joined him, that he has not met anybody who fulfils his Christian duty and who knows how to live as well as does Ivan Ivanovitch.

Heavens, how the time flies. More than ten years had already passed since he had become a widower. He had no children. Gapka has children and they often run about in the yard. Ivan Ivanovitch always gives each of them either a cracknel, or a small piece of melon or pear. Gapka keeps the keys of his granaries and cellars. But the key of the large trunk which stands in his bedroom, and of the middle granary, Ivan Ivanovitch keeps himself and does not like anybody to come near them. Gapka is a healthy girl. She wears a blouse and has fresh calves and cheeks.

And what a pious man Ivan Ivanovitch is! Every Sunday he puts on the fur coat and goes to church. As soon as he is inside Ivan Ivanovitch bows in all directions, usually seats himself in the choir and accompanies the tune very well with his bass. And when the service is finished, nothing can prevent Ivan Ivanovitch from making the round of the beggars. No doubt it is only his inborn goodness that impells him to undertake such a tedious duty.

"Hello, beggar!" he would say, having selected the most crippled woman in a torn dress composed of patches. "Where d'you come from, beggar?"

"I come from the village, Your Honour. It's three days

since I've had any food or drink. My own children have driven me out."

"Your poor soul! Why, then, have you come here?"

"To beg, Your Honour, for enough money to buy bread."

"Ahem! D'you want some bread then?" Ivan Ivanovitch would usually enquire.

"Yes, sir! I'm as hungry as a dog."

"Ahem!" Ivan Ivanovitch would usually reply. "Perhaps you want some meat as well?"

"Anything Your Honour gives me. I'll be grateful for anything."

"Ahem! Is meat better than bread?"

"Hungry beggars aren't choosers. Anything you give is good."

"Well, go along then, God be with you," Ivan Ivanovitch would say. "What're you waiting for? I'm not beating you, am I?"

And, having made similar inquiries from another and a third, he finally either returns home or drops in for a drink of vodka on his neighbour Ivan Nikiforovitch, or on the judge, or on the provost.

Ivan Ivanovitch likes it very much when somebody gives him a present or some gift. It pleases him enormously.

Ivan Nikiforovitch is also a very good man. His yard borders on Ivan Ivanovitch's yard. They are friends, such as the world has never produced before.

Anton Prokofyevitch Pupopuz, who still wears a brown jacket with light blue sleeves and lunches with the judge on Sundays, used to say that the Devil himself had tied Ivan Nikiforovitch to Ivan Ivanovitch with a string. Where the one goes, the other drags himself, too.

Ivan Nikiforovitch has never been married. They used to say that he had been married, but that is an absolute lie. I know Ivan Nikiforovitch very well and can say that he never even had any intention of marrying. Where does such gossip originate? For example, the rumour was spread at one time that Ivan Nikiforovitch was born with a tail at his back. But that invention is so incongruous and at the same time so base and indecent, that I do not even deem it necessary to repudiate it to my enlightened readers, who, I have no doubt, know that only witches, and very few of them, have a tail at the back. Witches, by the way, tend to belong more to the feminine sex than to the musculine.

Despite their great intimacy, these rare friends were not

quite alike. One can best learn to know their characters from comparison. Ivan Ivanovitch possesses the unusual gift of talking extremely pleasantly. My God, how he talks! This sensation can be compared only with the one you feel when somebody looks for something in your hair, or gently presses a finger along your heel. You listen, listen—and hang your head. Agreeable! Amazingly agreeable! Like sleep after a hot bath.

Ivan Nikiforovitch, on the contrary, is more taciturn. On the other hand, if he throws in a word, then just you look out. It will cut you closer than any razor.

Ivan Ivanovitch is thinnish and tall. Ivan Nikiforovitch is slightly smaller, but, on the other hand, he spreads out in width.

Ivan Ivanovitch's head resembles a radish with its tail down. Ivan Nikiforovitch's head resembles a radish with its tail up.

After lunch Ivan Ivanovitch lies under the awning clad only in his shirt, but towards evening he puts on the fur coat and goes somewhere, either to the town store, which he supplies with flour, or into the fields to catch quails.

Ivan Nikiforovitch lies on the porch the whole day—if the day is not too hot. There he usually exhibits his back to the sun—and does not want to go anywhere. If it comes into his head in the morning he will walk across the yard, survey his household and go back again to rest. Formerly he used to drop in on Ivan Ivanovitch.

Ivan Ivanovitch is an extremely refined man and in ordinary conversation will never use an indecorous word and takes immediate offence if he hears one.

Ivan Nikiforovitch will never take enough care. On such occasions Ivan Ivanovitch usually gets up from his seat and says, "That's enough, enough, Ivan Nikiforovitch. It is better for you to leave than to use such ungodly language."

Ivan Ivanovitch gets very angry if he finds a fly in his borshtch. Then he loses his self-control and will smash the plate and the host will suffer.

Ivan Nikiforovitch is very fond of taking a bath. When he is sitting up to his neck in water, he orders a table and a samovar, and loves to drink tea in such coolness.

Ivan Ivanovitch trims his beard twice a week. Ivan Nikiforovitch only once.

Ivan Ivanovitch is extremely curious. God forbid if you begin telling him anything and do not finish it! And if he is displeased with anything, then he immediately shows it.

It is extremely difficult to tell from Ivan Nikiforovitch's expression whether he is pleased or annoyed. Even if he is delighted with anything, he will not show it.

Ivan Ivanovitch's character is somewhat timorous. Whereas Ivan Nikiforovitch's loose trousers possess such wide pleats that, if they were inflated, his whole yard, with its granaries and buildings complete, could be put into them.

Ivan Ivanovitch's eyes are large and expressive and are the colour of tobacco, and his mouth somewhat resembles the letter "I". Ivan Nikiforovitch's eyes are small and yellowish and disappear completely between thick eyebrows and plump cheeks, and his nose resembles a ripe plum.

If Ivan Ivanovitch treats you to some tobacco, he will always lick the lid of the snuff-box first, then rap it with his finger, and offering it to you, will say—that is, if you are acquainted with him—"May I, sir, ask you to do me the honour," and, if you are not an acquaintance of his, then he will ask, "Sir, without having the privilege of knowing your rank, name and surname, may I ask you to do me the honour ?"

Ivan Nikiforovitch, on the other hand, puts his pouch straight into your hands and only adds, "Help yourself !"

Ivan Ivanovitch, as well as Ivan Nikiforovitch, strongly dislikes fleas and so neither Ivan Ivanovitch nor Ivan Nikiforovitch will ever allow a Jew to pass with his merchandise, without buying from him various pots of elixirs against such insects, first having scolded him properly for embracing the Jewish religion.

By the way, despite some disparity, both Ivan Ivanovitch and Ivan Nikiforovitch are wonderful people.

2

From which one learns what Ivan Ivanovitch suddenly desired, what conversation took place between Ivan Ivanovitch and Ivan Nikiforovitch and how it ended.

One morning—in the month of July—Ivan Ivanovitch was lying under the awning. The day was hot, the air dry and transfused with rays of sunlight. Ivan Ivanovitch had already managed to see the reapers outside town and in the village, to inquire from some peasants and peasant women he had met, where they came from, where they were going to and how and why. Having completely tired himself with walking, he lay down to rest. For a long time, lying there, he surveyed the granaries, the yard, the barns and the hens, which ran about the yard, and thought to himself :—

"God Almighty, what a good landowner I am ! What is there that I haven't got ? Birds, a building, granaries, every luxury, distilled vodka, liquor, pears and plums in the garden, poppy seed, cabbage and peas in the kitchen garden. What else is there that I haven't got . . . I should like to know, what there is that I don't possess ?"

Having put such a deep question to himself, Ivan Ivanovitch fell into a reverie and, in the meantime, his eyes found new objects, stepped over the fence into Ivan Nikiforovitch's yard and occupied themselves involuntarily with a curious spectacle.

An emaciated peasant woman was carrying out, one after another, clothes that had long been laid up and was hanging them out to air on a line. Soon an old uniform, with worn cuffs, stretched out its sleeves in the air and embraced a lamé blouse. Behind it peeped out a nobleman's coat with emblem buttons and a moth-eaten collar. Then followed white spotted pantaloons, which a long time ago would have been pulled on Ivan Nikiforovitch's legs and which now could be, perhaps, pulled on his fingers. Soon another pair of pantaloons was suspended, shaped like the letter "H". Then came a blue Cossack jacket, which Ivan Nikiforovitch had had made for himself about twenty years ago, when he was on the verge of entering the militia and had for that reason grown a moustache. Finally, there followed a sword, which, on the line, looked like a spire jutting out into the air. The tails of something resembling a peasant's coat began to whirl, grassy green with brass buttons the size of a five kopek piece. From behind the tails peeped out a waistcoat mounted with gold braid, cut low in front. The waistcoat was soon covered by a deceased grandmother's old skirt, with pockets, each spacious enough to hold a water melon. All this hotchpotch presented a very entertaining spectacle to Ivan Ivanovitch, as the sunrays successively seized now a blue, now a green sleeve, or a red cuff or a piece of gold braid. Playing on the sword-spire, they brought memories of a puppet show, presented in the villages by wandering scoundrels, particularly of the moments when the crowd, closely packed, looks at King Herod in his golden crown, or at Anthony leading a goat. Behind the puppet theatre a fiddle squeaks, a gypsy strums on his lips in place of a drum, the sun goes down and the fresh cold of a Southern night imperceptibly presses itself closer to the fresh shoulders and breasts of the plump village girls.

Soon the old woman crept out again from the storeroom and, groaning, dragged an ancient saddle with torn stirrups, worn leather pistol pockets, and a saddle-cloth, formerly red, with golden embroidery and brass plates.

"That's a silly woman," thought Ivan Ivanovitch, "for all I know she might drag Ivan Nikiforovitch himself out for an airing."

And indeed, Ivan Ivanovitch was not far out in his conjecture. About five minutes later Ivan Nikiforovitch's loose nankeen trousers planted themselves in the yard and took up almost half of it. After that the woman brought out a cap and also a gun.

"What does it mean?" thought Ivan Ivanovitch. 'I've never known Ivan Nikiforovitch to have a gun! What does he intend to do? He doesn't shoot and yet he has a gun! What does he want with it? And it's a nice piece of work. I wanted to get one myself a long time ago. I'd very much like to have that nice gun. I like toying with a gun. Hey, woman, woman!" shouted Ivan Ivanovitch, beckoning with his finger.

The old woman approached the fence.

"What have you there, granny?"

"You can see for yourself—a gun."

"What sort of a gun?"

"Who knows what kind it is? If it was mine, then perhaps I'd know what it's made of, but it's the master's."

Ivan Ivanovitch got up and began to inspect the gun from all angles and forgot to tell the old woman off for hanging it out to air along with the sword.

"I think it's made of iron," continued the old woman.

"Ahem! Of iron. Why is it made of iron?" Ivan Ivanovitch asked himself. "And has your master had it a long time?"

"May be."

"Nice little thing. I'll ask him to give it to me. What could he do with it? Or I'll exchange it for something. Granny, is the master at home? What?"

"He is."

"Is he lying down?"

"He is."

"All right then, I'll go to him."

Ivan Ivanovitch dressed, took a gnarled stick in his hand,

to protect himself against the dogs, for many more of them are encountered in the streets of Mirgorod than people, and left.

Although Ivan Nikiforovitch's yard was near Ivan Ivanovitch's yard, and one could climb from one into the other over the wattle hedge, Ivan Ivanovitch, nevertheless, went by way of the street. From this street one had to cross a side street, which was so narrow that if two one-horse carts happened to meet in it they could not pass, and had to remain in the same position until they were dragged out into the main street in opposite directions by their back wheels. And the pedestrian would adorn himself, as if with flowers, with buds of burdock which grew at both sides of the fence. Into this side street Ivan Ivanovitch's barn jutted out from one side and Ivan Nikiforovitch's granary, gates and dove-cote from the other. Ivan Ivanovitch approached the gates and rattled the latch. Dogs began to bark inside, but, seeing a familiar face, the variegated pack soon ran back wagging their tails. Ivan Ivanovitch crossed the yard which was streaked with multi-coloured Indian pigeons (usually fed by Ivan Nikiforovitch personally), skins of water melons and melons and in some places with grass ; in other places there would be a broken wheel, or a hoop from a cask or a boy lolling about in a dirtied shirt : a picture which painters love ! The shadow of the airing clothes covered almost the whole of the yard and imparted to it some coolness. A peasant woman met him with a bow and remained gaping in the same spot. A porch with an awning on two oak posts preened itself before the house—an unreliable protection against the sun, which at this time in Little Russia does not like joking and floods the pedestrian from head to foot with hot perspiration. How strong was Ivan Ivanovitch's desire to acquire an indispensable object is proved by his decision to go out at such a time and to break his daily rule of going for a stroll only in the evening.

The shutters were closed in the room which Ivan Ivanovitch entered and a ray of sunlight, which pierced a hole in the shutters, assumed a rainbow colour and painted on the opposite wall a multi-coloured picture of thatched roofs, trees, and the clothing hung out in the yard, but all upside down. This created a wonderful semi-darkness in the room.

"God be with you," said Ivan Ivanovitch.

"Oh, hello, Ivan Ivanovitch," answered a voice from a corner of the room.

Only then did Ivan Ivanovitch notice Ivan Nikiforovitch, who was lying on a rug spread out on the floor.

"Forgive me for appearing before you as nature made me"—Ivan Nikiforovitch was lying with nothing on, not even a shirt.

"That's all right. Have you had a rest to-day, Ivan Nikiforovitch ?"

"I have. And have you, Ivan Ivanovitch ?"

"I have."

"Have you only just got up, then ?"

"Have I just got up ? For Heaven's sake, Ivan Nikiforovitch ! How can one sleep until this time ? I've just returned from the village. The corn is wonderful all along the road. Magnificent ! And the hay is fully grown, so soft, so smooth."

"Gorpina !" shouted Ivan Nikiforovitch, "bring some vodka and some pies and sour cream for Ivan Ivanovitch."

"Nice weather we have to-day."

"Don't praise it, Ivan Ivanovitch. May the Devil take it ! There's no hiding from the heat."

"You would mention the Devil ! Listen, Ivan Nikiforovitch. You'll remember what I told you, but it'll be too late. You'll suffer in the next world for blasphemous words."

"Why have I offended you, Ivan Ivanovitch ? I didn't refer to your father or your mother. I don't know why I offended you."

"That's enough, now. That'll do, Ivan Nikiforovitch."

"By God, I haven't insulted you, Ivan Ivanovitch ?"

"It's strange that quails can't be caught with bird-calls."

"As you wish. Think what you like, but I didn't insult you in any way."

"I don't know why they don't come," Ivan Ivanovitch was saying, as if not listening to Ivan Nikiforovitch. "Perhaps the time isn't ripe yet . . . but it seems that the weather is right."

"You were saying that the corn is good ?"

"The corn is magnificent, magnificent !"

Silence followed after this.

"Ivan Nikiforovitch, why are you hanging out your clothes ?" Ivan Ivanovitch said at last.

"Because the blasted woman has allowed wonderful, almost new, clothing to rot. Now I'm airing it. The cloth is fine, it's excellent, you merely have to turn it—and it can be worn again."

"I liked one thing there, Ivan Nikiforovitch."

"Which ?"

"Tell me, please, what d'you want with the gun, which

has been put out to air with the clothes ?" Ivan Ivanovitch then offered some tobacco to Ivan Nikiforovitch and said: "May I ask you to do me the honour ?"

"That's all right. Have mine. I'd rather have a pinch of my own." Ivan Nikiforovitch felt beside him on the rug and produced his tobacco-pouch.

"What a silly woman ! So she's hung the gun out there as well. The Jew from Sorochintsy makes good tobacco. I don't know what he puts into it, it's so fragrant ! Tastes somewhat like grass. Take some, please. Chew a little of it. Isn't it like grass ? Here you are, help yourself."

"Tell me, please, Ivan Nikiforovitch, I'm still talking about the gun. What will you do with it ? After all, you don't need it."

"Why don't I ? And supposing I have to shoot ?"

"God protect you, Ivan Nikiforovitch. When will you have occasion to shoot ? Unless it be at the Second Advent. As far as I know and others remember, you haven't killed a single duck yet, and your nature wasn't designed by God Almighty so that you could shoot. You have the bearing and figure of a weighty man. How can you trail across marshes, when your clothes, which I'm too polite to mention by name, are being aired at this very moment ? What ? No, you need rest, relaxation" (Ivan Ivanovitch, as has been mentioned above, expressed himself unusually colourfully, when persuasion was imperative. How he talked ! My God, how he talked !) "Yes, you should behave decently. Listen, give it to me."

"How can I ? It's an expensive gun. You'll not find its like anywhere now. I bought it from a Turk when I intended to join the militia. How can I give it away now, suddenly ? How can I ? It's an indispensable article."

"Why is it indispensable ?"

"What d'you mean, why ? Supposing robbers attack the house . . . Of course it's indispensable ! God be praised ! Now I'm calm and afraid of nobody. And why ? because I know that there's a gun standing in my store-room."

"Is it a good gun ? But its lock is spoilt, Ivan Nikiforovitch !"

"What if it is spoilt ? It can be mended. You've only to grease it with hemp oil to keep the rust off."

"For the life of me, Ivan Nikiforovitch, I can see no signs of a friendly disposition on your part towards me. You won't do anything for me as a mark of friendship."

"How can you say, Ivan Ivanovitch, that I don't show

any signs of my friendship towards you ? Aren't you ashamed of yourself ? Your oxen graze on my field, and I haven't borrowed them once. When you travel to Poltava, you always ask for my cart. And have I ever refused it ? Your boys climb over the wattle hedge into my yard and play with my dogs—I don't say anything. Let them play, so long as they don't touch anything. Let them play !"

"If you won't give it to me, perhaps we could make an exchange ?"

"What will you give me for it ?" Having said this, Ivan Nikiforovitch propped himself up on his elbow and looked at Ivan Ivanovitch.

"I'll give you the brown pig, the one I've fattened up. It's a nice pig. Next year, you'll see, it'll produce piglets for you."

"How can you make such a suggestion, Ivan Ivanovitch ? What good is your pig to me ? Unless I use it for a funeral feast in honour of the Devil."

"There you go again ! You can't do without the Devil ! It's a sin you're committing. By God, it's a sin, Ivan Nikiforovitch."

"What d'you mean, Ivan Ivanovitch ? You want to give me in exchange for the gun—the Devil knows what—a pig !"

"Why is a pig 'the Devil knows what,' Ivan Nikiforovitch ?"

"And why not ? I'd think it over if I were you. A gun—that's a well-known thing, but a pig—is the Devil knows what. If it wasn't you who'd said it, I might have thought it was intended as an insult."

"And what bad things have you noticed about a pig ?"

"What do you really take me for ? That I should take a pig . . ."

"Sit down, sit down ! I'll stop . . . let your gun stay with you, let it rot and get rusty standing in the corner of the store-room. I don't want to talk about it any more."

After that silence ensued.

"They say," began Ivan Nikiforovitch, "that three kings have declared war on our Tsar."

"Yes, Peter Feodorovitch told me. What is this war ? And why is it on ?"

"One can't say for certain why it's on, Ivan Nikiforovitch. I suppose the kings want us all to embrace the Turkish religion."

"So that's what the fools have taken into their heads," said Iavn Nikiforovitch raising his head.

"You see, that's why our Tsar declared war on them. 'No,' he says, 'you'd better embrace the Christian religion.'"

"What of it? We'll beat them anyway, Ivan Ivanovitch."

"We will. So you don't want to exchange the gun, Ivan Nikiforovitch?"

"It seems strange to me, Ivan Ivanovitch, that you, a man with a reputation for learning, should talk like a schoolboy. Am I such a fool . . ."

"Sit down, sit down! Forget it. Let it rot. I shan't talk about it any more."

At that moment the snack was brought in.

Ivan Ivanovitch drank a glass of vodka and took a portion of the pie with some sour cream.

"Listen, Ivan Nikiforovitch. I'll give you two sacks of oats in addition to the pig You haven't sown any oats yet and you'll have to buy some this year in any case."

"By God, Ivan Ivanovitch . . . One should have a stiff drink before talking to you." (That was put comparatively mildly. Ivan Nikiforovitch lets off phrases worse than that.) "Where have you heard of a gun being exchanged for two sacks of oats? I bet you won't give your fur coat for it."

"But you forget, Ivan Nikiforovitch, that I'm giving you a pig as well."

"What! Two sacks of oats and a pig for a gun!"

"What about it. Isn't it enough?"

"For a gun?"

"Of course, for a gun."

"Two sacks for a gun?"

"Two sacks, not empty ones, but filled with oats, and have you forgotten the pig?"

"You can kiss your pig, and if you don't want to, then kiss the Devil!"

"Oh, why are you so quick tempered? In the next world they'll sew up your tongue with hot needles for such impious words. After a talk with you one has to wash one's face and hands and then one should fumigate oneself."

"Permit me, Ivan Ivanovitch. A gun—that's a noble thing, the finest means of recreation and in addition it's a pleasant ornament in a room . . ."

"Ivan Nikiforovitch, you fuss over your gun like a child over a new toy," said Ivan Ivanovitch with annoyance, as he was becoming really angry.

"And you, Ivan Ivanovitch, behave like a real gander."

If Ivan Nikiforovitch had not said these words, then they

would have argued a little with each other, and then, as always, parted good friends. But now things took quite a different turn. Ivan Ivanovitch flared up.

"What did you say, Ivan Nikiforovitch ?" he asked raising his voice.

"I said that you resemble a gander, Ivan Ivanovitch."

"How could you dare, sir, forgetting decency and respect for the rank and the family of a man, to dishonour him with such abuse ?"

"What's abusive about it ? And why, indeed, have you begun to wave your hands about so much, Ivan Ivanovitch ?"

"I repeat, how did you dare, against all propriety, to call me a gander ?"

"I snap my fingers at you, Ivan Ivanovitch ! Why are cackling so much ?"

Ivan Ivanovitch could no longer control himself. His lips began to tremble. His mouth changed its usual shape of the letter "I" and assumed the shape of the letter "O." He blinked his eyes so much, that it was frightening. This happened very rarely to Ivan Ivanovitch. One had to annoy him very seriously to cause that.

"I should like to inform you," said Ivan Ivanovitch, "that I don't want to know you."

"What a terrible misfortune ! By God, I won't weep because of that," answered Ivan Nikiforovitch.

He was lying, lying, by God he was ! He was very sorry about it.

"I won't cross your threshold."

"Ehe," said Ivan Nikiforovitch with vexation, not knowing what to do, and against his usual wont, rose to his feet : "Hey woman, boy !"

At this the same emaciated woman with a smallish boy, entangled in a long wide jacket, appeared at the door.

"Take hold of Ivan Ivanovitch's arms and put him out of the house !"

"What ! To do that to a nobleman !" shouted Ivan Ivanovitch with a feeling of dignity and indignation. "You just dare ! Try and approach me ! I'll annihilate you together with your silly master ! A crow won't find your burying place !" Ivan Ivanovitch spoke unusually strongly when his soul was stirred to its depths.

The whole group formed an expressive picture. Ivan Nikiforovitch stood in the middle of the room in all his beauty, absolutely unadorned. The peasant-woman, her mouth agape, bore on her face an expression at once vacant and terror-stricken. Ivan Ivanovitch's hand was raised, in the manner in which we depict Roman tribunes. What an unusual moment! What a wonderful spectacle! But it had an audience of only one. This was the boy in the immeasurable jacket, who stood unmoved and was picking his nose with his finger.

At last Ivan Ivanovitch took up his cap.

"You're behaving very well, Ivan Nikiforovitch! Wonderfully well! I'll remind you of this."

"Get out, Ivan Ivanovitch, get out! And see that I don't come across you. Or else—Ivan Ivanovitch, I'll smash your face in."

"This is what I think of you, Ivan Nikiforovitch," answered Ivan Ivanovitch, snapping his fingers at him and slamming the door, which with a rattle and a yelp opened up again.

Ivan Nikiforovitch appeared in the doorway and wanted to add something, but Ivan Ivanovitch did not turn round and flew from the yard.

3

What happened after the quarrel of Ivan Ivanovitch with Ivan Nikiforovitch.

And thus two respectable men, the pride and ornament of Mirgorod, quarrelled with each other! And why? For some absurd reason, because of a gander. They no longer wanted to see each other and severed all connections between themselves. Yet previously they were known as the most inseparable of friends. Every day Ivan Ivanovitch and Ivan Nikiforovitch would send someone to enquire after each other's health, and they would often converse across their balconies and say such pleasant things that it rejoiced one's heart to hear them. On Sundays Ivan Ivanovitch in his fur coat and Ivan Nikiforovitch in a yellowish-brown nankeen Cossack coat would depart together, almost arm in arm, for church. And if Ivan Ivanovitch, who had very good eyesight, was the first to notice in the middle of the street a puddle or some uncleanliness, which is sometimes to be encountered in Mirgorod, he would always say to Ivan Nikiforovitch: "Be careful, put your foot here, for there's something bad there." Ivan Nikiforovitch, on his part, also displayed most touching signs of friendship. However far off he might be standing somewhere, he would always stretch out his hand with the tobacco pouch to Ivan Ivanovitch adding: "Help yourself." And what wonderful households they both had! And these two friends . . . When I heard about it, I was thunderstruck. For a long time I did not want to believe it. God Almighty! Ivan Ivanovitch quarrelling with Ivan Nikiforovitch! Such worthy people! Is there any permanence left in this world?

For a long time after his arrival home Ivan Ivanovitch was greatly agitated. Formerly he would first drop into the stables to see if the mare was eating her straw (Ivan Ivanovitch's mare is a roan with a bald patch on the forehead, a very good little horse), then with his own hands he would feed his turkeys and pigs and only afterwards would he go to his rooms where he either makes wooden dishes (he can produce many things out of wood very skilfully, not worse than a carpenter) or he reads a book printed by Liuby, Gary and Popov (Ivan Ivanovitch does not remember its name, because one of the servant girls tore off the top of the title-page a long time ago, when she was amusing a child) or he rests under the awning. But on this occasion he did not embark on any of his usual occupations. Instead, meeting Gapka, he began to scold her for strolling about doing nothing, although she was dragging a sack of maize into the kitchen. He threw his stick at the cockerel, which came to the porch for its usual offering, and when a dirty boy in a small torn shirt came running up to him shouting: "Daddy, daddy, give me some gingerbread," he threatened him so terrifyingly and stamped so much with his feet, that the frightened child ran away God knows where.

Nevertheless he finally regained his composure and began to occupy himself with the usual matters. He had his lunch very late and did not lie down under the awning till it was almost evening. The good borshtch with pigeons cooked by Gapka, completely drove the morning's incident from his mind. Ivan Ivanovitch again began to survey his possessions with pleasure. Finally his eyes stopped on the neighbouring yard and he said to himself: "I haven't been to see Ivan Nikiforovitch to-day. I'll go to him." Having said this, Ivan Ivanovitch took his stick and his cap and departed into the street. But hardly had he stepped out of the gates, when he remembered the quarrel, spat out and turned back. Almost the same procedure occurred in Ivan Nikiforovitch's yard. Ivan Ivanovitch saw that a peasant woman had already put a leg on the wattle hedge with the intention of climbing over into his yard, when suddenly Ivan Nikiforovitch's voice was heard: "Back, back! There's no need for it!"

However, Ivan Ivanovitch became very bored. It was extremely likely that these worthy men would have made peace the very next day, if a special occurrence in Ivan Nikiforovitch's house had not destroyed every hope and poured fat on the fire of enmity which was on the point of dying out.

Agafya Fedosyevna arrived at Ivan Nikiforovitch's towards the evening of the same day. Agafya Fedosyevna was neither Ivan Nikiforovitch's blood relative nor his sister-in-law, nor even his godmother. It would appear that there was no earthly reason for her to visit him, and he himself was none too glad to see her. Nevertheless she did visit him and used to stay in his house for weeks on end and sometimes even longer. On these occasions she would take possession of the keys and would take the burden of the household on her shoulders. This was very irksome to Ivan Nikiforovitch, yet, surprisingly, he listened to her like a child, and although he sometimes tried to argue with her, Agafya Fedosyevna always had her way.

I confess, I do not understand why it has been so arranged that women can seize and lead us by the nose as deftly as they manipulate the handle of a teapot. Either their hands have been created for this purpose, or our noses are no good for anything else. And despite the fact that Ivan Nikiforovitch's nose somewhat resembled a plum, she seized him by that organ and by it led him after her like a pet dog. During her stay he even involuntarily changed his usual course of life. He did not spend as much time in the sun as usual, and, if he did, then not as nature made him, but always in his shirt and loose trousers, although Agafya Fedosyevna did not make any such demands. She did not stand on ceremony and when Ivan Nikiforovitch suffered from fever, with her own hands she rubbed him with turpentine and vinegar from head to foot. Agafya Fedosyevna wore a cap on her head, three warts on her nose and a coffee-coloured dressing gown with small yellow flowers. Her whole figure resembled a tub, and consequently it was as difficult to find her waist, as to see one's nose without a mirror. Her little feet were short, formed on the pattern of two cushions. She gossiped and ate boiled beetroots in the mornings, and swore extremely well, and during all these diverse activities her face did not change its expression for a moment, an attainment that can be claimed only by women.

As soon as she arrived everything went the wrong way.

"Don't you make peace with him, Ivan Nikiforovitch, and don't you ask his forgiveness. He wants to destroy you. The scoundrel! You don't know him yet!"

The blasted woman whispered, whispered and succeeded well, for Ivan Nikiforovitch did not even want to hear about Ivan Ivanovitch.

Everything assumed a different character. If the neighbour's dog ran sometimes into the yard, it was thrashed with anything in sight. Small boys who climbed over the hedge, returned howling, with their small shirts raised up and marks of flogging on their backs. Even the peasant woman herself, when Ivan Ivanovitch was on the point of asking her a question, made such an indecent gesture, that Ivan Ivanovitch, who was an extremely refined man, spat out and only said: "What a rotten woman! Worse than her master!"

Finally, to crown all the insults, the odious neighbour built right in front of him, on the spot formerly used as a stile for climbing over the wattle hedge, a shed for geese, as if with the special intention of redoubling the abuse. This enclosure, so repugnant to Ivan Ivanovitch, was built with devilish speed —in one day.

This roused Ivan Ivanovitch's spite and the desire for revenge. However, he did not show any outward signs of wrath, despite the fact that the enclosure usurped part of his ground, but his heart pounded so much, that it was extremely difficult for him to retain his outward calm.

In this manner he spent the day. Night arrived . . . oh, if I were a painter, how wonderfully would I have depicted all the charm of the night. I would show how the whole of Mirgorod lies asleep; how immovably innumerable stars look down; how near and far the barking of the dogs resounds in the visible quietude. How past them the infatuated sexton races and climbs the wattle hedge with chivalrous intrepidity. How the white walls of the houses, embraced by moonlight, become whiter, the shadowing trees darker, their shadows blacker, the flowers and the hushed grass more fragrant, and the crickets, turbulent knights of the night, simultaneously from all sides, raise reverberating songs. I would show how in one of the low clay houses, on a lonely bed, a blackbrowed townsgirl with young trembling breasts, tosses and dreams of a hussar's moustache and spurs, while the moonlight laughs on her cheeks. I would show, how on the white road flutters the black shadow of a bat, which alights on the white chimneys of the houses . . .

But I could hardly have painted Ivan Ivanovitch, who appeared on that night with a saw in his hands. So many diverse feelings were written on his face! Quietly—quietly and stealthily he crept to the enclosure. Ivan Nikiforovitch's dogs as yet knew nothing about their quarrel and therefore allowed him, as an old friend, to approach the enclosure, the whole of which was supported by four oak posts. Having crept up to the nearest post, he placed his saw on it and began to saw. The noise caused by his work forced him to turn around every minute, but the thought of the insult restored his valour. The first post was sawn through and Ivan Ivanovitch set to work on another. His eyes burned and his fear prevented him from seeing anything. Suddenly Ivan Ivanovitch screamed and became rigid. He thought he saw a corpse, but he soon recovered, perceiving that it was a gander which had stretched out its neck towards him. Ivan Ivanovitch spat with indignation and resumed his work. The second post was sawn through as well, and the building swayed. Ivan Ivanovitch's heart pounded so terribly when he began to saw the third, that he had to interrupt his work several times. More than half of the post was sawn through, when suddenly the unsteady building tottered . . .

Ivan Ivanovitch hardly had time to jump away, when the structure collapsed with a crash. Seizing the saw he ran home in a terrible fright and threw himself on the bed, lacking even sufficient courage to look through the window at the result of his terrible deed. It seemed to him that Ivan Nikiforovitch's whole yard was teeming with people, that there was the old woman, Ivan Nikiforovitch, the boy in the endless jacket, all with clubs, and that, led by Agafya Fedosyevna, they were coming to ruin and destroy his house.

The whole of the next day Ivan Ivanovitch spent as if shaken by fever. He imagined that his hateful neighbour, in revenge for this, would, at least, set his house on fire, and so he ordered Gapka to search everywhere every minute to ascertain whether any dry straw had been placed with malignant intent. Finally, in order to forestall Ivan Nikiforovitch, he decided to issue a writ against him in the district court of Mirgorod. What it consisted of, can be learned from the next chapter.

4

Reports what happened at a sitting of Mirgorod's district court.

Mirgorod is a wonderful town! What buildings will you not find there! Buildings with straw roofs, with reed roofs and even with wooden roofs. There is a street to the right, there is a street to the left. A wonderful wattle hedge everywhere. Along it climb hops, on it hang pots, from behind it the sunflower shows its sunlike head, the poppy blushes, the fat marrows twinkle . . . Magnificent! The wattle hedge is always adorned with objects which make it even more colourful. There is either a petticoat on it, or a shirt or a pair of trousers. There is no thieving in Mirgorod, no pilfering, and so everybody hangs on the hedge whatever comes into his head. If you approach the town from the square, then, to be sure, you will stop for some time to admire its view. On the square is to be found a puddle, an amazing puddle! A unique puddle! Such as you have never dreamed of seeing before! It takes up almost the whole of the square. A wonderful puddle! Large and small houses, which from the distance could be taken for hayricks, gather around it and admire its beauty.

But in my opinion there is no better house than that occupied by the district court. Whether it is made of oak or birch—that is none of my business—but it has, dear sirs, eight windows! Eight windows in a row look straight into the square and into that space of water, about which I have already spoken and which the Provost calls a lake! It is the only one to be painted the colour of granite. All the other houses in Mirgorod are merely white. Its roof is all of timber and would have been painted red, if the butter prepared for that purpose had not been seasoned with onions by the court clerks and eaten by them during fast days, as if to ensure that the roof should remain unpainted. A porch juts out into the square. On this hens often strut, for it is usually littered with grain or other food, not deliberately by the way, but mainly through the carelessness of litigants. The house is divided into two parts: one constitutes the court and the other contains the guard room. The part containing the court consists of two rooms. They are clean, distempered white. The front room is intended for the petitioners. In the other there is a table adorned with inkstains. On the table there is a mirror of justice and round it stand four oak chairs with high backs. Near the walls stand boxes encased in iron in which are kept stacks of local slanders. On one of these boxes stands a waxed and polished boot.

The sitting commenced early in the morning. The judge, a rather corpulent man, although somewhat slimmer than Ivan Nikiforovitch, with a kindly expression on his face, in a greasy dressing gown, with a pipe and a cup of tea, talked to the prisoner at the bar. The judge's lips were placed immediately under his nose, and so his nose could smell his upper lip to its heart's content. This lip served him instead of a snuff box, because the tobacco directed to the nose, almost always scattered over it. And thus the judge talked to the prisoner at the bar. A barefooted country girl stood on one side holding a tray with cups. At the end of the table the secretary read out the decision of the court, but in such a monotonous and mournful voice, that the prisoner himself would have fallen asleep listening to it. The judge, no doubt, would have done so before anybody else, if in the meantime an interesting conversation had not arisen.

"I purposely tried to find out," the judge was saying, sipping his tea which had already gone cold, "what they do to make them sing well. I had a nice blackbird about two years ago. And then, suddenly, it became absolutely spoiled and began to sing—Heaven knows what! The longer it went on, the worse and worse it became. It began to drawl, to croak—the least you could do was to throw it out. And it sang absolute nonsense! For the following reason: under the little neck develops a swelling, smaller than a pea. All one has to do, is to pierce this tiny swelling with a needle. Zachar Prokofyevitch taught me this. As a matter of fact, if you want to hear about it, I'll tell you how it happened. I arrive at his place . . ."

"Would you, Demyan Demyanovitch, like me to read another?" interrupted the secretary, who had already finished reading several minutes ago.

"And have you read it out already? Imagine, how quickly! I couldn't hear anything! And where is it? Give it to me, I'll sign it. What else have you there?"

"Cossack Bokitko's case, about the stolen cow."

"All right, read! Yes, so I arrive at his place . . . I can even tell you in detail what he regaled me with. Excellent dried sturgeon was served with the vodka. Yes, not like ours" (the judge clicked his tongue and smiled, and his nose smelled its perpetual snuff-box) . . . "to which our grocery shop treats us. I didn't take any herring, because, as you know, I often get heartburn from it. But I sampled the caviare—wonderful caviare—I should say it was superb ! Then I drank some peach-brandy distilled with horse-knop. There was also some saffron-vodka, but, as you know, I don't take saffron vodka. You see, it's very good at first, as they say, to whet one's appetite, but afterwards it'll finish you . . . Ah ! That's a wonderful surprise ! . . ." suddenly exclaimed the judge, seeing Ivan Ivanovitch enter.

"God be with you ! Good morning to you !" said Ivan Ivanovitch, bowing in all directions with his characteristic charm. My God ! how he could bewitch everybody with his manners ! I have never seen such refinement. He knew his own value very well and therefore considered as his due the universal respect that was paid to him.

The judge offered Ivan Ivanovitch a chair and his nose drew all the tobacco from his upper lip, which was always a sign of great satisfaction.

"What can I offer you, Ivan Ivanovitch ?" he asked, "would you like a cup of tea ?"

"No, thank you very much indeed," answered Ivan Ivanovitch and he bowed and sat down.

"Do me the favour, just one cup," repeated the judge.

"No, thank you. I appreciate your hospitality very much," answered Ivan Ivanovitch and he bowed and sat down.

"One cup," repeated the judge.

"No, don't trouble, Demyan Demyanovitch." At this Ivan Ivanovitch bowed and sat down.

"A small cup."

"So be it, I might have a small cup," said Ivan Ivanovitch, and stretched out his hand to the tray.

My God ! What infinite refinement some men possess ! It is difficult to describe what a pleasant impression such behaviour makes !

"Won't you have another small cup ?"

"I thank you sincerely," answered Ivan Ivanovitch, putting the cup upside down on the tray and bowing.

"Do me the favour, Ivan Ivanovitch !"

"I can't, I'm very much obliged." At this Ivan Ivanovitch bowed and sat down.

"Ivan Ivanovitch ! For friendship's sake, one small cup !"

"No, I'm extremely obliged for the treat," having said this Ivan Ivanovitch bowed and sat down.

"Only one cup! A small cup!" Ivan Ivanovitch stretched out his hand to the tray and took a cup.

The deuce! How the man can, how the man succeeds in keeping up his dignity!

"Demyan Demyanovitch, I . . ." said Ivan Ivanovitch, swallowing the last gulp of tea, "I've come to you on urgent business. I'm issuing a summons." At this Ivan Ivanovitch put down the cup and took out from his pocket a closely written sheet of stamped paper, "a summons against my enemy, a sworn enemy of mine."

"Who would that be?"

"Ivan Nikiforovitch Dovgotchkhoon."

When the judge heard these words he almost fell from the chair.

"What are you saying?" he said in amazement, "Ivan Ivanovitch, is it you?"

"As you see, it is I."

"God be with you and all the Saints! How can it be! You, Ivan Ivanovitch, have become Ivan Nikiforovitch's enemy! Are your lips saying it? Say it again! Isn't there somebody hidden behind you and saying it instead of you?"

"What is there incredible about it? I can't look at him. He has given me mortal offence. He has hurt my dignity."

"Holy Trinity! How can I now make my mother believe it? And every day, as soon as my sister and I quarrel, the old thing says: 'My children, you live like cat and dog with each other. If only you took Ivan Ivanovitch's and Ivan Nikiforovitch's example: what friends they are, real friends! They are pals! They are worthy people!' There you are—friends! Tell me what's all this? How did it happen?"

"This is a delicate business, Demyan Demyanovitch! You can't tell it in words, you'd better order the petition to be read. Here, take it from this side, it's more polite."

"Read it, Taras Tichonovitch!" said the judge addressing the secretary.

Taras Tichonovitch took the petition, and having cleaned his nose in the manner in which all secretaries clean their noses in district courts—by means of his two fingers—began to read:

> "From the noblemen and landowner of the Mirgorod district, Ivan, son of Ivan, Pererepenko, a petition, the particulars whereof are as follows:—
>
> "I. Notorious to the whole world for his sacrilegious disgraceful actions, the nobleman Ivan, son of Nikifor, Dovgotch-

khoon, the measure of whose iniquities is full, did in this year 1810, on the 7th day of July, put a deadly affront on my personal honour, tending equally to the destruction and to the defilement of my rank and family. The same nobleman, who is in addition of base appearance, possesses a cantankerous character and abounds in blasphemies of all kinds and swear words . . ."

Here the reader stopped for a while to clean his nose again, and the judge folded his hands with reverence and said to himself: "What a vivacious pen! God Almighty! How this man writes!"

Ivan Ivanovitch asked that the reading should proceed and Taras Tichonovitch continued:

"The same nobleman Ivan, son of Nikifor, Dovgotchkhoon, when I came to him with friendly suggestions called me publicly by a name, which insults and slanders my reputation, namely, 'a gander.' Whereas as is well known to the whole of the district of Mirgorod, I have never called myself by this base animal's name and have no intention of calling myself so in the future. AND whereas in proof of my noble origin there is the following that is to say that in the register of births in the church of the Three Saints, there is entered the day of my birth as well as the baptismal name received by me. AND whereas 'a gander' as is known to everybody in the least conversant with science cannot be entered in the register of births, for 'a gander' is not a human being, but a bird, as is well known to every one even to a person who has never attended a seminary. Nevertheless the above-mentioned malignant nobleman, being conversant with all this, for no other purpose, but that of putting a deadly affront upon my rank and calling, abused me with the above mentioned base word.

"II. The above mentioned indecorous and indecent nobleman has in addition trespassed on my patrimonial estate inherited by me from my parent, blessed be his memory, Ivan, son of Onisy, Pererepenko, who appertained to the priestly calling since, contrary to all laws, he transported an enclosure of geese exactly opposite my porch, which was done with no other intention than that of intensifying the insult put upon me as up to that time the above mentioned enclosure stood in an appropriate place and was comparatively stable. But the repulsive action of the above mentioned nobleman was designed solely for the purpose of making me a witness of indecent and vulgar acts, for it is known that not every man will go on respectable business to an enclosure, especially one containing geese. During these said unlawful actions, two supporting posts were erected on ground received by me from my parent, blessed be his memory, Ivan, son of Onisy, Pererepenko, during his lifetime, which land begins from the granary and extends in a straight line to that place where the women wash pots.

"III. The above described nobleman, whose very name and surname instil the greatest repugnance of every kind, harbours in his heart an evil intention of setting me on fire in my own house. The indubitable proof of which is clear from the below-mentioned facts.

"1stly, the same malignant nobleman has begun to leave his chambers frequently, which he never undertook before, because of his laziness and the odious fatness of his body.

"2ndly, in the servant's room, which adjoins the same fence, which guards my own ground inherited by me from my deceased parent, blessed be his memory, Ivan, son of Onisy, Pererepenko, daily and for unusual length of time there burns a light which is an obvious proof of this, for until now, due to his vile avarice, not only the tallow-candle but even the lamp has always been extinguished.

"AND I therefore ask that the said nobleman, Ivan, son of Nikifor, Dovgotchkhoon, who is guilty of arson, of insulting my rank, name and surname and of rapacious annexation of my property and, most important of all, of base and wilful addition to my surname of the epithet 'gander' should be ordered to pay a fine, to pay costs and damages, and that the same, as a transgressor, be put into shackles, and having been chained be removed to the city prison, and that judgment on this my petition be given immediately and promptly. Written and composed by the nobleman and landowner of Mirgorod, Ivan, son of Ivan, Pererepenko."

After the reading of the petition, the judge came nearer to Ivan Ivanovitch, seized him by a button and began to talk to him practically in this vein: "What are you doing, Ivan Ivanovitch? Have some fear of God! Throw the petition away, let it perish! May it dream of Satan! You'd better take Ivan Nikiforovitch by the hands and kiss each other.

And buy some wine or just make some punch and invite me! We'll have a drink together and forget everything!"

"No, Demyan Demyanovitch! This matter is different," said Ivan Ivanovitch, with the dignity which always suited him so well. "This is different from an action which could be decided by a friendly agreement. Good-bye. Good-bye to you, too, gentlemen!" he continued with the same dignity, addressing everybody. "I hope that my petition will have the appropriate effect."

And he departed, leaving all the court in amazement.

The judge sat without saying a word. The secretary snuffed his tobacco. The clerks dropped the fragment of a bottle, used instead of an inkstand, and the judge himself absent-mindedly spread the ink puddle on the table with his finger.

"What do you say to this, Dorofey Trofimovitch?" said the judge after a prolonged silence, addressing the accused.

"I won't say anything," answered the accused.

"Strange things happen nowadays!" continued the judge.

Hardly had he the time to say this, when the door squeaked and the front half of Ivan Nikiforovitch appeared before the court. The remaining half was still in the hall. Ivan Nikiforovitch's appearance, especially in court, seemed so uncanny that the judge screamed, the secretary interrupted his reading, one clerk, in a semblance of a baize semi-dress coat, put his pen in his mouth. The other swallowed a fly. Even the invalid, who performed the duties of courier and guard, and who, until then, had been standing near the door scratching inside his dirty shirt, which had a badge on its sleeve, even that invalid's mouth gaped and he stepped on somebody's foot.

"What a surprise! What brought you here and how? How is your health, Ivan Nikiforovitch?"

But Ivan Nikiforovitch was semi-conscious, for he had become wedged in the door and could not make a step either forward or backward. In vain did the judge cry out into the hall for someone there to push Ivan Nikiforovitch out into the courtroom from the back. Only one old woman petitioner was in the hall and she, despite all the efforts of her old bony hands, could not do anything. Then one of the clerks, with fat lips, wide shoulders, a thick nose, with eyes that squinted slightly and looked drunken, and with torn elbows to his jacket, approached Ivan Nikiforovitch's front half and folded both his hands across like a child's. Then he winked at the old invalid, who pushed his knee into Ivan Nikiforovitch's stomach, and despite the latter's piteous groans, he was squeezed back into the hall. Then the bolts were pushed aside and the second half of the door opened. The clerk and his assistant, the invalid, spread such a strong smell with their breath during their harmonious collaboration, that the court room transformed itself for a time into a tavern.

"They haven't hurt you, Ivan Nikiforovitch, have they? I'll tell my dear mother about it, she'll send you some lotion. If you only rub it into your waist and back, everything will be well."

But Ivan Nikiforovitch flopped heavily into a chair, and, except for prolonged groans, could say nothing. Finally, in a voice weak with exhaustion and hardly audible, he gasped "Won't you?" and taking the pouch from his pocket added, "Have some, help yourself!"

"I'm extremely glad to see you," answered the judge, "but I still can't imagine what forced you to undergo such a strain and oblige us with such a pleasant surprise."

"A petition . . ." Ivan Nikiforovitch could only murmur.

"A petition? What petition?"

"A summons . . ." (Here breathlessness caused a long pause.) "Och! A summons against a scoundrel . . . Ivan, Ivan's Pererepenko."

"Heavens! You too! Such exceptional friends! Summons against such a worthy man . . . !"

"He is—Satan himself!" said Ivan Nikiforovitch abruptly.

The judge crossed himself.

"Take the petition, read it."

"Can't be helped, read it out, Taras Tikhonovitch," said the judge, addressing his secretary with a displeased air, while his nose involuntarily snuffed his upper lip, which he usually did only when experiencing great satisfaction. This wilfulness of his nose made the judge even more annoyed. He took out a handkerchief and swept all the tobacco from his upper lip, to punish it for its insolence.

The secretary, after the usual preliminaries performed by him before he began reading, i.e., the cleaning of his nose without the aid of a handkerchief, began to read in his usual voice, as follows:—

"Petition by a nobleman of the Mirgorod district, Ivan, son of Nikifor, Dovgotchkhoon, particulars whereof are as follows:—

"I. Because of his odious anger and obvious malevolence, Ivan, son of Ivan, Pererepenko, who calls himself a nobleman, inflicted upon me various iniquities and damages and committed other malicious and horrifying deeds in respect of me, and yesterday, like a robber and a thief, with axes, saws, chisels and other such instruments, stole into my yard at night and into my enclosure which is situate therein and with his own hands wilfully hacked it to pieces for which unlawful and rapacious deed, I, for my part, did not give him any provocation.

"11. The same nobleman, Pererepenko, harbours homicidal intentions against me and he kept these intentions secret until the 7th day of last month when he came to me and began to entreat me in a friendly and, at the same time, sly manner, to give him a gun, which was in my room and offered me for it (with the meanness characteristic of him) various paltry things such as a tawny pig and two measures of oats. But, guessing in advance his criminal intent, I tried by various means to deflect him, but the same crook and scoundrel, Ivan, Ivan's son, Pererepenko, swore at me like a peasant and since that time has nurtured implacable enmity towards me. Moreover, the same frequently mentioned mad nobleman and robber, Ivan, Ivan's son, Pererepenko, is of very base origin: his sister was known to the whole world as a hussy and followed a company of chasseurs which was stationed in Mirgorod about five years ago and she enrolled her husband into the peasant's class, while his father and mother were also extremely lawless people and were both incredible drunkards. Nevertheless, the above-mentioned nobleman and robber, Pererepenko, with his animal-like and immoral deeds has surpassed all his relations and under the guise of virtue commits the most atrocious crimes: he never observes fasts, for on the eve of Lent this atheist bought a sheep and the next day ordered his peasant woman paramour Gapka to slaughter it, making the excuse that he needed fat for lamps and candles.

"Therefore I ask that the same nobleman as a robber, sacrilegist, scoundrel, clearly guilty of theft and robbery, be put in fetters and removed to prison or the district gaol and there, if it be so decreed by the court, be soundly thrashed and, if necessary, sent to hard labour in Siberia, and further, that he be ordered to pay costs and damages and that a decision be made accordingly on this my petition.

"This petition is signed and delivered by the nobleman of the Mirgorod district, Ivan, Nikifor's son, Dovgotchkhoon."

As soon as the secretary finished reading, Ivan Nikiforovitch took his cap and bowed with the intention of leaving.

"Where are you off to, Ivan Nikiforovitch?" the judge called out to the departing Ivan Nikiforovitch, "Stay for a while! Have some tea! Orishko, what are you standing about for, you silly girl, and why are you winking at the clerks? Be off, and bring some tea!"

But Ivan Nikiforovitch, alarmed at being so far from home and at having passed through such a dangerous ordeal, had already managed to squeeze himself through the door, saying, "Don't worry, I will with pleasure . . ." and closed it behind him, leaving the whole court in amazement.

There was nothing to be done about it. Both petitions were accepted and the action was on the verge of assuming a very interesting aspect, when an unfortunate occurrence added an even greater sensation. After the judge had left the court with the accused and the secretary in attendance, and while the clerks were stuffing into a sack the hens, the eggs, the loaves of brown and white bread and the pastry and other rubbish brought by petitioners, a brown pig rushed into the room and, to the amazement of the spectators, grabbed not the pastry nor a bread crust, but Ivan Nikiforovitch's petition, which lay on the end of the table with its sheets hanging down. Having seized the papers, the brown pig ran away so quickly that despite the rulers and inkstands which were hurled, not one of the clerks could catch up with it.

This extraordinary occurrence caused a tremendous upheaval, because the petition had not even been copied. The judge, or rather his secretary, and the accused discussed for a long time this unprecedented occurrence. Finally, it was decided to write out a report to the Provost, as investigation of this matter appertained to the department of the town police. The report headed No. 389 was sent to him that very day. There was a very peculiar sequel, the nature of which the readers may learn from the following chapter.

5

In which is described the conference between two persons respected in Mirgorod.

As soon as Ivan Ivanovitch had dealt with his household affairs and had left as usual to rest under the awning, he saw, to his extreme amazement, something red twinkle at his gate. It was the red lapel of the Provost who, like his collar, had received a varnishing and at the edges had lacquered skin.

Ivan Ivanovitch thought to himself, "It's not bad, that Peter Fedorovitch has come to have a chat," but became very surprised when he saw that the Provost walked extremely quickly and waved his hands, a thing he did very seldom.

Eight buttons were placed on the Provost's uniform. The ninth, which tore itself away during a procession to consecrate a church two years ago, has still not been found by the police, although the Provost, when accepting the daily reports made to him by the police inspectors, always asks whether the button has yet been found. These eight buttons were planted on him in the manner in which the peasant women plant beans: one to the right, another to the left. His left foot had been shot through during the last campaign, and, in consequence, limping, he thrust this foot so far to the side that he almost frustrated the efforts of his right foot. The quicker the Provost manoeuvred his infantry, the slower he moved forward, and so, before he reached the awning, Ivan Ivanovitch had enough time to puzzle over the reason which made the Provost wave his hands so quickly. It was all the more intriguing, as the business appeared to be of unusual importance, since the Provost wore even his new sabre.

"Good morning, Peter Fedorovitch!" exclaimed Ivan Ivanovitch, who, as had been mentioned before, was extremely curious and could not restrain his impatience at the sight of the Provost, who stormed the porch without raising his eyes and quarrelled with his infantry, which on no account could climb up the step at one go.

"Good day to my dear friend and benefactor, Ivan Ivanovitch," answered the Provost.

"Do me the favour to sit down. I see you're tired, because your wounded foot is in the way . . ."

"My foot!" exclaimed the Provost, throwing at Ivan Ivanovitch one of those glances which a giant casts at a pigmy, a learned pedant at a dancing master. At this he stretched out his leg and stamped it on the floor. This audacity, however, cost him dear, for his whole body swayed and his nose pecked at the bannisters. The wise guardian of law and order, to hide this, immediately straightened himself out and put his hand into his pocket as if intending to get out his snuffbox.

"Let me tell you, my dear friend and benefactor, Ivan Ivanovitch, that in my time I've taken part in more difficult campaigns than this. Yes, I certainly have. For example, during the campaign of 1807. Ach, let me tell you how I climbed over a fence after a pretty German girl." At this the Provost closed one eye and a devilishly roguish smile spread over his lips.

"Where have you been to-day ?" asked Ivan Ivanovitch, wishing to interrupt the Provost and to lead him more quickly to the reason for his visit. He wanted very much to ask the Provost point blank about the object of this visit, but his expert knowledge of the ways of society confronted him with all the indecency of such a direct question and Ivan Ivanovitch, his heart beating with unusual vigour, had to contain himself and await the solution of the puzzle.

"With your permission, I'll tell you where I've been," answered the Provost. "Firstly, may I say, the weather is excellent to-day . . ."

Ivan Ivanovitch almost died on hearing the last words.

"With your permission," continued the Provost, "I have come to you to-day on important business."

The Provost's face and demeanour assumed the same preoccupied air with which he had stormed the porch.

Ivan Ivanovitch's spirits revived and he trembled as if shaken by fever. Without any delay, as was his wont, he put the question :

"What's important about it ? Is it really important ?"

"Well, you will see. First of all, let me tell you, dear friend and benefactor, Ivan Ivanovitch, that you . . . as far as I am concerned, please appreciate, I've nothing to do with it, it's the Government's requirement that makes it necessary. You've disturbed the good order of the parish."

"What are you saying, Peter Feodorovitch ? I can't understand a word."

"Have a heart, Ivan Ivanovitch. Why can't you understand ? Your own animal has stolen a very important Government paper and you can still maintain, after all this, that you don't understand anything ?"

"What animal ?"

"If I may say so, your brown pig."

"What has it got to do with me ? Why does the court caretaker keep the doors open ?"

"But, Ivan Ivanovitch, your own animal, that means that you're guilty !"

"I'm obliged to you for comparing me with a pig."

"But I didn't say that at all, Ivan Ivanovitch. By God, I didn't. Be kind, let your conscience be the judge. It's known to you, no doubt, that according to the decision of the authorities, it's prohibited for unclean animals to stroll about town, especially in the main street. You'll admit yourself, that this is prohibited."

"God knows what you're talking about. What if a pig did get out into the street!"

"Allow me to inform you, allow me, allow me, Ivan Ivanovitch, that that's quite impossible. What can be done? The authorities decide—we have to obey. I don't dispute that hens sometimes run into the street and even into the square and also geese. But please note: hens and geese. Only last year I ordered pigs and goats not to be let out into the squares, and I ordered that instruction to be read aloud, word for word, in assembly, before the whole of the people."

"No, Peter Feodorovitch, I can't understand anything except your attempts to offend me in every way."

"You can't say, dearest friend and benefactor, that I'm trying to offend you. Remember: I didn't say a word to you last year, when you built a roof a whole arshine* higher than the established height. On the contrary, I pretended not to notice it at all. Believe me, dearest friend, that now too I would absolutely, so to say . . . but my duty, in short, obligation demands that I ensure cleanliness. Judge for yourself, what, when suddenly in the main street . . ."

"And how good your main streets are! Every peasant woman goes there to throw out everything she doesn't need."

"May I inform you, Ivan Ivanovitch, that it's you who are offending me! It's true that it sometimes happens, but in the main only under the fences, the barns and the granaries, but for a sow with its young to barge into the main street, into the square, that is a grave matter . . ."

"What is this, Peter Feodorovitch! A pig, after all, is God's creation!"

"I agree. It's known to the whole world, that you're a learned man, who cultivates all sciences and various other subjects. Of course, I never cultivated any sciences. I began to learn shorthand in the thirtieth year of my life. After all, as you'll know, I'm from the common people."

"Ahem" said Ivan Ivanovitch.

"Yes," continued the Provost, "in the year 1801 I was a lieutenant in the 42 Chasseur Regiment, 4th Company. Our regimental commander, if you wish to know, was Captain Yeremeyev."

* Russian measure, twenty-eight inches.

At this the Provost dived with his fingers into the snuffbox which Ivan Ivanovitch held open and kneaded the tobacco.

Ivan Ivanovitch answered: "Ahem."

"But my duty," continued the Provost, "is to obey the orders of the Government. Do you know, Ivan Ivanovitch, that one who steals Government papers from courts is liable, as for other crimes, to trial at the criminal court ?"

"I know it so well, that if you wish, I could teach you something about it too. Namely: it applies to all human beings. It would apply to you for example had you stolen some papers. But a pig is an animal, God's creation."

"That is so, but the law says Guilty of robbery . . . I would ask you to listen more attentively ! Guilty ! Here, neither kind, sex, nor rank is denoted, which means an animal can be guilty as well. It is as you wish, but the animal has to be produced in court as a disturber of peace, for its punishment to be decided.

"No, Peter Feodorovitch," coolly contradicted Ivan Ivanovitch. "That shall not be."

"As you wish, but I have to follow the Government's instructions."

"Are you trying to intimidate me ? You probably want to send the handless soldier to fetch it ? I'll order the servant woman to show him out with a poker and to break his remaining hand."

"I don't dare to quarrel with you. If you don't want to produce it to the police, use it as you desire. Slaughter it, if you wish, for Christmas and make hams from it or eat it raw. Only I'd like to ask you, if you make any sausages, send me a couple of those that Gapka makes so well from pig's blood and fat. My Agrafena Trofimovna is very fond of them."

"You're welcome. I'll send you a couple of sausages."

"I'll be extremely grateful to you, dear friend and benefactor. Now allow me to tell you only one more thing. I've been instructed by the judge as well as by all your acquaintances, so to speak, to make peace between you and your friend Ivan Nikiforovitch."

"What ! With that boor ! That I should make peace with that churl ! Never ! It'll never be, never !" Ivan Ivanovitch was in an extremely resolute state of mind.

"As you wish," answered the Provost, treating both his nostrils to some tobacco, "I don't dare to advise you. Nevertheless allow me to tell you, you are quarrelling now, but when you make peace . . ."

But Ivan Ivanovitch began to talk about quail-catching, which he usually did when he wanted to change the subject.

And so the Provost had to depart home without achieving any success.

6

From which the reader can easily find out everything it contains.

Despite the efforts of the Court to hush the matter up, the very next day the whole of Mirgorod found out that Ivan Ivanovitch's pig had stolen Ivan Nikiforovitch's petition. The Provost, losing control over himself, was the first to blurt it out. When Ivan Nikiforovitch was told about it, he did not say anything and only asked : "Was it the brown one ?"

But Agafya Fedosyevna, who was present at the time, began to attack Ivan Nikiforovitch again : "What are you going to do about it, Ivan Nikiforovitch ? They'll laugh at you, call you a fool, if you let it go at this. What sort of a nobleman will you be after this ? You'll be worse than the peasant woman, who sells the sweets you like so much."

And the turbulent woman prevailed upon him ! She found somewhere a middle-aged, swarthy man, with spots all over his face, who wore a dark blue jacket patched at the elbows, who in all respects resembled an office inkstand. He greased his boots with tar, carried three quills behind his ear and had a glass phial, instead of an inkstand, tied to a button by a string. He would eat nine tarts at one sitting and would put the tenth in his pocket, and on one stamped sheet of paper wrote down such a miscellany of slander, that not a single clerk could read it at one sitting without interspersing his reading with coughing and sneezing. This miniature likeness of a man, rummaged, pondered, wrote, and, finally, concocted the following paper :—

"To the Mirgorod District Court from the Nobleman Ivan, Nikifor's son, Dovgotchkhoon, as a sequel to my petition which came from me the Nobleman Ivan, Nikifor's son, Dovgotchkhoon, and which related to the Nobleman Ivan, Ivan's son, Pererepenko, with whom the Mirgorod District Court has acted in collusion.

"WHEREAS it was sought to keep secret that the brown pig imprudently took the law in its hand, but the news has already reached the ears of the outside world, AND WHEREAS this collusion, being of evil design, should be immediately referred to the jurisdiction of the High Court since a pig is a foolish animal, all the less capable of stealing the document and it abviously follows that the before-mentioned pig must have been incited to this act by the same enemy, who calls himself the nobleman Ivan, Ivan's son, Pererepenko, who has been already detected in robbery, attempted murder and blasphemy. AND WHEREAS the Mirgorod Court with partiality characteristic of it, concluded a secret agreement, without which the pig could on no account gain entrance to steal the document, for the Mirgorod District Court is extremely well supplied with officials in proof of which one has only to name one soldier, who always stays in the outer room and who, although he squints in one eye and has a somewhat damaged hand, nevertheless is fully capable of driving out a pig and striking it with a cudgel, all which unquestionably proves connivance of the Mirgorod Court and that there was a prior agreement to divide a bribe. NOW THEREFORE I, the Nobleman Ivan, Nikifor's son, Dovgotchkhoon, hereby notify the District Court for its full information that if the said petition is not exacted from that brown pig or from the Nobleman, Pererepenko, its abettor, and if judgment is not given in my favour as is my due, then I, the Nobleman, Ivan, Nikifor's son, Dovgotchkhoon, will lodge in the High Court a complaint about such unlawful collusion by the District Court with all the necessary formalities.

"Nobleman of the Mirgorod District, Ivan, Nikifor's son, Dovgotchkhoon."

This petition had its effect. The judge was a man, as all good people usually are, of cowardly disposition. He turned to the secretary. But the secretary blew through his lips a thick "Ahem" and showed on his face that equivocal and devilishly ambiguous expression which Satan assumes when he sees his prey rush to fall at his feet. One remedy remained: to make peace between the two friends. How was it to be achieved, when all previous attempts had been so unsuccessful? Nevertheless, they decided to try. But Ivan Ivanovitch declared bluntly that he had no such desire, and even became extremely annoyed. Ivan Nikiforovitch, instead of answering, turned his back on them and did not say a single word.

After this the proceedings commenced with that amazing speed for which the law courts are famous. The document was marked, entered, numbered, sown up, signed—everything on the same day—and then put into a cupboard, where it lay for

a year, a second year, a third year. A multitude of brides had managed to get married in the meantime. A new street was cut through Mirgorod. The judge lost a double tooth and two incisors. More children ran about in Ivan Ivanovitch's yard than before (where they came from God alone knows).. To rebuke Ivan Ivanovitch, Ivan Nikiforovitch built a new enclosure for geese, although somewhat further away than the first one, and completely blocked himself off, so that these worthy people rarely saw each other face to face. And the document, taking the normal course, still lay in a cupboard, which had turned marble from ink stains.

In the meantime an event occurred of the greatest importance for the whole of Mirgorod. The Provost gave a party! Where can I obtain brush and paint to describe the variety of the assembly and the magnificent banquet? Take a watch, open it and look at what goes on inside! What tomfoolery, is it not? Well, now imagine almost as many, if not more, wheels standing in the middle of the Provost's yard. What a variety of britchkas and carts! One had a broad beam and a narrow front. Another—a narrow beam and a broad front. One was a combination of a britchka and a cart, another resembled neither a britchka nor a cart. One resembled a huge hay-rick or a fat merchant's wife. Another resembled a dishevelled Jew or a skeleton which had not yet freed itself from its skin. Another's profile was precisely like the stem of a pipe. Another did not resemble anything and looked a queer creature, quite hideous and extremely fantastic. From amid this chaos of wheels and coach-boxes towered a semblance of a coach fitted with an ordinary house window protected with thick window bars. The drivers, dressed in grey overcoats and jackets, with sheepskin caps and forage caps of various types, with pipes in their hands, attended to the unharnessed horses in the yard.

What a party the Provost gave! Allow me to enumerate all who were there. Taras Tarasovitch, Yevpl Akinfovitch, Yevtichy Yevtichyevitch, Ivan Ivanovitch—not our Ivan Ivanovitch, but another—Savva Gavrilovitch, our Ivan Ivanovitch, Yelefery Yeleferyevitch, Makar Nazaryevitch, Foma Grigoryevitch . . . I can't go on! The hand grows tired of writing them! And how many ladies there were! Swarthy and pale faced, long and short, fat, like Ivan Nikiforovitch, and some so thin that it seemed each of them could be hidden in the Provost's sword sheath. How many women's caps! How many dresses! Red, yellow, coffee-coloured, green, blue, new, turned, recut—scarves, ribbons, handbags! Good-bye, poor eyes! You will be good for nothing after this spectacle. And what a long table was stretched out! And how talkative everybody became. What a noise there was! In comparison what is a mill with all its grindstones, cog-wheels, driving wheels, mortars! I cannot tell you for certain what they talked about, but I should think they discussed many pleasant and useful things, such as the weather, dogs, wheat, women's caps, colts.

Finally, Ivan Ivanovitch—not our Ivan Ivanovitch, but another—whose one eye squints, said: "It seems very strange to me that my right eye" (the squinting Ivan Ivanovitch always referred to himself ironically), "doesn't see Ivan Nikiforovitch Dovgotchkhoon, Esq."

"He didn't want to come," said the Provost.

"Why is that?"

"God be praised, two years have passed now since they quarrelled, that is Ivan Ivanovitch with Ivan Nikiforovitch, and where one is, the other will on no account go."

"What are you saying?" As he spoke the squinting Ivan Ivanovitch raised his eyes to Heaven and folded his hands together: "If people with good eyes do not live in peace, how can I live peacefully with my squinting eye?"

Everybody laughed loudly at these words. Everybody was very fond of the squinting Ivan Ivanovitch, for he made jokes entirely in accordance with modern taste. Even the tall, thinnish man in a baize jacket with a plaster on his nose, who until then had sat in a corner and had not once changed the expression on his face, not even when a fly flew into his nose—that same gentleman rose from his seat and moved nearer to the crowd which surrounded the squinting Ivan Ivanovitch.

"Listen," said the squinting Ivan Ivanovitch, when he saw that a considerable crowd had encircled him: "Listen! Instead of peeping into my squinting eye, let's reconcile our two friends! Now that Ivan Ivanovitch is chatting to the women and girls—let's quietly send for Ivan Nikiforovitch and then let us push them together."

Ivan Ivanovitch's suggestion was unanimously accepted and it was decided immediately to send for Ivan Nikiforovitch, and to persuade him, at any cost, to drive to the Provost's dinner. But the important question: whom to entrust with this vital mission, perplexed everybody. They argued for a long time as to who was the most capable and skilled in diplomatic errands. Finally it was unanimously decided to entrust Anton Prokofyevitch Golopuzy with the whole task.

But it is necessary first to tell the reader something about this remarkable person. Anton Prokofyevitch was an absolutely virtuous man, in the full sense of the word. If any of the notables of Mirgorod gives him a scarf or some underwear—he expresses his thanks. If anyone raps his nose slightly—he will express his thanks too. When he was asked, "Why, Anton Prokofyevitch, is it that your jacket is brown, but its sleeves light blue?" he would always reply, "And haven't you got one like that? You wait. It'll wear down and it will all become the same colour!" And indeed, the light blue cloth began to turn brown from the effect of the sun and now it completely matches the colour of the jacket. But the strange thing is, that Anton Prokofyevitch is in the habit of wearing woollen clothes in the summer, and nankeen clothes in the winter. Anton Prokofyevitch does not possess a house of his own. He had one formerly at the end of the town, but he sold it and with the proceeds of the sale bought three bay horses and a smallish britchka, in which he drove to visit landowners. But as there was a lot of trouble connected with the horses and moreover money was needed for oats, Anton Prokofyevitch exchanged them for a violin and a servant girl, and a twenty-five rouble note. Then Anton Prokofyevitch sold the violin and exchanged the girl for a morocco leather tobacco pouch embroidered with gold and now he possesses a tobacco pouch such as nobody else has. Thanks to this luxury he can no longer drive about the village and has to remain in town and spends his nights in various houses, especially in those belonging to noblemen who find pleasure in rapping his nose. Anton Prokofyevitch likes to eat well and is proficient in all kinds of drawing room games. It was always his nature to obey, and therefore taking his cap and stick he immediately departed on his way.

As he walked he began to consider how he could induce Ivan Nikiforovitch to come to the party. The somewhat gruff character of that, by the way, worthy man made Anton Prokofyevitch's undertaking almost impossible. And then, really, how could Ivan Nikiforovitch decide to go, when even rising from bed presented great difficulty to him? And assuming that he would get up, how could he go where, as he undoubtedly knew, his implacable enemy would be? The longer Anton Prokofyevitch pondered the more obstacles he found. The day was fragrant. The sun scorched. Sweat poured from him in streams. Anton Prokofyevitch, despite being rapped on the nose, was rather a shrewd man in many ways, only he was not very lucky in bartering. He knew well when to act the fool and could sometimes disentangle himself from circumstances and situations, out of which an intelligent man can seldom extricate himself.

While his cunning mind was concocting means to persuade Ivan Nikiforovitch and he was already bravely perparing to meet any contingency, an unexpected occurrence somewhat demoralised him. At this point it would do no harm to inform the reader that one pair of Anton Prokofyevitch's pantaloons was of such a strange nature, that whenever he put them on the dogs invariably bit his legs. As ill luck would have it, on that day he had put on the very same pantaloons and so hardly had he abandoned himself to his meditations, when from all sides terrifying barks arose. Anton Prokofyevitch let out such screams (nobody could scream louder than he did) that a rush was made towards him not only by a woman he knew and the inmate of an immeasurable jacket, but even by the boys scattered about Ivan Ivanovitch's yard. Although the dogs had managed to bite only one of his legs, this considerably diminished his valour and it was a little fearfully that he advanced to the porch.

7

and the last

"Ah, hello! Why do you tease the dogs?" said Ivan Nikiforovitch when he saw Anton Prokofyevitch, for nobody talked to Anton Prokofyevitch except in a jocular way.

"May they all perish! Who's teasing them?" answered Anton Prokofyevitch.

"You're lying."

"By God, I'm not! Peter Feodorovitch wants you to come to dinner."

"Ahem!"

"By God, I can't tell you how insistent he was. 'Why,' he says, 'does Ivan Nikiforovitch shun me like an enemy? He never calls for a chat, or on a visit.'"

Ivan Nikiforovitch stroked his chin.

"He says 'If Ivan Nikiforovitch won't come even this time, then I know what to think. He probably has some evil intentions. Do me a favour, Anton Prokofyevitch, prevail upon him!' What about it, Ivan Nikiforovitch, shall we go? There's a fine crowd there!"

Ivan Nikiforovitch began to scrutinise a cockerel, which stood on the porch crowing with all its might.

"If you only knew, Ivan Nikiforovitch," continued the zealous deputy, "what sturgeon meat, what fresh caviare has been sent to Peter Feodorovitch."

Ivan Nikiforovitch turned his head and began to listen attentively.

This encouraged Anton Prokofyevitch: "Let's hurry. Foma Grigoryevitch is there as well! What about it?" he added, seeing that Ivan Nikiforovitch was still lying in the same position: "Are we going or aren't we?"

"Don't want to."

This "don't want to" stunned Anton Prokofyevitch. He had already thought that his persuasive description had entirely won over this, by the way, worthy man, but all he heard was a resolute "don't want to."

"Why don't you want to?" he asked almost with annoyance, an emotion he rarely displayed, not even when people put burning paper on his head, a pastime in which the judge and the Provost especially liked to indulge.

Ivan Nikiforovitch snuffed some tobacco.

"As you wish, Ivan Nikiforovitch, but I don't know what's keeping you back."

"Why should I go?" said Ivan Nikiforovitch, after a long pause. "The robber will be there." It was thus he usually referred to Ivan Ivanovitch . . . God Almighty! And not long ago . . .

"I swear he won't be! As God is Holy, he won't! May I be struck by thunder in this very spot!" answered Anton Prokofyevitch, who was ready to swear on oath ten times in an hour. "Let's go, Ivan Nikiforovitch."

"But you're lying, Anton Prokofyevitch. He must be there."

"By God, by God, he's not! May I never move from this place if he's there! Think for yourself, what reason have I to lie? May my hands and legs dry off . . . ! What, don't you believe me even now? May I drop dead right here before you! May neither my father nor my mother, nor I myself see Heaven! Don't you still believe me?"

Ivan Nikiforovitch was completely reassured by these protestations and ordered his personal attendant, in the limitless jacket, to bring him his loose trousers and his nankeen Cossack coat.

I assume that to describe how Ivan Nikiforovitch put on his loose trousers, how a tie was wound around him, and, lastly, how they put on him the Cossack coat which burst under the left sleeve, is entirely superfluous. It will suffice to say that during the whole of that time he retained a suitable composure and did not answer a word to Anton Prokofyevitch's proposals about exchanging something for the latter's Turkish tobacco pouch.

In the meantime, the assembly awaited with impatience the decisive moment . . . when Ivan Nikiforovitch would appear and when, at last, the universal wish would be realized and these two worthy people reconciled. Many were almost sure that Ivan Nikiforovitch would not come. The Provost even offered to bet with the squinting Ivan Ivanovitch, that he would not arrive. They failed to agree only because the squinting Ivan Ivanovitch demanded that the Provost should stake his wounded leg, and he would stake his squinting eye.

This hurt the Provost very much, at which the assembly laughed. Nobody had yet sat down at the table although it had long before struck two o'clock—the hour at which in Mirgorod, even on state occasions, dinner is over.

No sooner had Anton Prokofyevitch appeared in the doorway, than he was immediately surrounded. Anton Prokofyevitch shouted in reply to all questions a resolute, "He won't come !" As soon as he said this a flood of reproaches, swearing and possibly blows was about to fall on his head for his unsuccessful mission, when suddenly the door opened and Ivan Nikiforovitch walked in.

Had Satan himself or a corpse appeared they would not have caused such a stir as was caused by Ivan Nikiforovitch's unexpected arrival. And all Anton Prokofyevitch did was to break out into peals of laughter, holding his sides with joy at fooling the whole assembly.

Apart from anything else, everyone was astonished that Ivan Nikiforovitch should have dressed as behoves a nobleman in such a short time. Ivan Ivanovitch was not present at the time. He had gone out for some reason. Having recovered from amazement, the crowd took an interest in Ivan Nikiforovitch's health and expressed satisfaction at his spreading width. Ivan Nikiforovitch kissed everybody, saying, "Much obliged."

In the meantime, the smell of borshtch wafted across the room and tickled pleasantly the nostrils of the hungry guests.

All thronged into the dining room. A file of ladies, talkative and taciturn, emaciated and fat, trooped in front, and the long table began to scintillate in all colours.

I will not describe all the dishes which were on the table. I will say nothing about either the mnishki* with sour cream, or the utribka†, which were served with the borshtch, or about the turkey with plums and raisins, or about that dish which, in appearance, closely resembles high boots soaked in kvass, or about the sauce which is the swan song of an ancient chef, or about the sauce served embraced by a wine flame which very much entertained and at the same time frightened the ladies. I will not begin talking about these dishes, for I very much prefer eating them to enlarging upon them in conversation.

Ivan Ivanovitch was very pleased with the fish cooked with horse-radish. He became intently engaged in the useful and nourishing exercise of disposing of it. Selecting the thinnest fish bones, he was putting them on the plate and somehow inadvertently looked across the table. Heavenly Creator! How strange it was! Opposite him sat Ivan Nikiforovitch!

At the same moment Ivan Nikiforovitch looked up, too! No! . . . I cannot . . . Give me another quill! Mine has wilted, it is dead. It is too thinly split for this picture! Their faces, with amazement mirrored in them, became as if turned to stone. Each saw a familiar face, a face each was involuntarily ready to welcome like an unexpected friend, and to offer the tobacco pouch with the words, "Help yourself," or "May I ask you to do me the honour?" but at the same time a face of horror—like an evil omen! Perspiration poured in torrents from Ivan Ivanovitch and Ivan Nikiforovitch.

All those present, all who were at the table, became numb with attention and fixed their eyes on the former friends. The ladies who, until then had been engaged in a rather interesting conversation about how capons were made, suddenly ceased their chatter. Everything became quiet. It was a picture worthy of a great painter's brush.

At last Ivan Ivanovitch took out a handkerchief and began to blow his nose, and Ivan Nikiforovitch glanced around and fixed his eyes on the open door. The Provost immediately interpreted this movement and ordered the door to be closed more firmly. Then each of the friends began to eat and not once did they look at each other again.

* Dish of flour with cream cheese.

† Dish made with tripe.

As soon as dinner was finished both former friends jumped up from their seats and began to look for their caps in order to slip off. Then the Provost winked, and Ivan Ivanovitch—not our Ivan Ivanovitch, but the other, the one with the squinting eye—placed himself behind Ivan Nikiforovitch and the Provost went behind Ivan Ivanovitch's back, and both began to push from behind in order to force them together and not to release them until they shook hands. Ivan Ivanovitch—the one with the squinting eye—pushed Ivan Nikiforovitch, somewhat askew, but, nevertheless, quite successfully up to where Ivan Ivanovitch stood. But the Provost set a course too much to one side. For he was quite unable to control his own obstinate infantry, which on this occasion paid no heed to any command and, as if on purpose, stepped out so vigorously in the opposite direction (which may possibly have been due to the varied assortment of liqueurs on the table) that Ivan Ivanovitch was thrown on a lady in a red dress, who in her curiosity had pushed herself out into the very middle of the room. This seemed to be a bad omen. Nevertheless, the judge, in order to improve matters, took over the Provost's place and, drawing into his nose all the tobacco from his upper lip, pushed Ivan Ivanovitch in the other direction. This is the usual method of reconciliation in Mirgorod. It somewhat resembles a game of ball. As soon as the judge had pushed Ivan Ivanovitch, Ivan Ivanovitch with the squinting eye, heaving with all his strength, pushed Ivan Nikiforovitch, from whom perspiration poured like rainwater from a roof. Despite the fact that both friends resisted extremely strongly, they were finally pushed together, because both teams received considerable reinforcements from the other guests.

Immediately they were closely surrounded on all sides and were not released until they decided to shake hands with each other.

"God preserve you, Ivan Nikiforovitch and Ivan Ivanovitch! Admit frankly: why did you quarrel? Wasn't it over some trifle? Aren't you ashamed before people and God?"

"I don't know," said Ivan Nikiforovitch, puffing with weariness (it was noticeable that he was not at all disinclined to be reconciled). "I don't know what I've done to Ivan Ivanovitch or why he sawed down my enclosure and planned to destroy me."

"I'm not guilty of any evil intent," said Ivan Ivanovitch without directing his eyes at Ivan Nikiforovitch. "I swear before God and before you, honourable nobility, that I have done nothing to my enemy. Why, then, does he insult me and slander my rank and calling ?"

"What harm have I done to you, Ivan Ivanovitch ?" said Ivan Nikiforovitch.

One more minute of explanation—and the old feud would be ready to die. Ivan Nikiforovitch was already putting his hand in his pocket to get out his pouch and say, "Help yourself."

"Isn't it harmful," answered Ivan Ivanovitch, without raising his eyes, "dear sir, to have insulted my rank and family with a word, which it is indecent to mention in this place ?"

"Allow me to tell you as a friend, Ivan Ivanovitch" (at this Ivan Nikiforovitch touched with his finger Ivan Ivanovitch's button, which signified his complete benevolence), "that you took exception, the Devil knows why, because I called you a gander . . ."

Ivan Nikiforovitch suddenly perceived that by uttering this word he had committed an indiscretion. But it was too late, the word was said. Everything went to the Devil ! If Ivan Ivanovitch lost control of himself and became so furious —so furious that may God prevent you from seeing a man in such a rage—at the utterance of that word without witnesses, judge for yourselves, dear readers, what was the effect now, when that deadly word was pronounced in an assembly which included a multitude of ladies before whom Ivan Ivanovitch liked to be especially proper ? Had Ivan Nikiforovitch not acted in such a manner, had he said "a bird," and not "a gander," it could have been remedied. But—everything was finished !

Ivan Ivanovitch cast a glance at Ivan Nikiforovitch—and what a glance ! If this glance had been given executive power, it would have turned Ivan Nikiforovitch to dust. The guests understood that glance and hurried to separate them. And that man, an example of amiability, who did not let a single beggar-woman pass by without questioning her, ran out in a terrible rage. These strong storms bring out passions.

For a whole month nothing was heard of Ivan Ivanovitch. He locked himself up in his house. The inviolable trunk was opened. From the trunk were taken out—what ? Silver roubles ! Grandfather's old silver roubles ! These silver roubles passed over into the stained hands of inky hedge-lawyers. The case was transferred to the High Court. And only when Ivan Ivanovitch received the glad news that the next day the action would be heard in court, did he come out into the light and decided to leave the house. Alas! From that time on, he was informed daily for the next ten years that the case would be finished the next day.

About five years ago I passed through the town of Mirgorod. I travelled at a bad time. It was in the autumn, with its sadly damp weather, mud and fog. Some unnatural herbage—creation of tedious uninterrupted rains—covered with sparse net the meadows and the cornfields, which it suited as pranks befit an old man, or roses an old woman. At that time the weather influenced me greatly! I was sad, when it was sad. But despite this, when I began to approach Mirgorod I felt my heart beat faster. Heavens, how many memories! I had not seen Mirgorod for twelve years. Then there lived here in touching friendship two unique men, two unique friends. And how many famous people had passed away! The judge, Demyan Demyanovitch, was already a dead man. Ivan Ivanovitch, with the squinting eye, had also taken leave of the world. I arrived in the main street. Everywhere stood poles with bunches of straw tied at their tops: some new planning was in progress! Several houses were demolished. Remnants of fences and hedges protruded dismally.

It was a feast day. I ordered my matted kibitka* to stop before the church and I entered so quietly that nobody turned around. It is true there was nobody to do so: the church was almost empty. There was hardly anybody there. It was obvious that even the most devout had been frightened by the mud. Candles in the dull, or shall I better say, sick day, were somehow strangely unpleasant. The dark entrances were sad. The oblong windows with rounded glass were drenched with tears of rain. I stepped back into the entrance and accosted a venerable old man with hair gone grey.

"Allow me to ask you whether Ivan Nikiforovitch is alive?"

At that moment the image lamp flickered more vividly before the ikon and the light flashed straight into my neighbour's face. How amazed was I, when I looked closer, to see familiar features! It was Ivan Nikiforovitch himself! But how changed!

"How's your health, Ivan Nikiforovitch? You have aged!"

"Yes, I have aged. I've come to-day from Poltava," answered Ivan Nikiforovitch.

* Tilt-cart or covered cart.

"What are you saying? You travelled to Poltava in such bad weather?"

"What can I do? My case . . ."

At this I involuntarily sighed.

Ivan Nikiforovitch heard the sign and said, "Don't worry, I've reliable information that the action will be decided next week, in my favour."

I shrugged my shoulders and left to find out something about Ivan Ivanovitch.

"Ivan Ivanovitch is here," somebody told me, "he's in the choir."

Then I saw an emaciated figure. Was that truly Ivan Ivanovitch? His face was covered with wrinkles, his hair was entirely white, but the fur coat was still the same. After a preliminary greeting, Ivan Ivanovitch turned to me with the cheerful smile, which always so well suited his funnel-shaped face, and said:—

"Shall I impart some pleasant news to you?"

"What news?" I asked.

"To-morrow my action will be definitely decided. The tribunal said that was certain."

I sighed even deeper and hurriedly said good-bye—for I was travelling on some very important business—and sat down in the kibitka.

The emaciated horses, famous in Mirgorod under the name of courier horses, began to drag along, making with their hooves, steeped in the grey mass of mud, a sound unpleasant to the ears. The rain poured in buckets on the Jew who sat on the coach-box and who had covered himself with a mat. The damp went through me. The sad town gate with the sentry box, in which there was only an invalided serviceman mending his grey armour, passed slowly by. Again the same meadows, partly ploughed, black and in parts green, wet jackdaws and ravens, monotonous rain, a tearful sky without a chink of light. The world is a melancholy place, gentlemen!

The Nevsky Prospect

NOTHING is finer than the Nevsky Prospect, at least not in Petersburg. It is Petersburg. There is nothing that does not scintillate in this beautiful street of our capital, and I know that none of its pallid inhabitants and officials would exchange the Nevsky Prospect for all the blessings in the world. It is full of charm, not only for the twenty-five-year-old owner of a bristling moustache and daringly cut frock-coat, but even for him whose chin sprouts white hair and whose head is as smooth as a silver dish. And as for the ladies! They find it even more charming. But then, who is not charmed by the Nevsky Prospect? A gust of leisure blows into your face almost before you set foot in it. Even if you were on the most pressing, indispensable business, it would fly from your mind as soon as you entered the Nevsky Prospect. It is the only place in all Petersburg to which people do not go because they must, to which they are not driven by some private need or business interest. It is as if the people one meets on the Nevsky Prospect are not such egoists as those one meets in the Morskaya, the Gorochovaya, the Liteynaya, the Meshchanskaya and other streets, where greed, avarice and want are reflected from every coach and droshky, fast or slow.

The Nevsky Prospect is the universal means of communication in Petersburg. The inhabitant of the Petersburg or Viburg district, who has not visited his friend from the Pesky or the Moskovskaya Gate for a few years, can be certain of meeting him here. No address book or information bureau provides such certain particulars as the Nevsky Prospect. The omnipotent Nevsky Prospect! The only promenade in all Petersburg that is a place of recreation for the poor. How cleanly swept are its pavements, and Heavens, how many feet have left their marks on it! The clumsy dirty jackboot of the retired soldier under the weight of which the very granite seems to crack, the tiny miniature shoe, light as a wisp of smoke, of the demoiselle whose little head turns to the glittering windows of the stores like a sunflower to the sun, the thundering sword of the hopeful ensign which cuts a fine scratch in the pavement—all attack the street with the power of strength or the timidity of weakness. What a swift, what a fantastic series of illusive images passes over it in the course of one single day ! What changes it undergoes in the course of a whole day and night !

Let us begin with the very early morning, when the whole of Petersburg smells of hot, freshly baked bread and is filled with old women, in torn clothes and cloaks, effecting their incursions into churches and against compassionate passers by. Then the Nevsky Prospect is empty. The corpulent owners of shops and their salesmen are still asleep in their Dutch shirts, or are soaping their noble cheeks and drinking coffee. The beggars congregate near the doors of tea shops where the sleepy young servant, who yesterday flew with chocolate like the wind, now creeps out with a broom in his hand and without a tie, and throws them stale cake and scraps. Along the pavements drags the inevitable crowd : sometimes the street is crossed by Russian peasants, hurrying to work in high boots stained with lime which even the Yekaterininsky canal, famous for its cleanliness, would not wash off. At this time of day it is improper for ladies to be about, because the common Russian people are wont to use expressions ruder than any likely to be heard even in the theatre. Sometimes, if his way leads him to a department of a Ministry across the Nevsky Prospect, a sleepy official trails along with a portfolio under his arm. Certainly at this period, that is until noon, the Nevsky Prospect is nobody's destination. It merely serves as a route. The street gradually begins to fill with people, who are preoccupied with their own worries and troubles and are not interested in their surroundings.

The Russian peasant talks about a griven*, or seven groshi.† The old men and women wave their hands and talk to themselves, sometimes with quite remarkable gestures ; but nobody listens to them or laughs at them, except perhaps some small boys in canvas dressing gowns with empty bottles or repaired boots in their hands, who flash like lightning along the Nevsky Prospect. At this time of day you may wear what you like. Even if you sport a peaked cap instead of a hat or your collar protrudes too much from under your tie, nobody will take any notice.

* Ten kopek piece. † Half kopek pieces.

At 12 o'clock the Nevsky Prospect is raided by tutors of all nationalities with their lawn-collared charges. English Joneses and French Kokos walk arm in arm with the young entrusted to their paternal vigilance and in decorous platitudes explain that shop signs are used to describe what the shops contain. Governesses, pale Misses and pink Mademoiselles, walk majestically behind their slim restless little girls, ordering them to raise their shoulders more and to hold themselves straighter. In short, at this time the Nevsky Prospect is a pedagogical Nevsky Prospect. But the nearer it is to two o'clock, the more the number of tutors, pedagogues and children decreases. Finally they are dislodged by their tender parents, who walk arm in arm with their variegated, multicoloured, weak-nerved better halves. Little by little their society extends to all who have finished quite important household occupations, such as those who have talked with their doctor about the weather and the little pimple on their nose, those who have ascertained the health of their horses and their children—who, by the way, show great promise—those who have read the advertisements and an important article in the papers about arrivals and departures, and lastly those who have drunk a cup of coffee or tea. They are also joined by those who serve in the Foreign Office and are distinguished by the nobility of their occupation and of their habits.

Heavens, what wonderful appointments and jobs there are! How they raise the spirit and rejoice the heart! But alas, I do not hold one and I am deprived of the pleasure of experiencing the exquisite refinement of superior officials.

Everyone you meet on the Nevsky Prospect is full of propriety—the men in long frock-coats with hands in their pockets, the ladies wearing long pink, white, and pale blue satin coats and smart little hats. Here you will meet side-whiskers, unique sidewhiskers, slipped under the tie with amazing, incredible skill. Velvety, satin sidewhiskers, black as sable or as coal, but alas, these belong only to the Foreign Office. To those serving in other departments fate has refused black sidewhiskers. To their great displeasure they must be content with ginger whiskers. Here you will meet wonderful moustaches, which no pen, no brush can describe. Moustaches to which the better half of life is dedicated, the object of long vigilance by day and night. Moustaches upon which have been poured the most ravishing perfumes and scents and which have been anointed with the rarest and most precious pomades. Moustaches which are wrapped up for the night in thin vellum. Moustaches for which their possessors nurture the most touching attachment and which are the envy of all who behold them.

Hats of a thousand and one shapes, dresses, scarves of all shades and colours, the owners of which remain attached to them sometimes for two whole days, combine to dazzle you on the Nevsky Prospect. It is as if a whole sea of butterflies has suddenly arisen and flutters in a glittering cloud over the black beetles of the masculine sex. Here you will meet such waists as you have never even dreamed of. Thin, narrow waists, no thicker than the neck of a bottle, upon meeting which you reverently step aside, in case unwittingly you snap them with an impolite elbow. Your heart trembles with fear lest, through a mere incautious breath, the most enchanting work of nature and art will be broken. And what feminine sleeves you will encounter in the Nevsky Prospect! How charming! They are like two aeronautical balloons, which would quickly raise the wearer to the skies, were she not anchored to a man. For it is as easy and pleasant to raise a lady into the air, as it is to raise a glass of champagne to the mouth. Nowhere are bows made so nobly and so unconstrainedly as on the Nevsky Prospect when people meet there. Here you will come across a unique smile. A smile which is the height of art, a smile which sometimes makes you melt with pleasure, a smile which sometimes sinks you lower than the grass and forces you to bend your head, a smile which sometimes raises you higher than the Admiralty spire and makes you feel able to lift it off the ground.

Here you will meet those who discuss a concert or the weather with unusual gentility and an air of personal dignity. Here you will encounter a thousand and one inconceivable characters and phenomena. Heavenly Creator! What strange characters one meets on the Nevsky Prospect! There are many who, when they meet you, will unfailingly study your boots and, when you pass, look back to stare at them from the rear. I still cannot understand why they do this. At first I thought they were shoemakers. But they are nothing of the sort. Mostly they serve in Government offices—many of them can write an excellent memorandum from their department to another—or they spend their time strolling and reading newspapers in cafés. They are usually respectable people.

That blessed time—between two o'clock and three in the

afternoon—can be termed the panorama period of the Nevsky Prospect. It is then that the climax is reached in the exhibition of the finest creations of man. One person displays a smartly-cut jacket of the best beaver, another a wonderful Grecian nose, a third a pair of magnificent sidewhiskers, a fourth two pretty eyes and a daring little hat, a fifth a talisman ring on a little finger, a sixth a tiny foot in a charming shoe, a seventh a tie which creates a sensation, an eighth a moustache which is overwhelming. But as soon as three o'clock has struck the exhibition finishes, the crowd grows thinner.

A new change occurs at three o'clock. Spring suddenly comes to the Nevsky Prospect. It becomes covered with officials in green uniforms. Hungry Titular, Aulic and other Councillors are striving hard to quicken their steps. Young Collegiate Registrars, District and Collegiate Secretaries, hurry to make the best use of their time and to stroll along the Nevsky Prospect with a bearing which does not reveal that for six hours they have been sitting in court. But the old Collegiate Secretaries, Titular and Aulic Councillors walk fast, their heads low. They have no time for the passer by. It is not for them to tear themselves away from their worries. In their heads is a confusion, a whole archive of jobs begun and unfinished. For a long time they still see, instead of the sign boards, a cardboard box filled with papers or the fat face of their chief.

From four o'clock the Nevsky Prospect is empty, and you will scarcely meet a single official. A seamstress from one of the shops rushing across with a box in her hands; the pitiful object of a registrar's philanthropy let loose on the world in a baize overcoat; a newly arrived stranger for whom all hours are the same; a tall lanky Englishwoman with a bag and book in her hands; a labourer—a Russian—in a cotton jacket with the waistline on his shoulders and a small narrow beard, who lives in a panic of haste and who, as he passes hurriedly along the pavement, moves everything, his back, his hands, his legs and his head; occasionally an artisan; you will meet no-one else on the Nevsky Prospect.

But as soon as dusk falls on the houses and the streets and the watchman scrambles up the steps to light the lamps and, from the low windows of the shops, etchings begin to appear which would not dare display themselves in daylight, then the Nevsky Prospect becomes alive again and begins to move. Then comes that mysterious time when the lantern confers on everything an enticing miraclous light. Then you will

encounter many young people, mainly unmarried, in warm jackets and overcoats. It is then that a sense of purpose is in the air, or rather something resembling a purpose. Something quite unaccountable. The steps of all are quickened and become uneven. Long shadows flash along the walls and the pavement, their heads almost reaching the Pliceysky Bridge. Young Collegiate Registrars, District and Collegiate Secretaries walk continually up and down the street. But the Senior Collegiate Registrars, the Titular and Aulic Councillors mainly sit at home. This is either because they are married men or because the German cooks, who live in their houses, cook them excellent meals.

But you will also meet venerable old men, who at two o'clock stalked along the street with such dignity and nobility. You will see them race like the young Collegiate Registrars, to look under the tiny hat of a lady perceived from afar, a lady whose lips and cheeks thickly plastered with paint are so pleasing to those strollers—mainly shop assistants, workmen, merchants, always in German jackets—who walk in a crowd, usually arm in arm.

"Stop !"

It was at such a time that this word was shouted by Lieutenant Pirogov, as he tugged at the young man in a dress-coat and cloak, who was walking with him.

"Did you see her ?"

"I did. She's wonderful, absolutely like Peruggino's Bianca."

"Who are you talking about ?"

"About her, the one with the dark hair. What eyes, my God, what eyes ! Her carriage, her figure, her features—wonderful !"

"I'm talking about the blonde who passed behind her to the other side. Why don't you follow the brunette, if you like her so much ?"

"How can I ? " exclaimed the young man in the dress-coat blushing. "As if she was one of those who patrol the Nevsky Prospect in the evening. She must be a very distinguished lady," he continued sighing. "Her cloak alone must have cost about eighty roubles."

"Simpleton !" shouted Pirogov, forcefully pushing him in the direction from which her vivid cloak was fluttering. "Go on, nincompoop, you'll lose sight of her ! I'll follow the blonde.'

The friends separated.

"I know you all," thought Pirogov to himself with a conceited and self confident smile, convinced that there was no beauty who could withstand him.

With timorous steps the young man in the dress coat and cloak walked in the direction from which the multi-coloured cloak fluttered in the distance, glittering as it approached the lamplight and quickly merging with the darkness when withdrawing from it. His heart was pounding and he involuntarily quickened his steps. The idea of attracting the attention of the lady, who was flying away in the distance, did not even enter his head and he certainly had no such dark thoughts as those hinted to him by Lieutenant Pirogov. He wanted only to see the house, to observe the dwelling of this charming creature, who, it seemed, had flown straight from Heaven to the Nevsky Prospect and would surely fly away Heaven knows where. He rushed so quickly that he was continually pushing sedate grey-whiskered gentlemen off the pavement.

This young man belonged to that class of people who in our country constitute quite a strange phenomenon and fit in as little with the inhabitants of Petersburg as does a character from a dream with the material world. This exceptional class of people is most unusual in this city where everyone is either an official or a merchant or a German artisan. He was a painter. Is it not a strange phenomenon? A painter in Petersburg! A painter in the country of snow, a painter in the country of the Finns, where everything is wet, smooth, flat, pale, grey, foggy. These painters are not at all like the Italian painters—proud, fiery, like Italy and its sky. On the contrary, they are mostly kind folk, meek, shy, carefree, who love their art, boast of no wealth and modestly discuss their beloved subject as they drink tea with two friends in a small room. They are continually calling in some beggar woman and forcing her to sit for a solid six hours so that they may transfer to a canvas her pitiful, innate expression. They paint the perspective of their rooms, about which are scattered oddments of artistic rubbish, plaster hands and feet, coffee-coloured by time and dust, an upturned palette, broken picture frames, a friend playing the guitar, walls stained with paint, an open window through which glimmer the red shirts of some poor fishermen and the pale waters of the Neva. Theirs is almost invariably a greyish turbid colouring—the indelible imprint of the North. Nevertheless, they labour at their work with delight. They often harbour a true talent, and if only they had breathed the fresh air of Italy, this talent would probably have developed as freely, as vigorously and as vividly as a plant which, after a long time indoors, has been carried out into the fresh air. Generally, they are very timid. A star and a thick epaulette throw them into such confusion, that they involuntarily lower the price of their works. They sometimes like to act the dandy, but this foppishness always appears inharmonious on them.

They will sometimes wear an immaculate dress coat and a stained cloak, an expensive velvet waistcoat and a jacket full of paint smudges. It is rather like one of their own unfinished landscapes, on which you will sometimes see a nymph drawn upside down; the artist, lacking another canvas, having made his sketch on the stained background of an earlier work, which he had once painted with enthusiasm. He never looks straight into your eyes. If he does, then somehow turbidly, indefinitely. He does not pierce you with the vulture glance of a passer-by, or the falcon look of a cavalry officer. For when he is looking at your features he is also seeing the features of some plaster Hercules standing in his room, or a painting which he has not yet put on to a canvas. He, therefore, often answers disjointedly, sometimes inopportunely, and the medley of thoughts in his head increases his timidity.

To this class belonged the young man we have described, the painter Piskarev, bashful, timid, but one who in his heart carried sparks of feeling which at an opportune moment were ready to burst into flame. With secret trepidation he hurried after her, who had so severely wounded him, amazed himself, it seemed, at his own audacity. The unknown being, to whom his eyes, thoughts and feelings were directed, suddenly turned her head and glanced at him. God! What heavenly features! The loveliest forehead of dazzling white was shadowed by hair as beautiful as agate. It was coiled in wonderful curls, some of which protruded from under the little hat and touched a cheek tinged a pale, fresh pink by the evening's cold. Her lips were locked by a whole swarm of the most charming reveries. Everything that is left of childhood memories, that gives dreams and quiet inspiration by the light of a shining lamp, all this, it seemed, was combined, merged and reflected in her harmonious lips.

She glanced at Piskarev and his heart fluttered at that glance. She glanced sternly, indignation expressing itself on her face at the sight of such insolent pursuit. But on that lovely face wrath itself was enchanting. Thrown into shame and confusion he stopped and cast down his eyes. Yet how could he lose this Goddess without even discovering the sanctuary where she had alighted for a visit ? This thought came into the young dreamer's head and he decided to pursue. But to make his pursuit unnoticeable he drew further back, looked nonchalantly in all directions and inspected the shop signs, but without losing sight of the stranger's single step. Pedestrians flashed by less often ; the street became quieter. The beauty turned round and he thought he saw a faint smile appear on her lips. He began to tremble from head to foot and could not believe his eyes. No, it was the lantern which, with its delusive light, delineated on her face the semblance of a smile. No, his own dreams were laughing at him. But his breath froze in his breast, everything in him turned into a vague tremor, all his senses burned and everything around him became enveloped in a sort of mist. The pavement swayed under him, the coaches with galloping horses seemed motionless, an arched bridge seemed to stretch out and break, a house stood with its roof upside down, the sentry-box was tumbling towards him and the watchman's halberd and the golden words of a shop sign and the scissors painted on it glittered, it seemed, on the very lids of his eyes. And all this was caused by one glance, one turn of a pretty head. Without seeing or hearing or listening, he rushed along the light tracks of the lovely little feet, trying to restrain the quickness of his steps which flew in unison with the beating of his heart. Sometimes doubt would assail him. Was the expression on her face really so benign ? Then he would stop for a moment, but the palpitation of his heart, the irresistable force and turbulance of all his senses, drove him forward.

Suddenly, without his noticing it, a four-storied house arose before him. All its four rows of windows ablaze with light, looked down on him and he stumbled against the iron staircase at the entrance. He saw the stranger fly up the staircase, turn round, put her finger to her lips, and give him a sign to follow her. His knees shook, his senses and thoughts burned. Joy, like lightning, pierced his heart with unbearable poignance. No, it was no longer a dream ! God Almighty ! What happiness that moment bore ! How wonderful life became in two minutes !

But was it not all a dream ? Could it be that she, for one heavenly glance from whom he was prepared to give up his life, to approach whose dwelling he deemed an inexpressible happiness, that she was now so gracious to him. He flew up the stairs. He did not think a single earthly thought. No flame of earthly passion burned within him. No, like a virginal youth, still breathing the indefinable spiritual need of love, he was pure and innocent. And what would have roused in a depraved man an insolent intention, served on the contrary, to purify his feelings. The trust, which a weak wonderful being placed in him, that trust imposed on him a vow of chivalrous rectitude, a vow to fulfil slavishly all her orders. He only desired that these orders should be as difficult as possible and hard to execute, so that only by exerting his strength to the utmost would he be able to overcome all the difficulties. He did not doubt that some secret and, at the same time, important happening had forced the stranger to put herself in his charge. Probably considerable services would be demanded and he felt in himself already the strength and daring to do everything.

As they ascended the winding staircase a succession of thoughts raced through his head. "Walk more carefully!" sounded a voice like a harp, which filled his heart with new tremor. In the dark height of the fourth storey the stranger knocked at a door—it opened and they both entered. A woman of not unpleasant appearance met them with a candle in her hand, but she looked at Piskarev so strangely and insolently that he involuntarily lowered his eyes. They entered a room. Three feminine figures in various corners appeared before his eyes. One was laying cards, another sat at the piano playing with two fingers a pitiful semblance of an ancient Polonaise, a third sat before a mirror combing her long hair, and did not deem it in the least necessary to interrupt her toilet at the entrance of a stranger. An unpleasant disorder, which is only to be encountered in a bachelor's room, reigned everywhere. The furniture was covered with dust. A spider had spun its web on a sculptured cornice. Through a door, which stood ajar, shone a high boot and the flushed braid of a uniform. A loud masculine voice and feminine laughter sounded without restraint.

Heavens, where had he come! At first he did not want to believe it and he began to examine more closely the objects which filled the room. But the bare walls and the curtainless windows demonstrated the absence of any busy housewife. The worn faces of these pitiful creatures, one of whom sat down almost in front of his nose and surveyed him as calmly as if he were a spot on a stranger's dress—all this convinced him that he had come into a disgusting den, in which dwelt piteous lewdness born of superficial education and the terrible overcrowding of the capital ; one of those harbours of vice where man has sacrilegiously suppressed and ridiculed everything that is pure and holy and adorns life, where woman, the world's beauty and the crown of creation, has turned into some strange, ambiguous creature, where along with purity of heart she has stripped herself of all that is feminine and has odiously appropriated the manners and the insolence of man and has already ceased to be that weak, that lovely being, so different from us.

Piskarev surveyed her from head to foot with amazed eyes, as if still wanting to ascertain whether it was she who had so bewitched him and swept him off his feet on the Nevsky Prospect. But she stood before him as lovely as ever. Her hair was just as wonderful, her eyes still seemed to be heavenly. She was fresh, she was only seventeen years old. It was apparent that only recently had horrible vice caught up with her. As yet it had not dared to touch her cheeks. They were fresh and lightly shadowed by a pink flush. She was beautiful.

He stood motionless before her and was already prepared to forget himself as naively as he had done before, but the beautiful girl had become bored with such prolonged silence and smiled meaningly, looking right into his eyes. This smile was so piteously insolent, so horrible, that it was as appropriate on her face as an expression of piety on the ugly face of an extortioner or of calculation on the face of a poet.

He shivered. She opened her pretty lips and began to say something, but it was all so silly, so profane . . . As if along with purity, the brain too leaves a human being. He no longer wanted to hear anything. He was very foolish and as simple as a child. Instead of taking advantage of such benevolence, instead of being pleased with such an opportunity, as no doubt anybody else in his place would have been, he rushed out into the street like a wild goat as quickly as his feet would carry him.

Hanging his head and with his hands down, he sat in his room like a beggar who had found a priceless gem and accidentally dropped it into the sea. "What beauty, what goddess-like features, and where ? . . . In such a place ?". . . . That was all he could utter.

Indeed, never does pity move us more strongly than at the sight of beauty contaminated by the pernicious breath of vice. Let ugliness be its intimate, but beauty, tender beauty . . . it is linked only with purity in our thoughts.

The beautiful girl, who had so bewitched poor Piskarev,

was indeed a wonderful, an amazing phenomenon. Her existence in that despicable circle seemed even more unusual. All her features were formed so purely, the expression on her lovely face was marked by such nobility that it was impossible to think that the claws of vice were ready to seize her. She could have been the priceless pearl, the whole world, the whole paradise, all the treasures of a passionate husband. She could have been a lovely calm star in a family circle, giving sweet commands with a movement of her lovely lips. She could have been a goddess on the light parquet floor of a crowded ballroom, by the glitter of candles with a crowd of admirers in silent reverence at her feet. But, alas! The spirits of Hell, avid to destroy the harmony of life, had by the dreadful exercise of their will hurled her with laughter into the abyss.

Pierced to the heart with pity, he sat before the burnt-out candle. Midnight had passed, the bell of the tower struck half-past twelve, and he still sat motionless, without sleep, but without being consciously awake. Sleep, taking advantage of his immobility. had begun to steal quietly upon him. Already the room began to disappear, only the light of the candle shone through the dreams which began to overcome him, when suddenly a knock at the door made him start, and he opened his eyes. The door opened and a lackey in a rich uniform appeared. Never had a rich uniform peeped into his lonely room. Moreover, it was such an unusual time . . . He was perplexed and with impatient curiosity looked at the lackey as he entered.

"The lady," said the lackey with a polite bow, "whom Your Honour visited several hours ago, has ordered me to ask you to come to her and has sent a coach for you."

Piskarev stood in speechless amazement. "A coach, a lackey in uniform! No, there is probably some mistake . . ."

"Excuse me," he said timidly, "but haven't you come to the wrong place? Your mistress has probably sent you to fetch somebody else, not me."

"No, sir, I'm not mistaken. Did you, sir, escort my mistress on foot to the house which is on the Liteynaya, to the room on the fourth floor?"

"I did."

"Well, then, please hurry, sir, the mistress wants to see you without fail and asks you to come straight to her house."

Piskarev ran down the staircase. Indeed, a coach stood in the yard. He sat down in it, the doors were slammed, the stones of the street thundered under the wheels and hoofs—and an illuminated perspective of houses with vivid shop signs flew past the coach windows. Piskarev pondered throughout the whole journey and did not know how to interpret this adventure. Her own house, a coach, the lackey in a rich uniform . . . These things he could not reconcile with the room on the fourth floor, the dusty windows and the untuned piano.

The coach stopped in front of a brightly-lit entrance and he was momentarily stunned by the sight of the long row of coaches, by the chatter of the coachmen, the brilliant illuminations of the windows and by the sound of music. The lackey in the rich uniform helped him into a hall with marble columns where a hall-porter, emblazoned with gold, presided over cloaks and fur coats scattered beneath the lamps. From the hall a wide staircase with glittering bannisters, perfumed with scent, floated upwards. He found himself on the staircase, he entered the first room, but drew back frightened by the sight of the vast crowd of people. The medley of faces threw him into a complete confusion. It seemed to him that some demon had crumbled the whole world into a multitude of variegated pieces and then, without any rhyme or reason, jumbled the pieces together again. Sparkling feminine shoulders and black dress coats, candelabras, lamps, airy fleeting gauze, etherial ribbons and a fat double bass which looked out from behind the bannisters of a magnificent gallery—all this dazzled him. He saw so many venerable old men and ageing men with stars on their dress-coats, so many ladies moving so proudly, so lightly and so gracefully on the polished floor, or seated in rows. He heard so many French and English words. And young men in black dress-coats had such a noble bearing, talked and listened with such dignity and without a superfluous word, joked so majestically, smiled so respectfully, sported such wonderful sidewhiskers and exhibited their beautiful hands with such skill as they adjusted their ties. The ladies were so etherial, so full of conceit and ecstasy and lowered their eyes so charmingly, that . . .

But Piskarev, who leaned with fear on one of the columns, showed by his timid bearing that he was completely disconcerted.

He noticed that the greater part of the crowd thronged around some dancers who floated in dresses that seemed to to have been woven from the air itself. They carelessly touched the shining floor with their glittering little feet and seemed more etherial than if they had not touched it at all. But one among them was dressed better, more magnificently and more brilliantly than the others. Her dress was indefinably exquisite and as if it had created itself around her without any effort on her part. She looked at the crowd of spectators who surrounded her, but did not seem to see them. Her lovely long eyelashes were lowered indifferently and the shining whiteness of her face was even more dazzling when a faint shadow fell on her charming forehead as she lowered her head.

Piskarev made every effort to push through the crowd in order to see her fully. But to his distress some huge head with dark curly hair kept continually screening her from him. The crowd, too, pressed round him so closely, that he dared not move forward or back, fearful lest he should jostle a Councillor of State. But at last he managed to press forward and glanced at his clothes, to straighten them out. Heavenly Creator, what was this? He was wearing a jacket stained all over with paint! In his hurry to drive away he had even forgotten to change into suitable clothes. He blushed up to his very ears and lowered his head, wishing that the ground would swallow him. But there was absolutely nowhere to hide. Courtiers in glittering uniforms closed up behind him like a sheer wall. He now wanted to be as far as possible from the beautiful girl with the lovely forehead and eyes. Fearfully he raised his head to see if she was looking at him. Heavens! She stood before him . . . But what is this? What is it? "It is she!" he exclaimed almost aloud. Indeed it was she, she whom he had met on the Nevsky Prospect and whom he had escorted to her dwelling.

In the meantime she raised her eyes and looked at everybody with a clear glance. "Ai, ai, ai, how lovely she is! . . ." was all he could say holding his breath. She surveyed with her eyes the whole circle of people, who vied with each other to draw her attention, but almost sadly she was turning her glance away when it met Piskarev's eyes. Oh what Heaven! What Paradise! Heavenly Creator, give him strength to bear it! Life cannot hold it. It will destroy and carry away his soul.

She made a sign, but neither with her hand nor with a nod of her head. No, that sign was indicated by her wonderful eyes, with such an exquisite, imperceptible expression, that nobody else could see it. But he saw and understood. The dance lasted for a long, long time. The weary music seemed to be dying down and expiring, and then it would again break out squeaking and thundering. But at last—the end!

She sat down. Her breast rose under the fine smoke of gauze. Her hand (God Almighty, what a lovely hand!) fell on her knees, crumpling the etherial veil, and the dress beneath seemed to breathe music, the contrast of its fine lilac colour making even whiter the whiteness of that lovely hand. If one could only touch it—nothing more! No other desires—they are all insolent . . . He stood behind her chair, not daring to talk, not daring to breathe.

"Were you bored?" she said, "I was bored too. I see that you hate me . . ." she added, lowering her eyes.

"Hate you? I? I . . . ." Piskarev, completely confused, wanted to say and would probably have poured out a volley of disjointed words, but at that moment a courtier with a wonderful curled tuft of hair on his head, came up to them making some brilliant and pleasant remark. He exhibited rather pleasantly a row of quite good teeth and with each witticism hammered a sharp nail into Piskarev's heart. At last, fortunately, someone alongside turned to the courtier with a question.

"How unbearable it is," she said, raising her heavenly eyes at him. "I will sit down at the other end of the room. Come there."

She slipped through the crowd and vanished. Like one possessed he pushed his way through the crowd and he was at her side and was already with her.

Yes, it was she! She sat like a queen, finer than everybody, lovelier than everybody, and her eyes were searching for him.

"Are you here?" she asked quietly. "I will be frank with you. The circumstances of our meeting will probably have seemed strange to you. Can you really think that I can belong to that despised class of beings, with whom you met me? My actions seem strange to you, but I shall tell you a secret. Will you be able never to divulge it?" she said casting a piercing look at him.

"Oh, I will! I will! I will! . . ."

But at that moment a rather elderly gentlemen appeared and began to talk to her in some language incomprehensible to Piskarev and gave her his arm. With an imploring glance she looked at Piskarev and signed to him to remain in his place and await her return. But a fit of impatience made it beyond his power to obey any orders, even from her lips. He followed her, but the crowd parted them. He no longer saw the lilac dress. With anxiety he walked from room to room and without mercy pushed past everyone he encountered, but in the rooms he visited sat only important personages playing whist in deadly silence.

In one corner of a room several elderly people were arguing about the advantages of military service over civilian life; in another, people in immaculate dresscoats were lightly exchanging views about the voluminous works of an industrious poet. One elderly man of respectable appearance seized Piskarev by a button of his coat and submitted to his judgment a profound remark he had made but Piskarev rudely pushed him away without even noticing the quite significant medal the elderly gentleman wore round his neck.

He ran into another room—she was not there either. He ran into a third—she was not there. "Where is she? Give her to me! Oh, I cannot live without having seen her again! I must hear what she wanted to say,"—but all his search was in vain.

Anxious, weary, he pressed himself into a corner and looked at the crowd. But to his strained eyes everything began to appear in an indistinct light. At last the walls of his room arose clearly before him. In front of him stood a candlestick with an almost dying light in its depths. The whole candle had melted. Fat had splashed over the table.

Then he had been sleeping! God, what a dream! Why did he have to wake up! Why could he not have waited one more minute. She would probably have appeared again! The room was in such a mess, in such a wretched disorder . . . Oh, how disgusting reality is! What is it compared with a dream? He hurriedly undressed and went to bed, wrapping himself up in a blanket, wishing to recall for a moment the departed vision. Indeed sleep did not tarry in coming to him, but it brought nothing of all he desired to see: there appeared Lieutenant Pirogov with a pipe, or the academy watchman, or an Aulic Councillor of State, or the head of a Finnish girl of whom he once drew a portrait and similar nonsense.

He lay in bed until noon, longing to fall asleep. But she did not reappear. If she had only shown her lovely features for a moment, if he had only heard for a moment the rustling of her dress, if he had only caught a glimpse of her hand dazzlingly white like snow from beyond the clouds.

Having cast everything aside, having forgotten everything, he sat with a heartbroken, hopeless expression, filled only with thoughts of the vision. He did not think of touching any food. His eyes, without any consciousness, without any life, looked through the window, which was over a yard where a dirty watercarrier was pouring out water which froze in the air and a pedlar's goatlike voice was jarring "old clothes for sale." These everyday mundane sounds came strangely to his ears. In this manner he sat until the evening and then eagerly threw himself down on his bed. For a long time he fought with insomnia and finally overpowered it. Again some dream, some vulgar odious dream.

"God, have mercy! At least for one minute, at least for one minute show her to me."

He again waited until evening, fell asleep again and again dreamed of some official who was an official and a bassoon at the same time. Oh, it was unbearable. At last she appeared, her head and curls . . . she looks . . . Oh, for what a short time! Again fog, again some silly phantom.

At last the visions became his life and from that time on his whole existence took a strange turn. He slept when he was awake, and he was awake only in his sleep. If anybody had seen him sitting wordlessly in front of an empty table or walking in the street, he would probably have assumed him to be a lunatic or a man ruined by alcohol.

His glance was completely devoid of expression, his inborn absentmindedness had fully developed and mercilessly driven from his face all feeling, all movement. He became animated only at the approach of night.

This condition broke his strength and it was a dreadful torture for him when finally sleep began to leave him altogether. He was prepared to use any means to recapture his sole joy. He had heard that by means of opium sleep could be restored. But where could opium be obtained? He remembered a Persian who owned a shop where he sold shawls and who, when they met, almost invariably asked him to paint his beautiful girl friend. Piskarev decided to go to him, assuming that he, no doubt, would have opium. The Persian received him sitting crosslegged on a couch.

"What do you need opium for?" he asked Piskarev. Piskarev told him about his insomnia.

"All right, I'll give you some opium but you paint my beautiful girl friend! Make her look beautiful, with black eyebrows and eyes as large as olives, and I will be near her smoking my pipe! You understand, it must be good. She must look beautiful."

Piskarev promised everything. The Persian disappeared for a moment and returned with a small jar filled with a dark liquid. He carefully poured off part of it into another small jar which he gave to Piskarev with instructions not to use more than seven drops in water at a time. Avidly Piskarev seized the precious little jar, which he would not have given away for a heap of gold, and ran home as quickly as his feet would carry him.

At home, he poured off several drops into a glass of water and having swallowed the liquid, dropped down on the bed.

Heavens, what joy ! She ! Again she ! But how different ! Oh, how prettily she sits at the window of a small white cottage ! Her dress breathes simplicity, such as only a poet's thought is dressed in. Her hair style . . . Heavens, how simple that hair style is and how it suits her ! A short neckerchief is thrown lightly over her slim little neck. Everything about her is modest, everything about her holds a secret subtle expression of taste. How sweet is her graceful walk ! How musical is the rustle of her steps and of her simple dress ! How beautiful is her hand embraced by a hair-bracelet. She beseeches him with tears in her eyes, "Don't despise me. Look more closely and tell me. Am I capable of being what you think me to be ?"

"Oh ! No, no ! Let whoever dared think that, let him . . ."

But he awoke. Exhausted, tortured with emotion, tears in his eyes.

"It were better if you did not exist at all ! If you had not lived in the world, and were the creation of an inspired painter ! I would not have moved from the canvas. I would have looked at you eternally and kissed you. I would have lived and breathed through you ; I should have been so happy. I should not have had any other desires. I would call you like a guardian angel in my sleep and in my waking hours. I would await you when I wished to paint the Godly and the Holy. But now . . . how terrible is life ! What is the use of her being alive ? Is a madman's life pleasant to his relations and friends, who once loved him ?

These were almost the only thoughts which occupied him. He did not think about anything else. He hardly ate anything and with impatience, with a lover's passion, he awaited the evening and the desired apparition. The uninterrupted trend of his thoughts towards one object at last took such a hold over his whole existence and imagination, that the desired image appeared to him almost every day, always in circumstances contrary to reality, for his thoughts were quite pure, like the thoughts of a child. Through all these visions the object itself somehow became purer and was completely transformed.

The opium inflamed his thoughts even more and if there was ever a man in love to the last degree of insanity, impetuously, violently, destructively, dreadfully, then this unhappy man was he.

Of all these visions one was more delightful than the rest. He dreamed of his studio. He was so gay and sat so joyfully with his brush in his hand. She was there too. She was already his wife. She sat near him, leaning with her charming little elbow on the back of his chair and looked at his work. In her languid eyes was mirrored complete bliss: everything in his room breathed of Paradise. It was so light, so neat, Heavenly Creator! She bent her charming little head on his breast.

He never had a better dream. He rose after it somehow fresher and less absentminded than before. Strange thoughts swarmed in his head. "Perhaps," he thought, "she has been dragged by some involuntary dreadful incident into vice, perhaps her soul is bent on repentance, perhaps she desires to pull herself out from the dreadful state into which she has fallen. Should one complacently let her perish when one has only to offer a hand to rescue her from drowning?"

His thoughts went even further: "Nobody knows me," he would say to himself. "Nobody cares about me, and I don't care about anybody. If she shows real repentance and is ready to change her mode of life, I'll marry her. I must marry her. I shall probably be doing much better than those who marry their housekeepers and often even worse creatures. And my deed will be unselfish and even perhaps great. I shall be giving back to the world its loveliest flower."

Having resolved on this reckless plan, he felt the colour flame up on his face. He went up to the mirror and became frightened by the sight of his drawn cheeks. Carefully, he began to tidy himself up, washed, brushed his hair, put on a new frockcoat, a smart waistcoat, threw a cloak over his shoulders and left for the street. As he breathed in the fresh air he felt a freshness in his heart, like a convalescent, who has gone out for the first time after a prolonged illness. His heart pounded when he approached that street in which he had not set foot since the time of the fateful encounter.

He looked for a long time for the house. It seemed as if his memory had failed him. Twice he walked up and down the street. At last he saw a house that seemed to resemble the one he was looking for. He ran hurriedly up the staircase and knocked at the door. The door opened and there came out to greet him none other than his ideal, his mysterious image, the original of his dream pictures, she, who was his life, his terrible, tortured, sweet life. She herself stood before him. He began to tremble. He could hardly stay on his feet from weakness and the intensity of the joy which he felt. She stood before him just as beautiful although her eyes were sleepy and her face, no longer so fresh, was pale. But she was still lovely.

"Oh!" she exclaimed on seeing Piskarev, and rubbed her eyes although it was long past midday. "Why did you run away from us?"

He sat down, exhausted, on a chair and looked at her.

"I have only just got up. I did not get back until seven o'clock this morning. I was quite drunk," she added with a smile.

Oh it were better if you were a mute, incapable of speech than that you should utter such words. He felt as if she had suddenly revealed to him, as in a panorama, her whole life. Nevertheless, bracing himself, he determined to make an appeal to her. Gathering all his courage, he began, in a shaking and yet fierce voice, to depict to her the dreadful condition of her life. She listened to him attentively and with that feeling of amazement, which we experience at the sight of something unexpected and strange. She glanced with a faint smile at her friend, who was sitting in a corner of the room and had put aside the comb which she had been cleaning, to listen attentively to the new preacher.

"It is true that I am poor," said Piskarev at last, after a long and instructive harangue, "but we can work hard at first, and vie with each other in trying to better our position. There is nothing pleasanter than to be indebted only to oneself for everything. I will work at my paintings, and you will sit near me, giving me inspiration, while you work on your embroidery or some other handiwork—and we will never want for anything."

"You expect me to do this?" These words with which she interrupted his speech were spoken almost with contempt. "I am no laundress or seamstress to begin doing any work."

God in Heaven! Her words expressed all her low, all her

despicable life, filled with emptiness and leisure, the faithful attendants of vice.

"Marry me!" came an insolent shout from her friend, who until then had kept silent in the corner. "If I become your wife I'll sit like this!"

A silly grimace appeared on her wretched face which made her beautiful friend burst into a peal of laughter.

This was too much! He had no strength to bear this. He rushed out, losing control of his senses and his thoughts. His brain became dulled. Foolishly, aimlessly, seeing, hearing and feeling nothing, he wandered about the whole of the day. Nobody knew where he spent the night. Only the next day, guided by some foolish instinct, he returned to his room in a dreadful state, pale, his hair dishevelled and with signs of madness on his face. He locked himself up in his room. He allowed no-one to come in and asked for nothing. Four days passed but his locked room was not opened once. A week passed and his room still remained locked. People began to knock at his door, to call out to him, but there was no reply. At last the door was broken open and his dead body with its throat cut was found inside. A blood-stained razor lay on the floor. Judging by the convulsive way in which his arms were outstretched and his terribly mutilated appearance, his hand must have been unsteady and he must have suffered for a long time before his sinful soul left his body.

So perished the victim of a mad passion, poor Piskarev, a quiet, timid, modest, childishly innocent man, who carried within him the spark of genius, which in time might have blazed up into a vivid flame. But nobody wept over him and no-one was to be seen near his lifeless body, except the usual figure of the District Inspector and the complacent face of the City physician. Quickly, without even any religious ceremony, his coffin was taken to Ochta. Only one soldier watchman walked behind it weeping and he only because he had drunk one bottle of vodka too many. Even Lieutenant Pirogov did not come to take a last look at the luckless wretch to whom, in his lifetime, he extended his high patronage. The Lieutenant, in fact, could not be bothered with the matter at all. He was preoccupied with an extraordinary happening. We shall return to him later.

I do not like bodies or dead men and I always find it unpleasant when a long funeral procession crosses my path and I see an old soldier, wearing some sort of cloak, taking snuff with his left hand, because his right is occupied with the torch. I am always annoyed by the sight of a rich catafalque and a velvet coffin, but my annoyance is mixed with sadness when I see drawn on a cart the red coffin of a poor man, uncovered and with only some beggar woman, encountered by chance at the cross roads and having nothing else to do, dragging after it.

I think we left Lieutenant Pirogov when he parted from poor Piskarev to rush after a blonde. That blonde was a slim, rather interesting little creature. She stopped at every shop window to peep at the belts, scarves, ear-rings, gloves and other baubles exhibited in them, kept turning her head incessantly, staring in all directions and looking back over her shoulder.

"Little pigeon, you are mine," said Pirogov conceitedly to himself, as he continued his pursuit, with his face thrust into the collar of his overcoat to prevent any of his acquaintances from recognising him.

It would do no harm to tell the reader who Lieutenant Pirogov was. But before we describe him, it will do no harm to say something about the society to which he belonged. There are officers who form, in Petersburg, a kind of middle class in society. At a dance or dinner given by a Councillor of State, who has reached this rank as a result of the efforts of forty years, you will always find one of them. A number of pale daughters, as colourless as Petersburg itself, some of them overripe, a tea-table, a piano, dancing at home—all these are inseparable from a bright epaulette which glistens in the lamplight between a virtuous blonde and the black dresscoat of a brother or some male acquaintance of the household. It is very difficult to enliven these cool-blooded young ladies and make them laugh. For this, great ability is needed, or rather, no ability at all. One has to talk in a manner which is neither too clever nor too amusing, so that in everything there is that triviality, of which women are so fond. The abovementioned young gentlemen must be given their due in that respect. They have a special talent for making these colourless beauties laugh and for engaging their attention. Exclamations smothered by laughter: "Oh, stop it! Aren't you ashamed to make me laugh so much?"—are often their highest reward. They are seldom to be encountered among the upper classes, or rather, never. There they are completely ousted by what is called in that branch of society "the aristocracy." They are, by the way, considered educated and well bred. They like to chat about literature. They praise

Bulgarin, Pushkin, and Gretch and talk with contempt and witty sarcasm about Orlov. They do not miss a single public lecture, whether it be about book-keepers or even forestry. In the theatre, whatever the play, you will always find one of them; except perhaps when "Filatka," which offends their selective taste, is being played. They are always in the theatre. Theatre proprietors find them the most profitable of people. They are especially fond of a play with good verse and are also very fond of calling out actors loudly. Many of them, by teaching in Government institutions or coaching for Government positions, manage to provide themselves with a cabriolet and a pair of horses. Then their circle becomes wider. At last they get as far as marrying a merchant's daughter, who can play the piano, has a hundred thousand in cash, more or less, and a heap of bearded relations. But they cannot achieve that honour before attaining, at least, the rank of Colonel. For Russian beards, although they still smell somewhat of cabbage, are, on no account, content to see their daughters marry anybody beneath the rank of General or at least of Colonel. These are the main features of this class of young men.

But Lieutenant Pirogov was possessed of many gifts peculiar to himself. He was an excellent declaimer of verse from "Dimitry Donsky" and "Woe from Wit," and he had the special talent of being able to blow rings from his pipe, so skilfully, that he could thread ten of them at a time one over another. He could recount very pleasantly a joke about how the big gun exists for its own sake, but the rhinoceros is itself for itself. It is difficult, by the way, to enumerate all the talents with which Fate had endowed Pirogov. He liked talking about actresses and dancers, but not so crudely as a young Ensign usually discusses these subjects. He was very pleased with his rank, to which he had been recently promoted. Although sometimes, lying on his divan, he would say to himself: "Och, och! Vanity of vanities! What if I am a Lieutenant?" secretly he was very flattered by his new dignity. In conversation he often tried to hint at it indirectly and once, when he came across some clerk in the street, who seemed to him to be impolite, he immediately stopped him and, in a few but sharp words, impressed upon that clerk, that before him stood a Lieutenant and no lesser officer. He tried to put it all the more eloquently, as two ladies, by no means plain, were passing at the time. Generally speaking, Pirogov exhibited a passion for the fine arts and encouraged the painter Piskarev. By the way, this was perhaps due to to the fact that he had a strong desire to see his masculine physiognomy in a portrait.

But enough of Pirogov's traits. Man is such a wonderful being that one can never enumerate all his virtues at once and, the more you observe him, the more new peculiarities appear and their description would be infinite.

And thus Pirogov did not cease to pursue the stranger and from time to time he engaged her with questions to which she replied sharply, abruptly and with indistinct sounds. They passed through the dark Kazansky Gate into Meshchanskaya Street, the street of tobacconists and small shops, of German artisans and Finnish nymphs. The blonde ran more quickly and fluttered through the gate of a rather dirty house. Pirogov followed her. She ran up a narrow, dark staircase and entered through a door, through which Pirogov also bravely sidled in. He observed that he was in a large room with dark walls, and a ceiling blackened by smoke. A heap of iron screws, locksmith's tools, shining coffeepots and candlesticks was on a table. The floor was covered with brass and iron filings. Pirogov immediately understood that he was in an artisan's flat. The stranger fluttered further through a side door. He hesitated for a moment but, following the Russian rule, decided to go on. He entered a room which bore not the least resemblance to the first. It was arranged very tidily, a fact which indicated that the occupiers were Germans.

Pirogov was almost stunned by the amazing spectacle which met his eyes.

Before him sat Schiller, not the Schiller who wrote "William Tell" and the "History of the Thirty Years' War," but the famous Schiller, the ironworker of Meshchanskaya Street. Next to Schiller stood Hoffman, not the writer Hoffman, but Hoffman the shoemaker from Officerskaya Street, Schiller's close friend. Schiller was drunk and sat on a chair stamping his foot and saying something in an agitated voice. But it was not this which amazed Pirogov. He was amazed by the very strange postures of the two figures. Schiller sat with his rather fleshy nose stuck out and his head raised, while Hoffman held him by that nose with two fingers and was turning the blade of his shoemaker's knife on its surface. Both persons spoke in German and therefore Pirogov, who only knew "Gutmorgen" in German, could understand nothing of the story. This, by the way, is what Schiller was saying.

"I don't want it. I don't need this nose!" he shouted, waving his hands. "I spend three pounds of tobacco every month on this nose alone. And I pay for it in a rotten Russian shop because the German shop doesn't keep any Russian tobacco. I pay this rotten Russian shop 40 kopeks for every pound. That comes to one rouble twenty-five kopeks—which makes fourteen roubles forty kopeks in a year. Do you hear me, Hoffman, my friend? Fourteen roubles, forty kopeks on one nose! Yes, and on holidays I snuff Rapé, because I don't want to snuff rotten Russian tobacco on holidays. In one year I snuff two pounds of Rapé at two roubles a pound. Six and fourteen—twenty roubles forty kopeks on tobacco alone! That's robbery. I ask you, Hoffman, my friend, isn't it?"

Hoffman, who was drunk himself, answered in the affirmative.

"Twenty roubles forty kopeks! I'm a German from Swabia. I have a king in Germany. I don't want a nose! Cut off my nose! Here is my nose!"

And if it were not for Lieutenant Pirogov's sudden appearance, no doubt Hoffman would have cut off Schiller's nose for no reason at all. For he was already holding his knife as if he were about to cut a shoe-sole.

It seemed very annoying to Schiller that an uninvited stranger should without warning disturb them so inopportunely. Although he was dazed by beer and wine, he felt that it was quite unseemly for a stranger to be present in such circumstances and during such a ceremony. Pirogov bowed slightly in the pleasant way peculiar to him, and said, "Forgive me . . ."

"Go to Hell!" bawled Schiller.

This nonplussed Lieutenant Pirogov. Such treatment was entirely new to him. A faint smile, which was on the point of appearing on his face, suddenly vanished. With a feeling of hurt dignity he said: "I am afraid, my good man . . . you have probably not noticed . . . . I am an officer . . ."

"What is an officer? I am a German from Swabia." At this point Schiller hit the table with his fist. "I will be officer myself. A year and a half Junker, two years Ensign and then immediately officer. I don't want to serve. I do with officers like this. Tfu!" At this Schiller opened the palm of his hand and spat on it.

Lieutenant Pirogov perceived that there was nothing left to do but to retire. Nevertheless such treatment, which did not at all accord with his rank, was unpleasant to him. He stopped on the stairs several times as if to brace himself and to think out how to make Schiller realise his insolence. At last he decided that Schiller could be forgiven, for his head was filled with beer fumes. He also thought about the pretty blonde and decided to forget the insult.

The next day Lieutenant Pirogov appeared early in the morning in the ironworker's shop. In the front room he was met by the pretty blonde and, in rather a stern voice, which well suited her pretty face, she asked :

"What is it you wish ?"

"Ah, hello, my dear ! Don't you recognise me ? You little rascal, what pretty eyes you have !"

At this Lieutenant Pirogov wanted to chuck her prettily under the chin. But the blonde made a frightened exclamation and with the same sternness repeated :

"What is it you wish ?"

"To see you. I don't want anything else," said Lieutenant Pirogov, smiling rather pleasantly and coming nearer. But perceiving that the frightened blonde wanted to step away through the door, he added : "My dear, I want to order some spurs. Could you make spurs for me ? Although one needs no spurs whatever to love you, rather a bridle. What sweet little hands !"

Lieutenant Pirogov was always very gallant in expressions of this kind.

"I'll call my husband at once," screamed the girl and ran out. After a few minutes, Pirogov saw Schiller, who came in with sleepy eyes, as he had hardly recovered from the debauch of the night before. Looking at the officer he recalled, like some vague dream, the occurrence of the previous day. He could by no means remember what had happened, but he felt that he had committed some foolishness and he therefore received Pirogov with a grim air.

"I can't take less than fifteen roubles for the spurs," he said, intending to get rid of Pirogov. For, like the honest German he was, he found it very embarrassing to meet someone who had seen him in an indecent state. Schiller liked to drink with two or three friends but without witnesses of any kind and, on such occasions, would lock himself away even from his workmen.

"Why are they so expensive ?" tenderly asked Pirogov.

"German workmanship." coolly answered Schiller, stroking his chin. "A Russian will make them for two roubles."

"All right. In order to prove that I like you and want to make your acquaintance, I'll pay fifteen roubles."

Schiller remained thoughtful for a minute. As an honest German he was somewhat embarrassed. Deciding to discourage Pirogov from giving an order, he declared that the spurs could not be made in less than two weeks. But Pirogov, without any remonstrance, expressed his complete agreement.

The German began to think again and pondered how best to do the work so that it should really cost fifteen roubles. Just then the blonde entered the room and began to rummage on the table which was obstructed with coffeepots. The Lieutenant made use of Schiller's preoccupation to approach her and press her little arm, which was bare to the shoulder. Schiller did not care for this at all.

"Mein Frau !" he shouted.

"Was Vollen sie doch ?" answered the blonde.

"Go to the kitchen !"

The blonde departed.

"In two weeks' time then," said Pirogov.

"Yes, in two weeks," answered Schiller, deep in thought. "I have a lot of work to do now."

"Good-bye. I'll drop in."

"Good-bye," said Schiller, locking the door behind him.

Lieutenant Pirogov decided not to leave his quest, despite the fact that the German woman had given him an obvious rebuff. He could not conceive how anyone could resist him especially as his gallantry and his excellent rank gave him the full right to attention. Nevertheless, it should be also pointed out that Schiller's wife, despite her prettiness, was very silly. Silliness, by the way, constitutes a special charm in a pretty little wife. At least, I have known many husbands who were delighted with their wives' foolishness and saw in it all the signs of childlike innocence. Beauty performs absolute miracles. All the defects of character in a beautiful woman, instead of causing disgust, become somehow unusually attractive. Vice itself in them ceases to be ugly. But when her beauty vanishes—the woman has to be twenty times as clever as a man in order to inspire if not love, then at least respect.

By the way, Schiller's wife, despite all her foolishness, was always faithful to her duty and so it was rather difficult for Pirogov to be successful in his daring undertaking. But there is always an added delight in gaining a victory over obstacles, and the blonde became more and more interesting every day.

He began to enquire rather frequently about the spurs, so that in the end it began to annoy Schiller. He made every effort to finish the spurs more quickly. At last the spurs were ready.

"Ach, what excellent workmanship!" exclaimed Lieutenant Pirogov seeing the spurs. "God Almighty, how well they are made! Our General himself has no spurs like these."

A feeling of self satisfaction welled up in Schiller's heart. His eyes began to look quite merry and he became entirely reconciled with Pirogov. "This Russian officer is a clever man," he thought to himself.

"Then that means, that you can also make a sheath, for example, for a dagger or other things."

"Oh, I certainly can," said Schiller with a smile.

"Then make me a sheath for my dagger. I'll bring it to you. I have a very good Turkish dagger, but I should like you to make a new sheath for it."

This struck Schiller like a bomb. His forehead suddenly wrinkled.

"There you are!" he thought, swearing inwardly at having brought this on himself. A refusal he regarded as dishonourable, besides the Russian officer had praised his work.

He shook his head a little but expressed his consent. He was, however, quite perplexed by the kiss which Pirogov insolently plastered on the very lips of the pretty blonde, when leaving.

I deem it superfluous to tell the reader much about Schiller. Schiller was a complete German, in the full sense of the word. Since the time when he was only twenty, that happy time when a Russian lives without caring a damn about anything, Schiller had planned out his life and in no case ever made any exceptions. He had decided to rise at seven, to dine at two, to be methodical in everything and to be drunk every Sunday. He had set himself to accumulate a capital of fifty thousand in ten years, and it was already as certain and as unavoidable as fate, for an official will sooner forget to flatter his superior, than a German will go back on his decision. He never increased his expenses and if the price of potatoes rose above normal, he did not add a single kopek, but decreased the quantity, and although he sometimes remained somehwat hungry, he nevertheless became used to it. His planning went so far, that he permitted himself to kiss his wife not more than twice in twenty-four hours and, so as not to kiss her on extra occasions, he never put more than a teaspoonful of pepper in his soup. By the way, on Sundays this rule was not so strictly obeyed, for Schiller then drank two bottles of beer and one bottle of caraway vodka, which he nevertheless always swore at. He did not drink like an Englishman, who locks his door straight after lunch and gets drunk by himself. On the contrary, like a good German, he always drank in convivial company: either the shoemaker Hoffman or the joiner Kunz, also a German and a terrible drunkard. Such was the character of the noble Schiller, who was at last placed in an extremely difficult situation. Although Schiller was of a phlegmatic temperament, and a German, Pirogov's actions nevertheless roused in him something resembling jealousy. He puzzled his brains but could not decide how to get rid of that Russian officer. Meanwhile Pirogov, smoking his pipe in the circle of his friends—for fate has ordained that where there are officers there are pipes as well—hinted significantly and with a pleasant smile at an intrigue with a pretty German, with whom, according to his account, he was quite intimate and whom, as a matter of fact, he almost despaired of disposing in his favour.

One day he was strolling along Meshchanskaya Street and looked up at the house which flaunted Schiller's shop-sign with its coffee-pots and samovars. To his great joy he saw the little head of the blonde hanging out of the window, surveying the passersby. He stopped, waved his hand and said: "Gut morgen."

The blonde bowed to him as to an acquaintance.

"Is your husband at home?"

"He is," answered the blonde.

"And when is he not at home?"

"He is not at home on Sundays," said the foolish blonde.

"That's not bad," thought Pirogov to himself. "I must make use of that."

And the next Sunday, like a bolt from the blue, he appeared before the blonde. Schiller was indeed not at home. The pretty hostess became frightened, but Pirogov acted rather cautiously this time, treated her very respectfully and displayed all the beauty of his pliable corseted waist as he bowed to her. He joked very pleasantly and politely, but the silly German answered everything with monosyllables. Finally, having tried various approaches and realising that none of them had any success, he suggested some dancing. The German consented instantly, for German women are always ready to dance. Pirogov based great hopes on this. Firstly, it gave her pleasure, secondly, it would show off his figure and nimbleness, thirdly, he could come closer to her when dancing. He could embrace the pretty German and make a beginning for the rest. In short, he expected absolute success from this. He began to hum a gavotte, knowing that a slow tempo is necessary where German women are concerned. The pretty German stalked out into the middle of the room and raised a lovely little foot. This posture so enchanted Pirogov that he began to kiss her. The German began to scream and this even more enhanced her loveliness in Pirogov's eyes. He covered her with kisses. Then suddenly the door opened and Schiller appeared with Hoffman and the joiner, Kunz. All these respectable artisans were as drunk as owls.

I leave it to the reader to imagine Schiller's fury and indignation.

"You ruffian !" he shouted in great indignation. "How do you dare kiss my wife ! You are a pig, not a Russian officer. The Devil take it, am I not a German and not a pig of a Russian, Hoffman, my friend ?"

Hoffman replied in the affirmative.

"I want no horns ! Take him by the collar, Hoffman, my friend. I want no horns !" He waved his hands violently, and his face assumed the colour of the red cloth of his waistcoat. "I live for eight years in Petersburg," he continued, "I have my mother in Swabia and my uncle in Nurenberg. I am a German, not a horned piece of meat ! Off with everything from him, Hoffman, my friend ! Take hold of his hand and foot, Kunz, my kamerad."

And the Germans seized Pirogov by his arms and legs. He struggled violently but in vain. For these three were the strongest Germans in Petersburg and they handled Pirogov so roughly and rudely, that I confess I can find no words with which to describe this sad incident.

I am sure that the next day Schiller, in a fever of anxiety, trembled like a leaf, as he awaited from minute to minute the arrival of the police and he would have given Heaven knows what to have merely dreamed the happenings of the previous day. But what had happened had happened.

As for Pirogov, his fury and indignation beggared description. The mere thought of the insufferable affront to his dignity nearly drove him mad. Siberia and the knout seemed to him only the mildest punishment for Schiller. He had rushed back home to dress and then rushed out again to go straight to the General to describe in the most vivid colours the violence of the German artisans. He intended at the same time to lodge a written petition with the General Staff and, if the matter was not satisfactorily concluded, to take it further and further.

But it all ended in a strange fashion. On the way Pirogov dropped into a café, ate two puff pastries, read something from the "Severnaya Pchela," and when he left was no longer in such an outraged mood. Moreover the evening was cool and pleasant and Pirogov could not resist a short stroll on the Nevsky Prospect. By nine o'clock he calmed down and came to the conclusion that it was not wise to trouble a General on Sunday, and in any case no doubt the latter would have been called away somewhere. So Pirogov went to a dance given by a Government official, where there was a very pleasant gathering of officials and officers. There he passed an enjoyable evening and so excelled in a mazurka that he enchanted not only the ladies, but even their cavaliers

How mysteriously is this world of ours arranged! This is what I thought when I was walking along the Nevsky Prospect about three days ago, and recalled to my mind these two occurrences. How strangely, how incomprehensibly Fate plays with us! Do we ever get what we desire? Do we ever attain what we seem to be designed to achieve? Everything happens the other way round. He, to whom Fate has given the finest horses, rides them apathetically, quite unconscious of their beauty, while another, whose heart burns with a passion for horses, goes on foot and has to be content with merely clicking his tongue when he sees a race-horse. He who has an excellent chef, has, alas, a mouth so small, that it cannot possibly take in more than two little pieces. Another has a mouth the size of an Admiralty arch, but, alas, has to be content with a German lunch of nothing but potatoes. How strangely fate toys with us!

But strangest of all are the incidents which occur on the Nevsky Prospect. Do not trust this Nevsky Prospect. I always wrap myself more tightly in my cloak when I walk along it and I try not to look at the objects I encounter. It is all a delusion. It is all a dream. Nothing is what it seems to be. You think that the gentleman who strolls in an excellently cut little jacket is very rich—nothing of the sort. The little jacket is his only possession. You imagine that these two fat men, who stopped before a church in course of erection, are discussing its architecture? Not at all. They are talking about two ravens who have perched opposite each other in such a strange manner. You think that the enthusiast waving his hands is talking about his wife who threw from her window a little ball of paper at an officer who is a complete stranger to him? Not at all. He is talking about Lafayette. You think that those ladies . . . but trust the ladies least of all. Look less into shop-windows: the baubles they exhibit are lovely, but they smell of a terrible quantity of banknotes. And may God prevent you from looking under the ladies' hats. No matter how the cloak of a beautiful girl flutters in the distance, I will never follow her nor will it ever rouse my curiosity. Keep away, for Heaven's sake, keep away from the lampposts! And pass by them quickly, as quickly as possible! You will be lucky if you get away with only their smelly oil on your smart jacket. But everything, not only the lampposts, is redolent with deceit. It lies, at all times, this Nevsky Prospect, but more than ever when night falls heavily upon it and merges the white and the straw-coloured walls of the houses, when the whole town is turned into thunder and glitter, when myriads of coaches clatter over the bridges, when the coachmen shout and rise on their horses, and when the Demon himself lights the lamps only to show everything in colours that are false.

The Coach

THE small town of B . . . grew much more cheerful after the . . . cavalry regiment became stationed there. Until then it had been immeasurably boring to live in. If, when travelling through, you glance at the small, low, plastered houses, which stare at the street so sourly, then . . . but it is impossible to describe the feelings which rise in your heart, the intense distress as if you had ruined yourself at cards or cracked an ill-timed joke—in short: you do not feel well.

The clay on the houses has been crumbled away by the rain and the walls have changed their colour from white to piebald. As is customary in our Southern towns most of the roofs are thatched with rushes. A long time ago the Provost had ordered the small gardens to be dispensed with for better appearance's sake. Not a single living creature is to be encountered in the streets, save perhaps a cockerel crossing the pavement rendered as soft as a pillow by the thick dust. This the slightest rain turns to mud and then the streets of the small town of B . . . are filled with those corpulent animals, which the local Provost calls "Frenchmen." Raising their solemn snouts from their troughs, they grunt so loudly that the traveller has no choice but to speed on his horses.

It is difficult, by the way, to meet a traveller in the small town of B . . . Occasionally, very occasionally, some landowner, who owns twelve souls, will clatter down the street in a nankeen jacket, riding in something which is a cross between a two-wheeled cart and a truck, and just visible above heaps of flour sacks as he whips a piebald mare, behind which runs a colt.

The market square itself has a somewhat sad appearance: the tailor's house juts out very foolishly, not with its whole facade, but with a corner of it. Opposite, a stone building with two windows has been in the process of being built for about fifteen years. Further away, and quite isolated, stands a modern deal fence. It is painted grey to match the colour of dirt and, as an example to the other buildings, was erected by the Provost in his youth when he had not yet acquired the habit of going to sleep immediately after lunch and of taking as a nightcap a decoction dressed with dried gooseberries. Everywhere else there are only wattle hedges. In the middle of the square are the tiniest shops. In them one can always see a bundle of round cracknels, a peasant woman with a red scarf, a poud* of soap, several pounds of bitter almonds, small shot for shooting, cotton material and two shop assistants perpetually playing "svayka"† near the doors.

But when the cavalry regiment became stationed in the district town of B . . . everything changed. The streets became variegated and enlivened—in short, assumed an entirely different character. The small low houses often saw a nimble, well-shaped officer with a plume on his head, passing by on his way to a friend to talk about crops, about the best tobacco, and sometimes to stake on a card a droshky of the type which can be called regimental. For without leaving the regiment the droshky managed to pass through everybody's hands. To-day the Major rides in it, to-morrow it appears in the Lieutenant's stables, and in a week's time you will once more see the Major's batman greasing it with fat.

The whole of the wooden fences between the houses was littered with soldiers' caps hanging in the sun. A grey overcoat would be certain to protrude somewhere from the gates. In the side streets one came across soldiers with moustaches as hard as shoe-brushes. These moustaches were to be seen everywhere. Whenever the women gathered with baskets in the market, a moustache would be sure to look out from behind their shoulders.

The officers put new life into fasionable society, which until then comprised only the Judge, who shared a house with a deacon's wife, and the Provost, a sagacious man, but one who slept absolutely the whole day—from lunch-time to evening and from evening to lunch-time. High life became even more crowded and entertaining when the Brigadier General took up his quarters in the town. The district landowners, about whose existence, until then, nobody would have guessed, began to travel more frequently to the district town to meet the gentlemen officers and sometimes to play Banker, about

* A Russian weight of forty Russian pounds.
† A local game.

which their heads held very hazy ideas, preoccupied as they were with seed sowing, errands for the wife, and rabbits.

It is a great pity that I cannot remember the circumstances in which the Brigadier General happened to give a big dinner. Tremendous preparations were made for it. The clatter of the chef's knives in the General's kitchen could be heard at the town gates. The entire market was bought up for that dinner, so that the Judge with the deacon's wife was forced to eat only buckwheat cakes and starch kissel.* The smallish yard of the General's quarters was completely filled with carts and coaches. The gathering was confined to men—officers and some of the district landowners.

The most remarkable of the landowners was Piphagor Piphagorovich Chertokutski, one of the principal gentlemen of the B . . . district, who made the greatest noise at elections and travelled to them in a dashing carriage. At one time he served in one of the cavalry regiments and belonged to the category of important and eminent officers. That is to say, he was to be seen at many balls and gatherings wherever his regiment wandered By the way, inquiries can be made about this of the young ladies of the Tembovskaya and Simbirskaya provinces. It may very well be, that he would have acquired the same flattering reputation in other provinces too, had he not been cashiered as the result of an incident, usually termed "an unpleasant story." Whether he slapped some senior officer's face, or whether he was himself slapped, I do not remember with certainty. The main thing is, that he was asked to resign. This, by the way, caused him in no degreee to lose his importance: he wore a high-waisted dress-coat cut like a military uniform, spurs on his high boots and, under his nose, a moustache, because without that the nobility might have thought he had served in the infantry to which he always referred with contempt. He was present at all those crowded fairs, to which the backbone of Russia—mothers, children, daughters and fat landowners—travel for entertainment in britchkas, two-wheeled carts, tarantasses, and coaches, the like of which scarcely exist even in dreams.

He would ferret out where a cavalry regiment was to be stationed and always arrived to meet the gentlemen officers. Nimbly alighting in front of them from his small light barouche or droshky, he would speedily make their acquaintance. During the last elections he gave an excellent dinner for the

* A sour jelly.

nobility at which he declared that if he were only elected their marshal, he would set noblemen on the firmest footing. Generally speaking, he behaved like a nobleman, as they say in districts and provinces. He married quite a pretty girl, who brought him a dowry of two hundred souls and several thousands in cash. The cash was immediately invested in six really excellent horses, gilt locks on the doors, a tame monkey for the house and a French majordomo. The two hundred souls with the two hundred of his own were mortgaged for some commercial speculation. In short, he was a landowner as landowners should be . . . a substantial landowner.

At the General's dinner there were, besides him, several other landowners, but there is nothing to be said about them. The remainder were military gentlemen from the same regiment and two field officers, a Colonel and a somewhat corpulent Major. The General himself was very big and stout, a good leader, by the way, according to his officers' reports. He talked in rather a thick and significant bass.

The dinner was remarkable. Sturgeon, white sturgeon, sterlet, asparagus, quails, partridges, mushrooms, all proved that the chef had not touched any alcohol for as long as twenty-four hours, and four soldiers with knives in their hands helped him, throughout the night, to make the fricassée and the jelly. An infinite number of bottles—longnecked with lafitte and shortnecked with madeira—a wonderful summer's day, windows wide open, plates of ice on the tables, dishevelled shirtfronts on the owners of spacious dress-coats, cross talk drowned by the General's bass and watered with champagne, everything was as it should be.

After dinner all arose with a pleasant heaviness in their stomachs, and having lighted their pipes, long-stemmed and short-stemmed, left for the porch with cups of coffee in their hands.

"Now we might have a look at her," said the General. "Be so good, my dear fellow," he added, addressing his adjutant, quite an agile young man of pleasant appearance, "as to order the piebald mare to be brought here. You will judge for yourselves."

Here the General drew at his pipe and puffed out some smoke.

"She is not yet in very good shape. This blasted small town! There are no decent stables here. The horse"—puff, puff—"is pretty good."

"Has Your Excellency had her a long time?" said Chertokutski.

Puff, puff, puff, pu . . . puff. "Not so long. It is only about two years since I took her from the stud farm."

"And did you have the pleasure of receiving her broken in, or did you have the pleasure of breaking her in here ?"

Puff, puff, pu, pu, pu . . . u . . . u . . . ff. "Here!"

Having said this, the General completely disappeared in smoke.

In the meantime a soldier leapt out from the stables. A clatter of hoofs was heard. Finally another man appeared in a white peasant's overcoat, with a huge black moustache, leading by the bridle a frightened prancing horse, which suddenly raised his head and almost lifted up the soldier, who had crouched down on the ground.

"Come on then, come on, Agrafena Ivanovna," he was saying, leading her up to the porch.

The mare's name was Agrafena Ivanovna. Strong and wild like a beautiful girl from the South, she banged with her hoofs at the wooden porch and suddenly stopped.

The General took out his pipe and began to look at Agrafena Ivanovna with complete satisfaction. The Colonel himself stepped down from the porch and took Agrafena Ivanovna by the muzzle. The Major himself tapped Agrafena Ivanovna's leg slightly. The rest clicked their tongues.

Chertokutski stepped down from the porch and approached her from behind. The soldier stood upright holding the bridle and looked straight into the eyes of the visitors, as if he wanted to jump on them.

"Very, very good," said Chertokutski. "A superb horse! And may one ask Your Excellency how it walks ?"

"Her step is good, only . . . the devil knows . . . the fool of a surgeon's assistant gave her some pills and now she has been coughing for two days."

"She is very, very good! And has Your Excellency a suitable carriage to go with her ?"

"A carriage ? . . . But this is a riding horse."

"I know that, but I asked Your Excellency in order to find out whether you possess a carriage on a par with your horses."

"Well, I have not exactly a sufficient number of carriages. To tell you frankly, I have wanted to have a modern coach for a long time. I wrote about it to my brother, who is now in Petersburg, but I do not know whether he will send it or not."

"I think, Your Excellency," remarked the Colonel, "that there is no better coach than the Viennese."

"You think rightly"—puff, puff, puff.

"Your Excellency, I possess a remarkable coach, of real Viennese workmanship."

"Which is that? The one in which you arrived?"

"Oh, no. That is an ordinary one, expressly for the purpose of driving about on my journeys, but the other . . . it is amazing, as light as a feather and when you sit down in it, then—if Your Excellency will permit me to say so—you feel just as if you were being rocked in a cradle."

"It is restful then?"

"Very, very restful. Cushions, springs, it is all as if painted on a picture."

"It sounds good."

"And how spacious it is! Indeed, your Excellency, I have never seen anything like it yet. When I was serving, ten bottles of rum and twenty pounds of tobacco could be stowed away in its boxes. In addition I always carried with me about six uniforms, underwear and two pipes, Your Excellency, the very longest kind, and you can put a whole ox into the boot."

"It sounds good."

"I paid four thousand for it, Your Excellency."

"Judging by the price it should be good. And did you buy it yourself?"

"No, Your Excellency, I obtained it by chance. It was bought by my friend, an exceptional man, a companion of my youth, whom you would have liked very much. I am on such terms with him that what is his is mine. We share everything equally. I won it from him at cards. Would Your Excellency deign to do me the honour of coming to my house for lunch to-morrow? We could look at the coach at the same time . . ."

"I do not know what to say to that. Alone, I somehow . . . unless you will allow me to bring my gentlemen officers with me?"

"I humbly request the presence of the officers. Gentlemen! I would deem it a great honour to have the pleasure of welcoming you, too, in my house."

The Colonel, the Major and the rest of the officers expressed their thanks with courteous bows.

"Your Excellency, I personally am of the opinion that if you buy a thing, then always buy a good one. If it is mediocre, it is not worth acquiring. When you do me the honour of calling at my place to-morrow, I shall show you some of the things I have myself introduced into my household."

The General looked up and puffed out some smoke from his mouth.

Chertokutski was very pleased that he had invited the officers to his place. In his mind he was already ordering pies and sauces in anticipation, and from time to time he looked gayly at the gentlemen officers, who, for their part, somehow redoubled towards him their benevolence, which was apparent in their eyes and in the slight movements of their bodies in the shape of semi-bows. Chertokutski stalked about somehow more freely and his voice assumed weakness—the tone of a voice burdened by satisfaction.

"There you will make the acquaintance of the lady of the house, Your Excellency."

"It will give me great pleasure," said the General, stroking his moustache.

After this, Chertokutski wanted to go home immediately in order to prepare everything for the reception of his guests on the following day. He had already taken his hat in his hands, when somehow it unaccountably so happened that he lingered on. In the meantime card tables were set out in the room. Soon the whole gathering, divided into parties of four for whist, was placed in various corners of the General's room.

Candles were brought in. For a long time Chertokutski did not know whether he should or should not sit down to play whist. But when the gentleman officers began to invite him, it seemed to him completely incompatible with the rules of sociable behaviour to refuse—and he sat down just for a moment. A glass of punch suddenly appeared before him and, without thinking, he drank it. Having played two rubbers, Chertokutski again found a glass of punch within his reach, and again, without thinking, drank it, saying first, "Gentlemen, it is time for me to go home. It really is."

But again he sat down for a short time to play another game. In the meantime the conversation in various corners of the room assumed an entirely private character. Those playing whist were comparatively taciturn, but those who were not playing and were sitting aside on couches, held a conversation of their own.

In one corner the second captain of cavalry, having put a cushion under his side and with a pipe in his teeth, was discussing his love affairs quite freely and fluently and completely monopolised the attention of the circle which had gathered around him. One extremely fat landowner with short hands, somewhat resembling two overgrown potatoes, listened with an unusually sweet expression, only striving from time to time to put his short little hand behind his broad back to pull out his snuffbox.

In another corner quite a heated argument ensued about squadron instruction, and Chertokutski, who had already played a Queen twice instead of a Jack, would suddenly interpose in their discussion, and shout from his corner: "In what year?" or "Of which regiment?" without noticing that sometimes the questions were entirely irrelevant.

At last, several minutes before dinnertime, the whist stopped, but it still continued in words, and it seemed that all heads were filled with whist. Chertokutski remembered very well that he had won a lot, but did not recall taking any tricks. Getting up from the table, he stood for a long time in the posture of a man who has no handkerchief in his pocket.

Meanwhile dinner was served. Naturally, there was no lack of wine, and Chertokutski, almost involuntarily, had to fill his glass from time to time, as bottles stood to the right and left of him.

Conversation was protracted at the table, but, by the way, it was somewhat strangely conducted. One Colonel, who had served in the campaign of 1812, told of some battle which had never taken place, and afterwards, for some quite obscure reason, took the stopper out of a carafe and stuck it into a pastry. In short, it was already three o'clock when they began to disperse and the drivers had to carry out several persons bodily, as if they were parcels of merchandise. And Chertokutski, in spite of all his nobility, bowed so deeply sitting in the coach and with such a waving of his head that, when he arrived home, he brought back in his moustache two buds of burdock.

The whole house was asleep. The driver, after some difficulty, managed to find the valet de chambre who led his master through the lounge and turned him over to the chamber-maid. Following her, Chertokutski somehow reached the bedroom and dropped down near his pretty young wife, who lay delightfully asleep in a nightdress as white as snow.

The motion caused by the fall of her husband on the bed awakened her. Stretching herself, she raised her eyelashes and, quickly screwing up her eyes three times, she opened them with a half angry smile. But seeing that this time he decidedly did not want to impart any caress, she turned on the other side with annoyance. Putting her fresh little cheek on her hand she soon fell asleep again.

The time of day had already arrived which in villages is

not called early, when the young house-wife awoke beside her snoring husband. Remembering that he had returned home at about four o'clock in the morning, she felt loath to wake him, and, putting on her bedroom slippers, which her husband had ordered from Petersburg, and a white blouse, which draped itself around her like flowing water, she left for her dressing room. She washed with water as fresh as herself and approached her dressing table. She glanced at herself once or twice and saw that she did not look at all bad. This apparently insignificant conclusion compelled her to sit before the mirror for exactly two extra hours. At last she dressed very pleasantly and left for the garden to refresh herself.

As if by design the weather was wonderful, such as only a Southern summer's day can boast. The sun, which had come out at noon, scorched with all the power of its rays. But in the dark, thickly planted alleys it was quite cool to walk and the flowers, warmed by the sun, trebled their perfume. The pretty hostess completely forgot that it was already twelve o'clock and that her husband was still asleep. The snores of two cabdrivers and one postillion, who were sleeping in the stables behind the garden, reached her ears. But she continued to sit in the dark alley from which there opened a wide view of the road, and absentmindedly gazed at its emptiness, when suddenly dust, which appeared from afar, attracted her attention. Looking more closely, she soon saw several carriages.

In front drove an open two-seater, in which sat the General with his fat epaulettes which glittered in the sun, and next to him sat the Colonel. It was followed by a four-seater. In this sat the Major with the General's Adjutant and two other officers who sat opposite them. Behind that coach followed the droshky, known to the whole regiment, in which this time sat the corpulent Major. Behind the droshky drove a four-seater carriage, in which sat four officers, with a fifth sprawled across their knees. Behind this carriage three officers could be seen displaying themselves on magnificent dappled and piebald horses.

"Are they really coming to us?" thought Chertokutski's wife. "Ach Heavens! They are! They have turned on to the bridge."

She screamed, clasped her hands and ran over flower-beds and flowers straight into her husband's bedroom. He slept the sleep of the just.

"Get up! Get up! Hurry and get up!" she shouted, pulling at his hand.

"Eh?" uttered Chertokutski, and stretched himself without opening his eyes.

"Get up, darling! Can't you hear? Guests!"

"Guests? What guests?"

Having said this, he emitted a short braying, like a calf searching with its muzzle for its mother's teats.

"M'm . . ." he mumbled. "Stretch out your little neck, Cookums! Let me kiss you."

"Sweetheart, get up, for Heaven's sake, hurry! The General with the officers! Ach, my God, there is burdock in your moustache."

"The General? Is he coming already? And why the devil has nobody wakened me up? And lunch, what about lunch? Is everything prepared as it should be?"

"What lunch?"

"Didn't I tell you?"

"Tell me? You came back at four this morning and however much I asked you, you told me nothing. Therefore, Snookums, I did not wake you. I was sorry for you. You hadn't slept at all . . ."

The last words she said in an extremely languishing and imploring voice.

Chertokutski's eyes protruded. For a minute he lay in bed as if thunderstruck. At last he jumped out, dressed only in his shirt, forgetting that it was not altogether decent.

"Ach, what a horse I am!" he said, hitting himself on the forehead. "I asked them to lunch! What is there to be done? Are they far away?"

"I don't know . . . they should be here any minute."

"Sweetheart . . . hide! Hey, who's there? You, girl! Come here, you fool. What are you afraid of? Officers will arrive any minute. Say the master is not at home. Say that he will not be back at all, that he left early in the morning . . . D'you hear? And tell it to all the servants. Go on, hurry!"

Having said this, he hurriedly grabbed his dressing gown and ran to hide in the coach barn, assuming that there he would be quite free from danger. But, standing in the corner of the barn, he realised that even here he might somehow be spotted.

"Ah, this will be better!" flashed through his mind, and in a second he threw down the steps of a coach which stood near, jumped up and closed the door behind him. For greater safety he covered himself with the leather cover and remained absolutely quiet, doubled up in his dressing gown.

In the meantime the coaches drew up to the house.

The General alighted and shook himself. After him came the Colonel, attending with his hands to the plume on his hat. Then the fat Major jumped from the droshky, holding his sabre under his arm. Then from the four-seater leaped the thin Second Lieutenants and the Ensign who had been ensconced between them and finally the officers who had been displaying themselves on their horses alighted from their mounts.

"The master's not at home," said the lackey coming out on to the porch.

"What do you mean—not at home? Anyhow, he must be back here for lunch."

"Sorry, sir, he won't be. They drove away for the whole day. They might be back, perhaps, to-morrow at this time."

"This is a nuisance!" said the General. "What can have happened?"

"I admit it is awkward," said the Colonel laughing.

"But really, how can people act like this?" continued the General with displeasure. "What the devil . . . After all, if you cannot receive people, why force your hospitality on them?"

"Your Excellency, I cannot understand how any one could do that," said one young officer.

"What?" said the General, who was always in the habit of using this interrogative pronoun when talking to a subaltern.

"I was saying, Your Excellency, how can one act in such a manner."

"Naturally . . . if anything has gone wrong—at least let one know or do not issue an invitation."

"Your Excellency, there is nothing to be done now. Let us go back," said the Colonel.

"Naturally, there is no other course. By the way, we can have a look at the coach without him. He has probably not taken it with him. Hey, you there! Come here, man!"

"What is it you wish, sir?"

"Are you a groom?"

"I am, Your Excellency."

"Show us the new coach, which your master obtained recently."

"Yes, Sir. Would you come into the barn?"

The General and the officers went into the barn.

"If you'll wait, I'll wheel it out a little, it's a bit dark in here."

"Very good, very good! That will do."

"Well, there is nothing extraordinary about it," said the General, "the coach is quite commonplace."

"It seems to me, Your Excellency, it is not worth four thousand at all," said one of the young officers.

"What?"

"I was saying, Your Excellency, that it seems to me it is not worth four thousand."

"Never mind four thousand. It is not worth two. There is simply nothing in it. Unless there is something special inside . . . Be so good, dear fellow, as to unbutton the cover . . ."

And Chertokutski appeared before the officers' eyes, sitting doubled up in an extraordinary way in his dressing gown.

"Ah, you are here . . ." said the amazed General.

Having said this, the General instantly slammed the door, covered Chertokutski again and drove away with the gentlemen officers.

The Nose

ON the 25th of March an extraordinary thing happened in St. Petersburg. The barber Ivan Yakovlevitch, who lives on the Voznesiensky Prospect (his surname has been forgotten, and even on his sign-board, which depicts a gentleman with a soaped cheek and on which are inscribed the words, ". . . and blood is let," nothing else appears), barber Ivan Yakovlevitch woke early and smelled the odour of hot bread. Raising himself slightly on the bed, he saw that his spouse, a respectable lady who was very fond of coffee, was taking freshly baked bread out of the oven.

"To-day, Praskovya Osipovna, I shall not drink coffee," said Ivan Yakovlevitch, "but instead I'd like some hot bread and onion." (That is, Ivan Yakovlevitch would have liked both, but he knew that it was absolutely impossible to demand both things at once, as Praskovya Osipovna did not encourage such fancies).

"Let the fool eat the bread—suits me," thought the spouse, "there will be all the more coffee left," and she threw a loaf of black bread on the table.

For decency's sake, Ivan Yakovlevitch put on his frock-coat over his shirt and, sitting down at the table, took some salt, peeled two onions, took up a knife and, with an air of importance, began to cut the bread. Having cut the loaf in halves, he looked inside and, to his amazement, saw something white. Ivan Yakovlevitch cautiously poked the knife, at it and touched it with his finger. "It is firm," he said to himself, "what can it be ?" He pushed his fingers in and extracted—a nose !

Ivan Yakovlevitch was confounded. He began to rub his eyes and to feel the object. Yes, it was a nose, really a nose ! And there seemed to be something familiar about it. Ivan Yakovlevitch's face expressed terror, but this terror was nothing compared with the indignation which filled his wife.

"Animal, where have you cut this nose from ?" she shouted furiously. "Crook, drunkard ! I shall report you to the police myself. Robber ! I have already heard from three people that, while shaving them, you pull them about by their noses so much that they can hardly stay in their seats."

But Ivan Yakovlevitch felt half dead. He realised that the nose belonged to nobody else but the collegiate assessor Kovalev, whom he shaved every Wednesday and Sunday.

"Wait, Praskovya Osipovna, I'll wrap it in a little rag and put it in a corner. Let it lie there for a little while, and I will carry it out later on."

"I will not even hear of it. That I should allow a sliced nose to lie in my room ! Like a baked rusk ! All he knows is how to pull a razor along a strop, and he soon won't be fit to do even that, vagabond, blockhead ! Away with it. Out ! Take it wherever you wish—I won't have it in the place for a minute."

Ivan Yakovlevitch stood as if stunned. He thought and thought and did not know what to make of it. "The devil knows how it happened," he said at last, scratching behind his ear. "Can't make it out. Did I come home drunk yesterday or not ? Most likely I did, judging by all the signs. This thing is impossible. Bread is a matter for baking, but as far as a nose goes . . . no. Can't make it out."

Ivan Yakovlevitch stopped talking. The thought that a policeman might discover the nose on him and charge him made him feel quite faint. He could already see the blood-red collar, handsomely embroidered with silver, a sword . . . and began to tremble. Finally he grabbed his breeches and high boots, put all this rubbish on and, accompanied by violent exhortations from Praskovya Osipovna, he wrapped the nose in a rag and went out into the street.

He wanted to push it under a loose curb stone at somebody's gate or drop it somewhere without being noticed and then turn into a side street, but unfortunately he kept running into some acquaintance or other who would immediately begin asking : "Where are you going ?" or "Who have you come out to shave so early ?" So that Ivan Yakovlevitch could not possibly find an appropriate moment. Once he managed to drop it, but a sentry pointed with his halberd from the distance and shouted : "You've dropped something —pick it up !" and Ivan Yakovlevitch had to pick up the nose and hide it in his pocket.

He became desperate, especially as the crowds continued

to increase as the stores and shops began to open. He decided to go to the Isaaky Bridge. Perhaps he could succeed in throwing the nose into the Neva.

But I am somewhat at fault for not having yet said anything about Ivan Yakovlevitch, an honourable man in many respects. Ivan Yakovlevitch, like all honourable Russian artisans, was a terrible drunkard, and, although he shaved strange chins every day, his own was always unshaven. Ivan Yakovlevitch's frock-coat (Ivan Yakovlevitch never wore an ordinary jacket) was piebald—that is, it was black but dappled with brownish yellow and grey ; the collar was shiny and, in place of its three buttons, only the threads were hanging.

Ivan Yakovlevitch was a great cynic, and, when the collegiate assessor Kovalev used to tell him during shaving, "Your hands, Ivan Yakovlevitch, always stink !" Ivan Yakovlevitch would answer with the question, "Why shouldn't they stink ?" "I don't know, brother, but they stink !" the collegiate assessor would reply, and Ivan Yakovlevitch, after taking a pinch of snuff, would in revenge soap Kovalev's cheek as well as under his nose, behind his ear, under his beard—in short, wherever he fancied.

This honourable citizen now found himself on the Isaaky Bridge. First he looked round, then he leaned over the parapet as if to look under the bridge and to see whether there were any fish in the river, and quietly threw in the rag containing the nose. At once he felt as if a ton weight had fallen from his shoulders. Ivan Yakovlevitch even chuckled. Instead of going to shave the chins of officials, he was departing to an establishment bearing the inscription "Food and tea" in order to obtain a glass of punch, when he suddenly noticed at the end of the bridge a police officer, of noble appearance, with broad whiskers, a three-cornered hat and a sword. He stopped dead. The police officer, however, was beckoning him with his finger and calling, "Come here, friend."

Ivan Yakovlevitch, fully aware of how a man in this uniform should be treated, took off his cap at a distance, and, approaching him nimbly, said, "Good morning, your Honour."

"No, no, brother, don't be so formal. Tell me, what were you doing there on the bridge ?"

"As true as God is in Heaven, sir, I was on my way to shave somebody and only peeped at the river to see how fast it was running."

"You are lying, you are lying, brother. You will not get away with that ! Kindly answer me."

"I would willingly shave your Honour twice or even three times a week," answered Ivan Yakovlevitch.

"No, my friend, that's nonsense! Three barbers attend to me already and they regard it as a great honour. Now tell me, what were you doing there?"

Ivan Yakovlevitch became pale . . .

But here the scene becomes completely obscured by mist, and we know absolutely nothing else of what transpired.

2

Collegiate assessor Kovalev awoke comparatively early and made the sound, b-r-r-r with his lips, which he always did on waking, although he himself did not know the reason for it. Kovalev stretched himself and called to his servant to give him a mirror which was standing on the table. He wanted to look at a pimple which had suddenly appeared on his nose the night before, but, to his great amazement, he saw that there was a completely smooth place instead of the nose. Kovalev grew frightened and shouted for some water. He rubbed his eyes with a towel—still no nose! He began to feel his face with his hand, and pinched himself to find out whether he was asleep or not—apparently he was not. Collegiate assessor Kovalev jumped out of bed, shook himself —still no nose! He immediately ordered his clothes to be brought to him, and rushed off straight to the Chief of Police.

But in the meantime I should say something about Kovalev, so that the reader may see what kind of a collegiate assessor he was.

It is impossible to compare collegiate assessors who attain this rank by means of a certificate of learning with those who are being turned out in the Caucasus. They are two entirely different species. Learned collegiate assessors. . . . But Russia is such a peculiar country, that if you say something about one collegiate assessor, then all collegiate assessors from Riga to Kamchatka, without exception, will take it personally. The same applies to all other ranks and professions.

Kovalev was a Caucasian collegiate assessor. He had held this rank for only two years, and therefore could not forget it for a moment, and, in order to add more nobility and importance to himself, he never called himself just a collegiate assessor, but always a major. "Listen, little pigeon," he would say on meeting a woman in the street who was selling shirt-fronts, "call at my place, my flat is on the Sadovaja. You just ask 'Does Major Kovalev live here?'—anybody will direct you." If, however, he met a comely woman, he would, in addition, give her certain secret instructions, adding, "Darling, you ask for Major Kovalev's flat." Therefore, we too, shall in future call him a major.

Major Kovalev was in the habit of strolling along the Nevsky Prospect every day. The collar of his shirt-front was always extremely clean and well starched. His side whiskers were of the kind which are still to be seen on government and district land surveyors, on architects and regimental doctors, also on those performing various duties and, generally speaking, on all those men who have fat, rosy cheeks and are good boston players. These side whiskers grow along the very middle of the cheek and go straight up to the nose. Major Kovalev carried a multitude of little carnelian seals, some with coats of arms and some on which were engraved "Wednesday," "Thursday," "Monday," etc. Major Kovalev had come up to Petersburg on business, namely, to find an employment worthy of his profession. If possible he would have liked the post of Vice-Governor or, failing that, some executive position in an important department. Major Kovalev was also not averse to marriage, but only if the prospective bride happened to have a dowry of two hundred thousand roubles. Therefore, reader, you may judge for yourself what the Major's predicament was when, instead of a nose, not uncomely but of reasonable proportions, he saw a very silly plain and smooth place.

As bad luck would have it, not one cab driver showed himself in the street, and he had to walk, having wrapped himself in his cloak and covered his face with a handkerchief, as if his nose was bleeding.

"But perhaps I only imagined it—it is impossible that a nose should so stupidly disappear," he thought, and entered a pastry shop, where he intended to look at himself in a mirror.

Fortunately, there was nobody there. The boys were sweeping the rooms and replacing the chairs: some of them, with sleepy eyes, were carrying trays of hot pies. Yesterday's papers, wet with coffee, were scattered on tables and chairs.

"Well, thank Heaven, nobody's here," Kovalev muttered, "I can have a look now." He timidly approached the mirror and looked into it.

"The Devil take it—what a filthy mess," he said and spat.

"If there were only something in its place—but no, simply nothing there!"

He bit his lips in his grief and, on leaving the pastry shop, he decided, against his usual wont, not to look or smile at anybody.

Suddenly, as if thunderstruck, he stopped in front of a house. He beheld an inexplicable apparition. A coach stopped at the house entrance; the door opened and a gentleman in uniform jumped out and ran up the steps. How great was Kovalev's horror and at the same time his amazement when he recognised who it was—his very own nose! It seemed to him, witnessing this unusual sight, that everything swayed before him. He could hardly stand, but decided, whatever happened, to await the return of the nose to the coach. He was trembling as if with ague.

After two minutes the nose actually reappeared. It was in a uniform embroidered with gold and was wearing a stiff collar and suede breeches. A sword hung at its side. Judging by the plume on its hat, it held the rank of a State Councillor. Everything pointed to the fact that it was going to visit somebody. It looked around and, calling to the driver, "Let's go," sat down and was driven away.

Poor Kovalev nearly went mad. He did not know what to think of such a strange occurrence. How could the nose, which was yesterday on his face and could neither ride nor walk, wear a uniform? He ran after the coach, which, fortunately, did not go far and stopped in front of the bazaar. He hurried there, threading his way among a row of old beggar women, with bandaged faces and two holes for eyes, at whom he used to laugh. The crowd was not large. Kovalev was in such a bad state that he could not decide anything, and his eyes were searching for the gentleman in all the corners. Finally, he saw it standing in front of a shop. The nose's face was completely hidden in the large military collar and it was examining some merchandise with deep attention.

"How is the nose to be approached?" thought Kovalev. "Judging by everything—the uniform and the hat—it is obvious that it is a State Councillor. The Devil knows how it is to be done!"

Drawing nearer, Kovalev coughed, but the nose did not change its posture for a moment.

"Sir," said Kovalev, inwardly forcing himself to some courage, "dear sir . . ."

"What is it you wish?" answered the nose, turning round.

"It is strange, dear sir . . . it seems to me . . . you ought to know your place. And suddenly I find you—and where ? You will agree . . ."

"Forgive me, but I do not understand what you wish to say. Will you kindly explain ?"

"How shall I explain it ?" thought Kovalev, and, gathering courage, he began, "Of course, I . . . by the way, I am a major. You will agree that it is unseemly for me to walk about without a nose. Some beggar woman selling peeled oranges on the Voskresenski Bridge may sit there without a nose, but I have prospects of obtaining . . . and in addition, being acquainted with ladies in many households —Mrs. Chechatiroeva, State Councillor's wife, and others . . . Judge for yourself. I do not know, dear sir" (at this Major Kovalev shrugged his shoulders), "forgive me, whether this is in accordance with the rules of honour and duty. You yourself will understand . . ."

"I do not understand anything at all," answered the nose. "Kindly explain more clearly."

"My dear sir," said Kovalev, full of dignity, "I do not know how to interpret your words. It seems to me that the whole matter is quite obvious . . . or do you want . . . ? After all, you are my own nose !"

The nose looked at the major and raised its eyebrows slightly.

"You are mistaken, sir, I am myself. Besides, there can be no close relationship between us. Judging by the buttons on your uniform, you are serving in a different department." Having said this, the nose turned away.

Kovalev became completely confused, not knowing what to do, nor even what to think. At that moment a pleasant rustle of female dresses was heard. An elderly lady approached, her clothes profusely trimmed with lace, and with her was a slim girl in a white dress which clung attractively to her graceful waist. She was wearing a straw-coloured hat as light as a pastry. A tall man-in-waiting stopped behind them and opened a snuff-box. He wore large side whiskers and at least a dozen collars.

Kovalev moved nearer, pushed out the batiste collar of his shirt-front, re-arranged the seals which were hung on his gold chain, and, smiling in all directions, turned his attention to the slim lady, who, like a spring flower, was bending slightly and was holding her little white hand, with semi-transparent fingers, to her forehead. The smile on Kovalev's face broadened even more when he saw, under the hat, her round chin of lucid whiteness and part of her cheek, the shade of a rose in spring. Suddenly, however, he jumped away, as if burnt. He remembered that, instead of a nose, he had absolutely nothing at all, and tears sprang to his eyes. He turned round with the intention of telling the gentleman in uniform, quite frankly, that he was only impersonating a State Councillor—that he was a rogue and a scoundrel and was nothing but his, Kovalev's nose ; but the nose was no longer there. It had had time to drive away, probably to visit somebody else.

This drove Kovalev to despair. He went back and stood still for a moment against a pillar, looking carefully in every direction to see whether he could catch sight of the nose. He clearly remembered that its hat bore a plume and that its uniform had gold embroidery, but he had not noticed either the great-coat or the colour of the coach or the horses, nor even whether there was any footman behind it and what livery he wore. Moreover, such a multitude of coaches was driving so quickly backwards and forwards that it was difficult to pick one out ; and, even if he had recognised one of them, he had no means of stopping it.

The day was lovely and sunny. There were masses of people on the Nevski ; a whole flowery cascade of ladies was streaming along the pavement, which stretched from the Policeiski up to the Anichkin bridge. There went his acquaintance, the Court Councillor, whom he used to call a lieutenant-colonel, especially when strangers happened to be present. There also went Yarishkin, chief of a table in the senate, his great friend, who always lost when he played boston. There went another major, who had obtained his assessorship on the Caucasus. He was waving his hand and beckoning him.

"Oh, the Devil take it !" said Kovalev. "Hey there, cabman ! Drive me at once to the Chief of Police."

Kovalev sat in the carriage and kept shouting to the cabman, "Drive as fast as you can."

"Is the Chief of Police at home ?" he cried as he entered the hall.

"I am afraid not," answered the porter.

"What a nuisance !"

"Yes," replied the porter, and added, "and he only left a short time ago. Had you come a minute sooner, you might have found him in."

Kovalev returned to the carriage, without removing the handkerchief from his face, and shouted in a desperate voice : "Get a move on."

"Where to?" asked the driver.

"Straight on!"

"What do you mean, straight on? We've got to turn here—right or left?"

This question made Kovalev stop and think again. In his condition it behoved him to go to the police station, not because the matter directly concerned the police, but because their orders would be more quickly obeyed than those given by anyone else. It would, however, be senseless to seek satisfaction from the authorities of the place where the nose had declared it was serving, as one could see from the replies of the nose itself that it held nothing sacred and might lie as readily in that place as it had lied in assuring him that it had never met him before. Therefore, Kovalev had almost decided to order the driver to go to the police station, when the thought struck him that this rogue and scoundrel, who had behaved so dishonestly already at the first meeting, might again, conveniently making use of time, somehow slip out of town, and all the search would be in vain, and might, God forbid, last a whole month. Finally, it seemed that Heaven itself directed him. He decided to go straight to the newspaper office with a detailed description of the nose, so that anybody meeting it could immediately return it to Kovalev, or at least tell him of its abode. Therefore, having decided this, he ordered the driver to go to the newspaper office, and, during the whole of the journey, never stopped thumping the man's back with his fist and urging him on, crying, "Hurry, dastard! Hurry, crook!"

"I am doing my best, sir," the driver would say, shaking his head and striking the horse, whose coat was as long as a spaniel's.

At last the carriage stopped, and Kovalev, breathless, ran into the small reception room, where a grey-haired official, wearing an old frock-coat and glasses, was sitting at a table, with a pen in his teeth, counting copper coins.

"Who takes advertisements?" shouted Kovalev. "Oh, good morning."

"Good morning," said the grey-haired official, raising his eyes for a moment and then looking down again at the small piles of money.

"I want to inser . . ."

"Excuse me, will you kindly wait a little," murmured the official, writing a figure on a paper with his right hand, and, with a finger of his left hand, moving a bead on his counting board.

A footman, with gallooned livery, and of a comparatively clean appearance, denoting his employment in an aristocratic house, stood near the table, with a note in his hands, and deemed it appropriate to show his sociability by saying, "Believe me, sir, the dog is not worth eight griven. I would not have given even eight groshi for her, but the Countess loves her—I swear she loves her—and whoever finds her gets a hundred roubles ! It would be right to say between ourselves, that people's tastes are incompatible. If you so desire, then keep a setter or a poodle, and don't be sorry to give five hundred for it—give a thousand—but then you should get a good dog."

The respectable official listened to this with an air of importance, and at the same time busied himself calculating the numbers of letters in the note.

A crowd of old women stood at the side, as well as merchants' clerks and porters with notes. One announced that a horse-driver, of sober behaviour, was free for service ; another, that a good second-hand carriage, imported from Paris in 1814, was for sale. There was a 19-year old servant girl available, practised in laundry work and suitable for other work as well ; a solid droshky, with one spring missing ; a young and spirited horse, dappled grey, seventeen years old ; new turnip and radish seeds from London ; a country house, with all conveniences, two stables and a site suitable for growing a fine birch or fir grove. There was also a notice to those wishing to buy old shoes soles, with an invitation to appear at the second auction every day from 8 to 3.

The room in which all this company found itself was small, and the air in it was extremely thick, but the collegiate assessor could not smell anything, as he had covered his face with a handkerchief, and because his very own nose was—Heaven knew where.

"My dear sir, permit me to ask you . . . it is very important," he said at last impatiently.

"Just a moment, a moment . . . Two roubles forty three kopeks ! . . . Just a moment . . . One rouble sixty four kopeks !" the grey haired gentleman was saying, thrusting the notices in the faces of the old women and the porters.

"What is it you wish ?" he said at last, turning to Kovalev.

"I should like to ask . . ." Kovalev said, "a swindle, an outrage has taken place—up to now I have not been able to find out anything. I should only like to advertise that whoever will produce the dastard to me will receive an ample reward."

"May I ask your name ?"

"But why my name ? It is impossible for me to disclose it. I have many acquaintances—Chechtareva, State Councillor's wife ; Pelageya Grigorievna Podtochina, Staff Officer's wife. . . . They may suddenly find out ! God forbid ! You can simply write, a collegiate assessor—or, even better, a major."

"Has your house-servant run away ?"

"Who is talking about a house-servant ? That would not have been such an outrage ! My nose . . . has run away from me !"

"Ahem ! A peculiar name ! And has this Mr. Nosey stolen a large sum of money from you ?"

"My nose . . . that is . . . you are thinking of something different ! My nose, my own nose, disappeared—I don't know where to. Damme, are you trying to joke with me ?"

"But how has it disappeared ? I can't quite understand."

"I don't know how. The main thing is that it is now travelling about town in the disguise of a State Councillor. Therefore, I want to advertise, so that whoever catches it shall bring it to me in the shortest possible time. Judge for yourself ! Really, how can I manage without such a conspicuous part of my body ? It is not as if it were the small toe on my foot which has disappeared, and which I could hide in high boots, and nobody would see whether it were there or not ! On Thursdays I go to the State Councillor's wife, Chechtareva ; Podtochina Pelageya Grivorievna, Staff Officer's wife—she has a very pretty daughter : they are very good friends of mine, and judge for yourself—what can I do ? I cannot appear there now !"

The official began to think, which was demonstrated by his firmly compressed lips.

"No ! I cannot put such an advertisement in the paper," he said finally, after a long silence.

"Why ? Why not ?"

"For this reason—a newspaper may lose its reputation. If everybody began to write that his nose had run away from him, then . . . ! As it is, people say that many absurd and false rumours are being printed."

"But why is this matter absurd ? There is nothing absurd about it !"

"That is how you see it. But then last week a similar thing happened. An official came in, just as you came to-day, and brought a written notice. According to calculation, the cost amounted to 2 roubles 73, and all the advertisement consisted of was the fact that a black-haired poodle had run away. On the face of it, what is wrong with that ? But it resulted in a libel action. That poodle was a treasurer—I don't remember of what department."

"But I am not advertising for a poodle ! I am advertising for my own nose—therefore, almost about myself !"

"No ! On no account can I take such an advertisement."

"But my nose has really disappeared !"

"If it has disappeared, it is a matter for a medical man. They say that there are people who can give you any nose you desire. But, by the way, I realise that you must be a man with a gay nature and like to indulge in a joke when in company."

" I swear to you ! And, as things have gone so far, I'll show you."

"Why take the trouble ?" replied the official, taking snuff. "On the other hand, if it is not too much trouble," he added with curiosity, "it would be interesting to have a look at it."

The collegiate assessor removed the handkerchief from his face.

"And so it is—very strange !" said the official. "The place is quite smooth, like a freshly fried pancake. Yes, yes, incredibly smooth !"

"Will you stop arguing now ? You can see for yourself that it is impossible not to print it ! I shall be extremely grateful to you, and I am very glad that this incident has afforded me the pleasure of making your acquaintance."

You can see from this that the collegiate assessor had, by this time, decided to ingratiate himself a little.

"Of course, it is a small matter to print it," said the official, "but I cannot see any advantage in it for you. If you want to do it, give it to somebody, clever at writing, to describe it as a rare work of nature, and print an article about it in the 'Northern Bee' " (here he again took a pinch of snuff) "for instruction" (here he wiped his nose), "or generally for the sake of everybody's curiosity."

The collegiate assessor completely lost all hope. He let his glance travel over the newspaper, where various theatre performances were advertised. He was almost prepared to smile on seeing the name of an actress, of pretty appearance, and his hand went into his pocket to see whether he had on him a blue banknote, as Staff Officers, in Kovalev's opinion, should sit in the stalls: but the thought of the nose spoilt it all.

The official himself was apparently touched by Kovalev's

predicament. Wishing to lighten his sorrow somewhat, he thought it appropriate to show his sympathy in a few words. "It really grieves me very much that such a curious thing should have happened to you. Would you care for a pinch of snuff? That cures headaches and sorrowful moods: it is even good for hæmorrhoids." Saying this, the official offered Kovalev the snuff box, having very deftly turned up the lid bearing the portrait of some lady wearing a hat.

This unpremeditated action made Kovalev lose his patience. "I do not understand how you can find this a suitable time for joking," he said with feeling, "don't you see that I do not possess the very thing to sniff with? May the Devil take your snuff!" Having said this, he left the newspaper office, deeply upset, and departed to the Commissioner of Police.

Kovalev entered the Commissioner's office just when the latter had stretched himself and yawned and had said to himself, "Now I'll have a pleasant two hours' sleep," and, therefore, as may be supposed, the collegiate assessor's arrival was very badly timed. The Commissioner greatly encouraged art and industry, but he preferred Government banknotes to anything else. "This banknote," he used to say, "there is nothing better. It does not ask for food, takes up little space, will always go into the pocket and will not break if you drop it."

The Commissioner received Kovalev somewhat frigidly and said that after lunch was not the time to make investigations: that nature itself ordered some rest after a good meal: (from this the collegiate assessor could gather that the sayings of the ancient sages were not unknown to the Commissioner) that a nose could not be torn away from a decent man. This touched Kovalev on the raw.

It is necessary to point out that Kovalev was very easily offended. He could forgive anything said about him in his personal capacity, but any reflection on his rank or profession was unpardonable. He acquiesced in the privilege of the stage to ridicule subalterns, but would countenance no reference to the Officers of the Staff. The Commissioner's reception embarrassed him so much that he shook his head and said, with dignity, slightly extending his hands, "I confess I can say nothing more after such insulting remarks . . ." and left.

He arrived home, hardly able to drag one foot after the other. Dusk was falling. His flat seemed to him wretched and extremely odious after all these unsuccessful searches.

Entering the hall, he saw his man-servant, Ivan, lying on his back on a dirty leather settee, spitting methodically at the ceiling, and quite successfully hitting the same spot every time. The man's indifference infuriated him: he struck him on the head with his hand, crying, "Pig! You are always doing something idiotic!"

Ivan immediately jumped up and rushed to take off Kovalev's cloak.

The Major entered his room, weary and sad, threw himself on a chair and, finally, after several sighs, said, "My God! My God! Why have I deserved such misfortune? If I were without a hand or a foot, it would be bearable; but without a nose, a citizen is no citizen: you might just as well take him and throw him out of the window! If it had been cut off in battle or a duel, or if it had gone through some fault of my own! But it has gone for no reason at all—voluntarily, without any cause. But no, it cannot be true," he added after some thought, "it is impossible for a nose to disappear—absolutely impossible! I am probably either dreaming or raving. Perhaps, by some mistake, instead of water, I drank the vodka with which I wipe my beard after shaving. Ivan, the fool, forgot to take it away, and I probably swallowed it."

To assure himself that he was not drunk, the Major pinched himself so hard that he screamed. This pain quite persuaded him that it was all very real. He quietly approached the mirror, first screwing up his eyes, hoping that his nose might have appeared in its proper place; but the next minute he jumped back, saying, "What a dreadful sight!"

It was certainly incongruous. If a button, silver spoon, watch or anything similar had disappeared . . . but, for a nose to disappear! And, in addition, in one's own flat! Major Kovalev, considering all the circumstances, conjectured, perhaps nearer the truth than ever before, that the person responsible was none other than the Staff Officers' wife, Podtochina, who wanted him to marry her daughter. He had liked to flirt with her, but had evaded the final issue. When the Staff Officer's wife told him plainly that she would like him to marry the girl, he had quietly withdrawn with compliments, saying that he was still young; that he had to serve for another five years, after which he would be exactly forty years old. No doubt the Staff Officer's wife had decided to ruin him out of revenge and had employed some sorceress to that end, as it was impossible to suppose that the nose had been cut off. Nobody had entered his room, and the barber, Ivan Yakovlevitch, had shaved him as recently as Wednesday; and during the whole of Wednesday, and even Thursday, his nose was all there—he remembered distinctly. In any case, he would have felt pain, and the wound could not have healed so quickly and become as smooth as a pancake. He thought out plans. Should he start formal legal proceedings against the Staff Officer's wife, or go to her himself and accuse her personally? His meditation was interrupted by the sight of a light gleaming through the chink of the door, indicating that the candle in the hall had already been lit by Ivan. Soon Ivan himself appeared, carrying it before him and illuminating the whole room. Kovalev's first movement was to snatch the handkerchief and cover that part of his face where, yesterday, his nose had been, to avoid his stupid servant's gaping at the curious sight which his master's face presented.

Ivan had hardly had time to reach his dirty palliasse, when a strange voice was heard in the hall, saying, "Does the collegiate assessor Kovalev live here?"

"Come in. Major Kovalev is here," said Kovalev hurriedly, jumping up and opening the door.

A police official entered; a handsome man, with side whiskers not too light nor too dark, and plump cheeked; the same who had stood at the end of the Isaaky Bridge at the beginning of the story.

"Have you lost your nose?"

"That's right."

"It has been found."

"What are you saying?" exclaimed Major Kovalev. Joy robbed him of speech. He gaped at the officer, who was standing in front of him and on whose full lips and cheeks the trembling light of the candle twinkled brightly.

"By a strange coincidence, it was intercepted almost on the road. It was already seated in the coach and intended to travel to Riga. Its passport had been issued a long time ago in the name of an official. The strange thing is that I, myself, had at first taken it for a gentleman, but, luckily, I had my glasses with me, and, when I put them on, I saw at once that it was a nose. I am short-sighted, and, if you stand up in front of me, I can only see that you have a face, but cannot distinguish either nose or beard. My mother-in-law—that is, my wife's mother—does not see anything either."

Kovalev was beside himself. "Where is it? Where? I shall rush to it immediately."

"Don't bother. Knowing that you needed it, I have brought it with me. Strangely enough, the chief accomplice in this matter is the scoundrel barber from the Vosnesenski Street, who is at present sitting in a cell. I have suspected him for a long time of drunkenness and theft, and even two days ago he stole a card of buttons from a shop. Your nose is as good as new." Thereupon, the District Officer delved into his pocket and extracted from it the nose, wrapped in a piece of paper.

"Yes, that's it!" exclaimed Kovalev. "That's it alright! Have a cup of tea with me."

"I should deem it a great pleasure, but on no account can I do so. I have to drive from here to the gaol . . . The price of food has risen a lot . . . I have also my mother-in-law —that is, my wife's mother—living with me, and children: the eldest especially is promising; a very clever youngster, but there are no means at all for education . . ."

For some minutes after the police officer's departure, the collegiate assessor remained almost in a trance, and only regained his senses after another few minutes. He was overwhelmed by the intensity of this unexpected joy. Then, cautiously, he took his restored nose in the palms of his hands and studied it closely.

"It's it—it's it alright," Major Kovalev cried. "Here is the little pimple on the left which appeared yesterday." The Major nearly laughed aloud with joy.

But nothing is permanent in this world, and even joy, after the first few minutes, becomes less vivid, its intensity waning until, finally, imperceptibly, it merges into the ordinary state of mind, as a ripple in a pool, born of the fall of a stone, merges finally with the smooth surface. Kovalev began to meditate, and the realisation dawned upon him that the matter was not yet settled: the nose had been found, but it had still to be attached—to be put back in its place.

"And what if it will not stick?" Having put this question to himself, the Major became pale. Filled with inexplicable dread, he dashed to the table and moved as near as possible to the mirror, so as not to misplace the nose. His hands were trembling. Carefully and warily, he put his nose in its former place. Oh, horror! The nose would not stick! He put it to his mouth, warmed it a little with his breath, and again moved it to the smooth space between his two cheeks; but nothing would make the nose stick.

"Come on, cling, you fool!" he cried to the nose; but the

nose was as lifeless as a piece of wood, and kept falling on to the table and producing the sound of a falling cork. The Major's face twisted into a grimace. "It must stick!" he cried, frightened. But all his efforts were in vain.

He called Ivan and sent him for the doctor, who occupied the best flat on the second floor of the same house. The doctor was a handsome man and possessed beautiful, pitch-black side whiskers and a fresh, healthy wife. He ate fresh apples every morning, and kept his mouth unusually clean, washing it out every morning for almost three-quarters-of-an-hour, and polishing his teeth with five different kinds of tooth-brushes.

The doctor arrived almost at once. Having enquired when the misfortune had occurred, he lifted Major Kovalev by his chin and rapped with his thumb on the place where the nose used to be, so that the Major had to throw back his head with such force that he hit the wall with the back of his head. The medical man said that this was nothing to worry about, and, having advised the Major to move slightly from the wall, ordered him to bend his head to the right. Having felt the place where the nose used to be, he said "Ahem!" Then he ordered the Major to bend his head to the left, and said "Ahem!" Finally, he again rapped him with his thumb, so that Major Kovalev jerked his head like a horse whose teeth are being inspected. After this examination, the doctor shook his head and said, "No, impossible! You'd better stay as you are, or you may be worse off. Of course, it is possible to fix it; I could even fix it on now; but I assure you that it would be worse for you."

"I like that! How can I remain without a nose?" said Kovalev. "It could not be worse than it is now. The Devil knows what I am to do! How can I show myself in this idiotic state? I have important acquaintances. . . . For example, to-day I am invited to receptions at two houses. I know many people, the State Councillor's wife, Chechatareva, the Staff Officer's wife, Podtochina . . . after this occurrence I shall have nothing more to do with her, unless it be through the police. Please help me," continued Kovalev in an imploring tone, "isn't there some remedy? Fix it somehow, however badly, if it will only stay put. I could even support it slightly with my hand on dangerous occasions. And I don't dance, so that I can't harm it with some incautious movement. Any recompense for your visit, be assured, as far as my means will allow . . ."

"Believe it or not," said the doctor, neither loudly nor

quietly, but extremely soothingly and convincingly, "I never visit for gain: it's against my convictions and my art. It is true that I charge for my visits, but merely in order not to hurt by refusal. I could, of course, fix your nose; but I can assure you, upon my honour, if you do not believe my word, that it would be the worse for you. Leave it to the work of nature herself. Wash the place frequently with cold water, and I assure you that, even without a nose, you will be as healthy as if you had one. As for the nose, I would advise you to put it in a jar with spirit, or, even better, with a mixture of two tablespoons of strong vodka and warmed vinegar, and then you may get a considerable sum for it. I will buy it myself if you won't overcharge."

"No, no! Nothing would induce me to sell it!" cried Major Kovalev in desperation, "I'd rather it perished!"

"What is there to be done? At least, you can see that I have tried." Having said this, the elegant doctor left the room.

Kovalev had not even noticed the doctor's face, and, in his deep preoccupation, had only seen the cuffs of his white shirt, as clean as snow, which peeped out from the sleeves of his black frock-coat.

The next day he decided, before starting formal proceedings, to write to the Staff Officer's wife in order to find out whether she would, without a legal struggle, undo the wrong done to him. The letter was as follows:

"Dear Madam,

Alexandra Grigorievna,

I cannot understand the strange deed you have perpetrated.

I assure you that, by acting in this manner, you will gain nothing, and will never force me to marry your daughter.

Believe me, the story about my nose is well known, as is also the fact that you are the principal person responsible, and nobody else. Its sudden departure from its place, its flight and masquerade, first as an official, and finally as itself, has been caused only by sorcery, practised by you, or by those who, like you, engage in such dishonourable occupations. It is my duty to warn you that, if the above mentioned nose does not return to its place in the course of to-day, I shall have no alternative but to seek the protection of the law.

I have the honour to be, incidentally with the deepest respect for you,

Your obedient servant,

PLATON KOVALEV."

"Dear Sir,

Platon Kuzmich,

I was extremely astonished by your letter. I confess, frankly, I never expected it, especially the unwarranted rebuke it contains.

I must advise you that I never received the official whom you mention, either disguised or undisguised.

"It is true that Philip Ivanovitch used to visit me. It is also true that he sought my daughter's hand, and, although he is a man of good and steady habits and very learned, I never offered him any hope.

You also refer to a nose. If, by this, you imply that I wanted to lead you by the nose and then give you a formal refusal, then you surprise me. As you yourself imply, I was, on the contrary, of an entirely different opinion, and, even now, if you would seek my daughter in marriage in the proper way, I am prepared to accept you at once, as this has always been my greatest desire. Hoping which, I remain ever at your service.

ALEXANDRA PODROCHINA."

"No!" said Kovalev, having read the letter, "she really is not guilty. Impossible! The letter is written in a way in which a person guilty of a crime could never write." The collegiate assessor was wise in such matters, as he had been several times detailed to attend inquests while he was still in the Caucasus.

"How on earth could it have happened? Only the Devil can know," he finally concluded, disheartened.

In the meantime, the news about this unusual occurrence —and, as usual, some additional details—had spread. It was at a time when everybody's thoughts had been directed to the supernatural. Only a short time before, the public had been engrossed with experiments in spiritualism. The story about the dancing chairs on Konuishenaja Street was still quite fresh, and so it was little wonder that people soon began to say that the collegiate assessor Kovalev's nose paraded on the Nevsky Prospect at precisely three o'clock. A crowd of curious people congregated there every day. Somebody said that the nose was inside the Junker Stores: and such a crowd collected near Junker's that even the police had to interfere. One opportunist of honourable appearance, with side whiskers, who sold stale pastries at the theatre entrance, constructed some wonderful solid wooden benches especially for the purpose of inviting the curious to stand on them at the price of eighty kopeks a head. One very worthy colonel left his house early for that very reason, and, with great difficulty, threaded his way through the crowd; but, to his great indignation, he saw in the shop window, instead of the nose, an ordinary woollen vest and a lithographic picture depicting a girl straightening her stocking and a dandy, in a fancy waistcoat and with a small beard, looking at her from behind a tree—a picture which had been hanging in the same place for more than ten years. He moved away and said, with annoyance, "How can people mislead the crowd with such foolish and incredible rumours?" Then he said, loudly, that the Major's nose was promenading, not on the Nevsky Prospect, but in the Tavricheski Gardens; that apparently it had been there for some time; that, even when Chozrev-Mirza used to live there, he was very much surprised at this strange trick of nature. Some of the students from the Surgical Academy departed there. One eminent and respectable lady asked the superintendent of the Gardens in a special letter to show her children this rare phenomenon and, if possible, to give an explanation which would instruct and edify youth.

All the indispensable social guests at balls and receptions, who like to make the ladies laugh and whose stock at this time was completely exhausted, were extremely pleased by these happenings. A small party of honourable and well intentioned people showed extreme displeasure. One gentleman said, with indignation, that he could not understand how, in the present enlightened age, such absurd stories could spread and that he was amazed that the Government had not done something about it. This gentleman apparently belonged to those who would entangle the Government in everything—even their daily squabbles with their wives.

After that . . . but here again the whole affair is obscured by mist, and what followed is unknown.

3

The world is full of absolute nonsense. Sometimes there is no way of understanding it. Suddenly the very same nose, which had travelled about in the guise of a State Councillor and made such a noise in the town, found itself, as if nothing had happened, back in its place—that is, between Major

Kovalev's two cheeks. This had already happened by the 7th day of April.

Having awoken, and automatically glanced in the mirror, Kovalev saw—the nose! He grasped it with his hand—yes, it was really his nose! "Well!" said Kovalev, and, barefoot as he was, nearly began to dance a trepak with joy. The entrance of Ivan restrained him. He immediately ordered a wash basin and towel, and, washing himself, looked again in the mirror—the nose was still there. Wiping himself with the towel, he again looked into the mirror—he still had a nose.

"Ivan, look here. I think I have a little pimple on my nose," he said, and thought, "How terrible if Ivan says, 'No, sir, there is not only no pimple there—there is no nose either.'" But Ivan said, "No, sir, there's no pimple. Your nose is clear."

"Dash it—that's good!" the Major said to himself, and snapped his fingers.

At that moment the barber, Ivan Yakovlevitch peeped through the door, but timidly, like a cat which has just been beaten for stealing some fat.

"Tell me first—are your hands clean?" shouted Kovalev to him from the distance.

"Quite clean, your Honour."

"You liar!"

"I swear by the Almighty, sir, they are clean."

"Well, be careful."

Kovalev sat down. Ivan Yakovlevitch covered him with a serviette and, in a moment, with the aid of a brush, transformed his beard and part of his cheek into a froth of snowy whiteness like that offered on merchants' birthdays.

"Am I dreaming?" Ivan Yakovlevitch said to himself, suddenly seeing the nose, and, bending his head, looked at it from the other side. "Upon my soul, can it really be?" he continued, and looked at the nose for a long time. At last, gently and with the greatest care imaginable, he raised two fingers to take it by its tip, such being Ivan Yakovlevitch's method.

"Go carefully!" shouted Kovalev.

Ivan Yakovlevitch lowered his hand. He became panic-stricken and embarrassed, as he had never been before. Finally, he began to scrape carefully with the razor under Kovalev's chin and beard, and, although it was awkward and difficult to shave without support from that part of the body with which one smells, nevertheless, managing to press his rough thumb against the Major's cheek and lower jaw, he at last surmounted all obstacles and finished the shaving.

When everything was ready, Kovalev hurriedly dressed and immediately took a cab and drove straight to the café. As soon as he entered, he shouted from afar, "Boy, a cup of chocolate!" and immediately rushed to a mirror—the nose was still there. He turned round gaily and looked patronisingly, slightly closing his eyes, at two army men, one of whom had a nose no larger than a waistcoat button.

He then left for the office of the department where he had applied for a Vice-Governor's post, or, in case of failure, an executive. one. Passing through the reception room, he glanced at the mirror—he still had a nose.

Then he drove to the house of another collegiate assessor, or major—a great humourist. On his way there he thought, "If even the Major refrains from bursting his sides with laughing on seeing me, then it will be a sure sign that everything is in its right place." The collegiate assessor did not, however, even bat an eye-lid. "That's good, that's good dammit!" thought Kovalev to himself.

Proceeding on his way, he met the Staff Officer's wife, Podtochina, with her daughter. He bowed to them and was greeted with joyous cries—apparently there was nothing wrong with him. He talked to them for a long time, and, taking out his snuff-box with deliberation, slowly filled both nostrils with snuff, thinking, "Serves you right, women hens! I still shan't marry the daughter. All you can have is a flirtation."

Thereafter Major Kovalev gallivanted, as if nothing had happened, on the Nevsky Prospect, in the theatres and everywhere. And the nose, too, as if nothing had happened, sat on his face without the slightest hint that it had ever strayed in various directions. And ever after Major Kovalev was to be seen, eternally good humoured and smiling and pursuing pretty women—even, on one occasion, entering a shop on the market-place and buying some official ribbon, although for reasons unknown, as he himself was no Knight of any Order.

Such is the story of what happened in the Northern capital of our spacious State. Only now can we realise that, taking everything into consideration, there is much in it that is incredible. Apart from the supernatural departure of the nose—strange as that was—and its appearance in various places in the shape of a State Councillor, why on earth did not Kovalev tumble to the fact that it is impossible to advertise for a nose through a newspaper office? I do not mean this in the sense that I think it too extravagant to pay for an advertisement—that would be nonsense, and I am by no means one for misers—but it is unseemly, awkward, bad. Again, how did the nose happen to turn up in the baked bread, and how could Ivan Yakovlevitch himself . . . ? No, I cannot understand this at all—definitely not! But even stranger and more incomprehensible is that authors should choose such subjects. I will confess that it is entirely inconceivable—that it is really . . . No, no! I do not understand it at all. First of all, it is of absolutely no value to the Fatherland; secondly . . . and secondly too, it is of no use at all. I simply do not know what the . . .

Yet, taking everything into account—although, of course, one can assume one thing and another and a third—perhaps even . . . Well, yes—and yet, what happening is without some absurdity? When you come to think of it, there is really something in all this. Whatever anybody may say, such things do happen in the world—seldom, but they do happen.